THE ÆTHER COLLECTION

Thomas H. Brand

<u>**Also available from the author**</u>

<u>Fiction</u>
The Serpent's Eye

<u>Non-Fiction</u>
A Basic Guide to Ethical Non-Monogamy

To Sue and Robin

My parents.
For raising me in a home filled with books enough to last a childhood. And only complaining occasionally at how much of my time was spent reading rather than paying them any attention.

Contents

We should never assume we know everything there is to know. There will always be hidden aspects of the world yet to be discovered, and discoveries to change the very idea of who we are and the world we live in.

- Professor Thomas Goldfarn
Theoretics of the Ætheric, and their Implications in Modern Science (1861)

Eyes in the Glass

1898

Despite a night of troubled rest, I awoke that morning both energised and exhilarated, filled with a childish excitement that undercut my lack of sleep. After thankless years of study and research; long weeks spent designing and procuring equipment; nights spent labouring over calculations and equations by guttering candlelight, now at last the day was finally here.

I dressed quickly and made my way downstairs, entering the dining room to find David, my nephew and assistant, already waiting for me. He was, and remains, a tall, intelligent boy, who since joining me in my research had considerably hastened the pace of my work. His sharp mind had proven able to grasp and advance the concepts of my theories as easily as my own, if not more. Even by that point he may have already had a greater understanding of the nature of the æther than I. And with him available to undertake the task of travelling about the country to procure the equipment we required, each piece ordered to the strictest specifications, I had been free to remain at home and work on the theoretical side. Each aspect of the experiment had to be exactly constructed to the most minute detail, with every element checked and rechecked. Nothing could be left to chance.

Neither of us spoke. We made a hasty breakfast, then made our way out across the courtyard to my workshop. There were none of the meteorological conditions that I feared could interfere with the experiment. The day was cool, with pale clouds hanging low and still in the sky to prevent any glaring sunlight that might have obscured our observations.

I locked the stout wooden door behind us. We did not expect visitors, but I had no wish to be disturbed by a chance guest on this of all days. The workshop was just as we had left it the previous evening, with all miscellaneous equipment tidied away in preparation for today's experiment. Along one wall ran the bench covered with chemicals and mixing apparatus. On the main table, which we had cleared and placed in the centre of the room, sat the Bowl.

The Æther Bowl. This one piece of equipment had taken over a year to design and commission. The cost had been enough to make me reconsider my plans more than once, but there had been no other way I could see to obtain my predicted results. The expense had to be borne. A masterpiece of the glassmaker's art, the Bowl consisted of two spheres, one within the other. The outer was a little over two feet in diameter, with a gap of about five inches between it and its interior twin. These were connected only by narrow rubber pipes sealed with brass valves that allowed for the attachment of the vacuum pump. Sitting in the centre of the Bowl, inserted by detaching the valves, the small swab of chemicals sat within the wire mesh that hung between two electrical nodes. It was these chemicals that would, if my theories and calculations were correct, draw in and store the æther.

Æther. What possibilities it held! Plato's fifth element; eternal and unreadable. He wrote of it with such little understanding, yet had been able to deduce its existence by thought alone. Throughout my university studies, I had read and reread every theory and idea that had ever been speculated over the intervening centuries. It was these that had set me on my path, certain of its existence and the possibilities it offered. I knew that, given the correct conditions, it should be possible to harness. Æther is a force, a substance as real as electricity or oxygen. Before that day I had possessed no proof, but held an utter certainty it could be done. And that I could be the one to do it.

Many mocked me for my choice of study. Most men of science dismissed my theories completely, but my young mind had been caught by the ideas of those past philosophers. I marvelled at how such men who, with only the primitive tools of their age at their disposal, had deduced so much of our world. What a study they made of the universe, building the bedrock of knowledge that forms the foundation of our modern lives. If so many of their ideas had been proven correct, why not æther? Plato knew of it. Aristotle knew of it. Newton knew of it. It had simply taken two thousand years before mankind had the technology to prove its existence. It would be my masterpiece. My vindication. The culmination of a life's work.

The two of us quickly went about preparing the equipment. First we carefully attached the tubes to the fastenings on the Bowl, connecting the seals to the vacuum pump. Then David carried over the voltaic cell and methodically attached the wires. I relied on him for most of the fine work. My hands were shaking too much with excitement. I watched in fevered anticipation as the connections were made. Soon the thumping vibrations of the pump filled the room as it began the process of extracting air from the outer chamber of the Bowl.

Time passed at a crawl. Both of us sat staring intently into the glass, despite the fact that there was yet no visible signal of progress. After what seemed an eternity, the dials at last indicated that the outer chamber was empty. Pure vacuum. We set the valves and disconnected the pump. David then set the pump to the connecting tubes of the inner chamber and we began the wait afresh.

As the air slowly drained from the second chamber I remember how I was unable to pull my eyes from the cotton swab sitting in the thin wire mesh. The mixture that soaked the raw cotton had literally been years in the making; years spent poring over texts both modern and ancient, searching for clues in the work of every scientist of the last two millennia. Even then I could not be sure that the formula would work. The solution was entirely theoretical. Æther is all around us, but mostly flows in a great flood above us. If my mathematics and chemistry were correct, igniting the prepared solution within a vacuum should draw the æther forth into a state so concentrated it would be visible to the naked eye. If anything was to go wrong that day, it would have been that mixture. If I had been incorrect in my amalgamations, if any of my estimations were off, then the work and preparation of the last few weeks would have been for nothing and we would have had to begin again from the first principles of our theory.

At last the inner chamber emptied. Nothing but pure vacuum surrounded the swab. David set the seals and disconnected the voltaic cell. Now had come the final moment of truth. I took up in my hand the end of the wire that trailed out through the valves. One end connected to the swab. The other I held over the cell. Once the connection was made the electric current would, if all went well, cause the chemicals to ignite and the experiment to begin. My hands were shaking, but I could not pass the wire to my companion. This one task was mine alone. I could no more have handed it to David than he could have accepted it. This was the climax of a lifetime's work and study.

I glanced at David and saw my own excitement reflected in his eyes. Gingerly, I touched the wire to the final connector. In an instant, the charge flew along the conductive wire. The thin mesh flashed out of existence, taking the swab with it. There was an intense orange flame which caused us both to flinch away. Then nothing. When I turned back the swab and wire were utterly consumed, without even a crumb of ash remaining from the brief ignition. The Bowl was empty.

I leant in, yearning for some sign, some indication. All I had in that moment was hope. Hope that my calculations and formulas had been correct. Hope that the Bowl had been built to the correct specifications. Hope that my life's work was not about to come to naught. My heart thumped against my chest. While I stared, David busied himself extinguishing the lights and drawing the curtains across the windows until the room was shrouded in expectant darkness.

Ah! But not quite. A spark of light hovered at the very centre of the Bowl. Faint, but growing stronger. I was afraid to breathe as I stared wide-eyed at this miracle taking form before me. A gentle, eggshell blue illumination began to show across the darkened surface of the table, highlighting the tools upon it in subtle shadows that slowly grew to encompass the entire workshop. Soon the inner chamber of the bowl was filled with a uniform glow that bathed the room in a light strong and clear enough to see by, yet not so bright as to hurt the eye even though I stared into its heart.

Tears ran down my cheeks. This was it. We two were the first men ever to look upon pure, concentrated æther. David stood beside me, writing furiously into a notebook. I had not even thought of making any record of this moment. For me the joy was too great. I could not bring myself to believe my own eyes. I was a man of science. I had dedicated my life to wrestling with one of the mysteries of the universe, seeking reason and proof of concepts first espoused by Plato himself, and yet here I was, gazing open mouthed as if regarding an angel.

For those first moments I could do nothing but gaze into the Bowl. Then I noticed a clean, sterile smell. The permeating hints of dust and chemicals that normally filled the interior of my workshop were now replaced by an emptiness. Not an odour in itself, more its opposite. One did not really acknowledge it, but rather noted the absence of that to which you had grown so accustomed to that you do not notice until it is removed.

Overcome by what I was experiencing, my legs began to shake and I sat down heavily into my chair. From this new angle I saw, staring straight back at me from the bowl, a pair of striking blue eyes.

Startled, I straightened up and looked across the table. There was nobody there. David and I were alone in the room as we had always been. Shaking my head, I looked back into the Bowl.

There again; a pair of eyes, the rich blue of a distant summer ocean, regarding me through the glass.

At first I thought them nothing more than a reflection, and that some property of the light caused my own dark brown eyes to appear blue. I searched around the interior of the Bowl, hunting for some glint or sign of refraction that might explain the appearance of this phenomenon. I could find nothing, but did notice that when I tilted my own head, the eyes did not mirror my movements. Curious, I purposely moved my head about, keeping the eyes in my field of vision at all times. Then I proceeded to carefully blink each of my own eyes one after the other. Not once did they move. For all the world it appeared as if they were the eyes of one sitting stationary on the opposite side of the table to me.

At last the light within the Bowl began to dim. I stared, desperate to take in every last second of this life-changing moment, until the room was once again shrouded in darkness.

David and I remained in place, without speaking, for some time. Eventually, David stood and lit the lamps while I simply sat there, staring into the empty Bowl. My mind was reeling from the enormity of what we had just accomplished. The physical proof of my theories. Easily replicable. Plans for the next stage in our work could now begin, plans that I had not dared hope might become necessary. Yet more than anything I was haunted by the memory of those striking, blue eyes.

Once the initial exhilaration had worn off, we busied ourselves with note making; recording the entire process in minute detail. We were as giddy as schoolboys. David was barely able to keep still, pacing around the room and speaking in a most animated manner. His elation mirrored my own, though I remained seated for fear of my shaking legs. We discussed and dissected each and every aspect; the hue of the light, the time each step of the process had taken, and of course the appearance of those eyes. Though we agreed that it must have been some mundane reflection, something about them continued to nag at my thoughts. We began detailing possible improvements for the repeat experiment. This absorbed the remainder of the morning, and we were still deep in our business when the cook's girl came knocking cautiously upon the door to inform us that luncheon was ready.

Not wishing to be away from the workshop for more than absolutely necessary, the two of us hurried to the house and set about our meal. David would have ordered the food brought to us, but I have never held with food in my workshop: the chance of contamination is far too great. Additionally, I have always insisted on the benefits to the scientific mind of regular meal times, yet on that day it was all I could do not to break my own prohibition. Once at the table a stillness settled over me. David continued to think out loud, detailing his plans for the afternoon. As for myself, despite the excitement of the morning, for the first time in days my mind was not filled with formulae and equations and chemical mixtures. The sight of those mysterious eyes in the glass overwhelmed every other thought in my head.

The meal done, we began the afternoon readying the Bowl for the repeat of that morning's experiment. The apparatus was disconnected, cleared and cleaned. Carefully, under my exacting eye, David mixed up the chemicals, soaked a fresh swab, placed this in a wire mesh and inserted it into the Bowl. Then each of the seals was reattached and the equipment readied.

Before we began, I fetched three more chairs and arranged them around the table. Now one could sit and view the results from each cardinal point. Despite all the possibilities for the manipulation of æther I had planned on studying that day, all I could think on during those moments was the mystery of the eyes. I *needed* to know what they meant.

Extinguishing the lights, we once again set the pumps to work. When all was ready, at the touch of the wire to the voltaic cell, the soaked swab burst into brief incandescence. The appearance of the flame was different than before. The swab, being freshly soaked, burned slower and with a wet, yellow flame. I feared that this might cause a fault in the test, but to my relief the pale blue light returned and began to grow in the centre of the vacuum. Within a few moments we were once more staring into a cloud of captured and condensed æther.

My hands gripped the wooden bench as I stared into the glass. There they were! This time the eyes were visible almost as soon as the light had filled the inner chamber. I breathed in, again noticing how the dust and chemicals were eclipsed by the sterile scent of nothing.

I reached out and touched the glass surface of the bowl. At the moment my fingers made contact, the eyes vanished, as if obscured by some cloud. Instantly I removed my hand. As soon as the contact was lost the eyes reappeared.

What marvel was this? What strange illusion did this ethereal light cast? Without moving, I ordered David to put his head close to mine and tell me what he saw. Reluctantly setting aside his pen, he crouched behind me. The eyes remained clearly in my vision the whole time, yet he reported that he saw nothing but the Bowl and the light within. I insisted; could he not make out the pair of eyes in the light? Again, he claimed he saw nothing.

What then was this vision? There had to be some explanation, and I was determined to deduce the answer before this experiment ran its course. David did not dismiss my insistence of this vision. He knew that æther would hold innumerable strange qualities, the listing of which would occupy us for many months ahead. He simply did not find this one thing as compelling as I and quickly returned to his notes.

I continued to stare into those eyes and could feel that they, in turn, regarded me. They had a life about them that belied rational possibility. I had thought they must be some strange reflection, yet as I looked I saw that they could not possibly be the mirror of my own. Even discounting the disparity in colour, I knew my own face well enough to recognise the eyes of an old man. These were young eyes, yet with a sense of depth behind them that sat in contrast with their apparent youth. There was a feminine tilt to them, and also something

I could not place. A sadness perhaps? Some aspect of recognition maybe? A subtle familiarity that gnawed at me like an unasked question.

I stood and moved to sit in the chair I had placed opposite my own, where one would have expected the owner of the eyes to be seated had they been of the physical world. From this angle the Bowl appeared empty. I did the same with the other seats. Each time I saw only the muted outline of the room through the concave glass of the Bowl. Only on returning to my original seat did I see the eyes again, staring back at me as before. For all intent and purpose it seemed as if a spectre sat in the chair opposite me, visible only through the light in the glass.

All too soon that light began to fade. Though their manifestation fled, the haunting sensation of regard remained with me.

I attempted to drag my mind back to the material world. Comparing the notes from the two experiments, David and I saw that this second attempt had lasted a good minute longer than the first. While the Bowl had not been designed with the intention of storing the æther indefinitely, our hope was that in the future this would be a real possibility. The change in duration therefore caused great speculation between us about the chemical mixture being fresher, and the swab being still wet. The remainder of the afternoon and evening was dedicated to poring over the formula that had taken me so long to create. The day sped by in a flurry of mathematics and chemistry, and by nightfall we had a selection of solutions sitting waiting for the next morning's work. David wished to continue on, but I insisted upon rest. Night-time work was another self-imposed prohibition. I had learned long ago of the importance of a fresh mind and the risks of missing some vital fact due to fatigue. Instead we cleaned and laid out the equipment for the following day before returning to the house.

While David's excitement had only grown as the day wore on, I had become more sober. I could not shake the vision of those eyes from my head. There was something about them, some fact that I was missing. I was sure of it. The sight of these eyes was no simple trick of the light through the curvature of the glass. This was proven by David's inability to see them whilst at the same time I could observe them clearly. In truth, my nephew seemed to care very little about this visual manifestation. His mind, driven by the excitement of youth, was already racing along the paths of rational scientific application, filled with visions of all the possibilities that lay ahead.

We bade each other good night and retired to our own rooms. I had instructed the cook not to disturb us at dinner time - for even I had been unable to drag myself away from our work that evening for our usual mealtime - but to leave a tray in our rooms for when we returned. This awaited me now, but I could not eat. My appetite had been extinguished by mystery.

I sat by the dying light of my fire and pondered over the day's events. On this of all days, why could I not drag my thoughts from this one thing? I was the man who had proven, after centuries of debate, the certain existence of æther, something that most considered only a crackpot theory. I would be the toast of London. Invited to lecture across the world. So why could I summon up no excitement? So many questions had been answered through today's work and many more now stood ready to be addressed, yet all I could do was picture those two sapphire blue eyes. If I closed my eyes I could still see them, hanging ghostlike in the air before me.

I did not feel even close to sleep and sat up until well after midnight. These blue, hauntingly familiar eyes would not leave my thoughts. Each time I closed my eyes they hovered in my memory until I could take it no longer. I had to know. I resolved to break my own convention on taking rest at night and undertake the experiment once again. Alone.

Carefully, making as little sound as possible lest I alert David to my endeavour, I crept from my room and along the corridor. Navigating through the house without a lamp or candle I reached the door to the courtyard. Outside, the clouds had passed and an ethereal moon bathed the ground with silver light. It was not so cold, but I had brought neither coat nor jacket and shivered in the night air.

Once inside I lit the lamps and began to prepare the Bowl. It took longer alone, but soon enough all was ready. I turned to the bench where that evening David and I had mixed the various different chemical solutions. There was one I was most convinced would grant a stronger reaction. If it failed I would return to my room and in the morning beg David's forgiveness for working through the night without him. Thus resolved, I soaked a fresh swab in the solution, set it within its wire mesh and fixed it in place.

As the vacuum pump whirred and thumped, emptying each chamber in turn, I sat in dread that its noise would draw David from the house. I knew, for reasons I could not put into words, that I had to be alone for this experiment. That there was something I would not be able to recognise were someone with me.

After an indeterminable length of time, the gauges at last registered that both chambers were finally empty. I set the seals, with only my own force of will keeping my hands from shaking too hard to do so. Wiping my palms on the coarse fabric of my shirt, I carefully extinguished the lamp. With my eyes fixed on the swab, I touched the wire to the voltaic cell's connector.

There was a wet burst of lazy yellow fire, still bright

enough to cause me to flinch from where I leant in close, my face almost touching the smooth glass. I sat there, my breath caught in my throat. For a while nothing happened. My heart began to sink. Had this mixture been the wrong choice? Had this entire night's clandestine work been for nothing?

Then a speck of blue light! I watched, transfixed, as it slowly grew; seeming to draw upon itself, swelling from the exact centre of the Bowl as the carefully constructed conditions gradually drew in the æther from the great flow far above.

I believe that the process was slower that time, but so focused was I on the opposite side of the glass, so impatient, that I cannot be sure. Every sense was straining, desperate to see and deduce the cause of that alluring phenomenon.

There! There they were, staring back at me; those two striking, feminine blue eyes. Definitely no reflection of my own. I shook and angled my head but never once did they mirror my actions. I moved to all four chairs in turn, and still they were only visible from that one angle. I leant in, careful not to touch the glass for fear this would once more banish the image. The haunting familiarity remained, but for the life of me I could not place it.

The eyes blinked.

I jumped, and clasped my hand over my mouth to stifle my exclamation of excitement. They had not done this before. Suddenly they seemed alive in a way which hitherto had alluded them. Now more than ever I knew they were so much more than simple illusion or some trick of the light. I was convinced that they regarded me as much as I regarded them. Again! Once more the eyes closed and opened. Nothing could have been more real unless somebody had in truth been sitting across the Bowl from me.

I leant in. Their movement had only increased the sense of familiarity. There was something itching at the back of my mind. Something I could not quite...

Elizabeth!

The realisation struck me like a physical blow, strong enough that I almost fell from my chair. Those eyes! Those striking blue eyes were the eyes of Elizabeth! Now I had seen it I could see nothing else. How had it taken me so long? It was beyond all doubt. How many times had I stared into those deep, beautiful sea blue eyes in the years before that final sickness had taken her from me?

My fingers gripped the hard wooden grain of the table, seeking an anchor to the real world which had been so suddenly pulled from beneath me. Nothing seemed true. This thing could not be, yet here it was before me. I could not look away. Those eyes, which had always reflected the love shown her by a poor, youthful student of science and the joy that we had found in one another, now mirrored that deep, hollow sensation I recalled when I knew that with all my knowledge I was still unable to save her. The sorrow of parting had finally dulled the light of those eyes I had never thought to see again.

I do not know how long we remained there before the light began to fade. A brief forever, snatched away by the inadequacies of science. As the blue glow receded I stared hungrily, hanging on to every fading second, just as I had when I had sat at her bedside that night all those years ago.

David found me later that morning sitting in the old chair in the courtyard, staring up at the clear blue of the morning sky. He wasn't angry, but found it funny that I had been unable to resist working alone through the night. He attributed my malaise to exhaustion and escorted me to my room, leaving me to rest while he set about with the day's planned experiments. I lay on the bedclothes for hours, utterly unable to sleep. Elizabeth's eyes floated in my memory until at last I slipped into a bitter, unrestful slumber.

* * *

I have not worked since that day. David, of course, has taken my prepared place as the foremost expert and pioneer of the field. He has already gathered about him a group of likeminded young men, burning with enthusiasm to further this new science. I am glad. For all my enervation I still see the good that æther could bring to the world. If any man is to take the leading role in that task, I am pleased it is David.

I no longer feel any passion for either science or society. Something within me stopped that night, as Elizabeth's eyes faded away with the light. The momentum that drives us, the push and desire to do and create has left me. I have retired from public and professional life. People call on me, those who wish to learn more of the lifetime of work that led to my discovery. Most leave disappointed, for I have no desire to speak about it. I find no joy in the things that once enthralled me.

Many believe this apathy has come about from finally reaching my life's goal. They believe that having now proven the existence of æther's physical substance, I have nothing to live for. They assume I am happy having proven my theory and have no interest in continuing a study that, at my age, I will never see developed much further. That I seek to enjoy a peaceful retirement in the knowledge that my place in history is assured.

Perhaps they are right. Perhaps I am simply an old man who recognises that I have achieved that which I sought to do, and having done so loses the drive that keeps us going in this life.

But the truth of the matter is that the world and its mysteries no longer hold any interest for me. Whatever I put my mind to, always it returns to the memory of Elizabeth, and those sapphire blue eyes in the glass.

Distortions

1908

What am I doing wrong?

The image in his hand showed himself and Claire, his wife, standing together in the lounge downstairs. The light was perfect, falling across her face like silk, highlighting and enhancing the slender lines of her features. Yet while his own image stood out in bright colour, as clear and precise as he could have hoped, hers was faded, pale, and speckled with blotches of discolouration.

Groaning, Andrew threw the failed æthergraph down onto the counter. It landed face up, mocking him with its divided nature; one half clear and bright, the other so distorted. He sat back in his chair, the wood creaking as he rubbed at his temples. He had tried everything. He had altered the mixture, taken fresh images with different quality papers, taken images under different lighting. What was he missing?

Mr. Andrew Barnes had long been an enthusiast of photography. He and Claire had been holidaying in Bournemouth when, while strolling together on the promenade one afternoon, they chanced to meet a gentleman by the name of Barnaby Miller, who had been setting up a camera of a build and design Andrew had never seen before. Wandering over and introducing himself, Andrew had enquired about the new equipment which Mr. Miller had been more than happy to acquaint him with.

Mr. Miller's photographic gear had been one of a new design based on ætheric technology. Andrew was faintly aware of the field of æther. Its discovery had been in all the papers some years ago, but of little note to those not of a scientific inclination. His interest had been mere curiosity, until Miller had drawn out of his folder a photograph of such vivid and realistic colours that even Claire had been unable to hide her astonishment. The image, that Miller insisted had been created with remarkably little effort, was so bright and enthralling, so in contrast to the dull greys Andrew was used to achieving using his photochemical process. Before long he had set himself upon procuring similar equipment.

Once they returned home from their holiday, he had done just that. The new camera was not so different from those he had used before, and had been relatively inexpensive. Only the chemicals and the ætherbowl required for the development of the images were harder to obtain. The Bowl had been expensive, but they were rapidly becoming cheaper as more and more companies were granted licenses to produce them. Unfortunately, the chemicals required for exposure were not so simple. As they lost their potency over time if left unused it was not possible to acquire them ready mixed, and so Andrew was required to create the emulsion himself, following the published instructions.

In theory, the process was simple. You inserted the paper into the camera, shut the box, and then fixed the atomiser in place. Spraying inside covered one side of the paper in an even coating of the chemical mixture which, when exposed to a burst of normal light, would fix the image upon the sheet.

Then, given a few moments to dry, the paper could be safely removed and stored. Only when later exposed to the light from an ætherbowl would the picture then develop.

This was, at least, the theory. The æthergraphs Andrew developed, while bright and colourful as could be expected, repeatedly showed these blights and distortions that he could not remove. The problem did not affect every picture. He had yet to encounter any such issues with individual portraits. It was only group pictures that developed so unevenly, and even then the issue was never uniform. He had taken a number of group portraits, both of he and Claire and of friends who had requested it, and while some would have only subtle variations in hue and quality, others would be so bad as to be unusable.

The equipment had been checked, and the manufacturer insisted that there were no defects, which left the quality of the chemical solution. Andrew had tweaked and adjusted it over and over again, but he was no chemist. He had a workroom on the top floor of the house, not a laboratory. While quite capable of following instructions to mix the chemicals and prepare the equipment, he wasn't cut out for all this fiddly experimental stuff. All he wanted was to create photographs. Beautiful images that reflected life. He didn't want to develop the technology, he just wanted to use it. He had written to the company that manufactured the equipment, but they insisted that no one else had reported this fault. He had contacted Barnaby Miller, who in turn had put him in contact with other enthusiasts. Yet none of them reported having the same trouble. He had even written to David Goldfarn himself, asking for assistance, but had little hope that he would receive a response from such a prominent man.

He sighed, looking at the collection of pictures that lay on the desk in front of him. A collection of the various failures he had encountered over the past few weeks. He didn't wish to destroy them until he had solved the problem in case they might hold some clue to the eventual solution. Each had been developed using a slightly different mixture, and all showed the same flaw. There were several of himself and Claire. There were a couple he had taken of Mr. and Mrs. Sharp with their newborn. Where the parents themselves were in perfect focus the small child they held between them had a dark smear across its chest, almost as if the image had been placed near a flame. Another of Captain Goddard who had asked for a portrait of himself and his family to celebrate his promotion. The soldier stood out in the centre of the image, his full dress uniform a rich, blazing red, and while he and his young sons were clear and bright, the same distortions as affected Claire's image marred the place where Mrs. Goddard stood.

With such clear divisions to these images Andrew could have hoped that the issue might have been nothing more than an uneven covering of the chemical on the paper, but the portrait he had taken of the family of his friend, Samuel Penwood, had fully scuppered that theory. It stood out as the worst picture he had taken so far. Samuel and his wife, Joanna, were fine, as were their two eldest children. Yet the black smears of discolouration wiped across the image, obscuring the forms of his youngest son and elderly mother. The way in which the family were arranged made it impossible to believe that the atomiser had covered the paper so unevenly. The distortions were utterly chaotic, yet somehow defined to each figure.

The most frustrating aspect of the whole thing was that so many of the æthergraphs, as Claire had jokingly coined them, came out perfectly. Every individual portrait he had taken had developed on the paper in full glorious colour when exposed to the soft blue æther-light. Even some group shots would be fine. While she had not said anything directly,

Andrew knew that Claire was annoyed that he had managed to produce a beautiful colour portrait of Samuel and Joanna, which now hung in pride of place in their drawing room, but still could not create the same for his own wife.

Andrew glanced at the carriage clock that sat over the fireplace. It was getting late. He had spent almost the whole of the afternoon working on his last batch of exposures and still had no new ideas as to the cause of this problem. Grumbling, he shuffled the useless pictures into their folder and shoved it back into one of the drawers in his desk. He set about tidying his equipment and storing the expensive chemicals. He was all but ready to give up on this whole venture. Were it not for the fact that he had invested so much money into the equipment he most likely would have just packed it all away and gone back to traditional photography. That, and the fact that the focused portions of the photos showed he was at least close to getting it right.

Claire's voice called up the stairs. It was late, and the two of them were due to visit the Penwoods that evening for dinner and cards. Andrew put the last items away and picked up his jacket from where it hung on the back of his chair. As he left the room Claire was walking up the stairs towards him. As always, the sight of his wife made him smile despite his frustrations. As she reached the top she met him with a kiss, and he allowed himself to forget his problems as she led him off to dress for dinner.

* * *

Andrew had been friends with Samuel Penwood since they had attended school together. Upon leaving they had managed to remain in sporadic contact, and when chance had seen fit to lead Andrew and Claire to purchase a house in the same town as Samuel and his wife Joanna, they had quickly rekindled that friendship. Claire had also become good friends with Joanna, so now the group were regular guests in each other's homes.

That night, Andrew and Claire arrived in good time and were ushered into the parlour. Andrew's gaze was immediately drawn to the fireplace, above which hung the beautiful æthergraph of Samuel and Joanna. Seeing his work displayed in such a way should have brought out some level of pride in him, but now it just seemed to mock him with its uniform colour and perfect focus. Why on earth could he not get that result every time? He felt rather than saw Claire's sideways glance.

The evening was a pleasant one, though the mood seemed a little muted; Samuel remained as effusive as always, but Joanna was quiet. She showed dark rings under her eyes and a complexion paler than usual. Her mother, who lived with them, also appeared unwell, though Andrew knew that her constitution was weak in general. She was a woman happy to sit quietly during these gatherings, enjoying the company and allowing her children to take the duties of hosting, but while she had never been the most talkative person tonight she barely said a word.

After the meal, when the women had left the two of them alone, he enquired with Samuel as to Joanna's health. The two men were lounging in their chairs, smoking and enjoying a rather fine brandy Samuel had managed to acquire. The windows were open and the warm evening air blew the blue fug of cigar smoke into twisting and dancing shapes above them.

"She's not been sleeping well these last few weeks, I'm afraid," answered Samuel. For the first time all evening, he too seemed to deflate a little. "It's Edward. He's been ill again."

"Oh my dear chap, I'm sorry," said Andrew. Edward was

Samuel's youngest. A sickly child from birth, he had never been as strong as his two elder sisters who were a pair of as stoically robust girls as you could hope for. He seemed always to be suffering from some ailment or another, no matter what preventatives the family procured. This did not, however, stop him being the apple of his father's eye. Andrew knew that Sam adored all his children, but was especially fond of Edward.

"Is it serious?"

"We didn't think so," Sam answered, "But he's had this cough now for two weeks and it's only growing worse. Poor thing. Coughs throughout the night and gets no rest."

"What has the doctor said?"

"'Here's my bill', mostly," Samuel sighed. The bitterness in his tone honestly surprised Andrew. Normally his friend would be loath to speak ill of anyone. The fact he would make such a comment showed just how worried he must have been. "Claims that there's nothing he can do other than prescribe different medicines, each one more useless and more expensive than the last. Joanna's taken to sitting up with the boy, trying to help him sleep. I try to get her to rest, but she says that she simply won't be able to until Edward can."

"Is there anything we can do?" Andrew asked. He was concerned. Edward was often ill, but Samuel was the font of optimism for his family. Seeing him so downcast was worrying.

Samuel finished his drink. "Thanks, old man, but I don't think so. We've just got to wait it out I'm afraid. The little devil will pull through. He always does."

* * *

It was a little less than a week later when the telegram arrived informing Andrew and Claire that Edward had passed away in the night. They went straight over to offer what condolences they could. They were let in by the maid, and while Claire set about comforting the inconsolable Joanna, Andrew went to find Samuel. He found him in his study, stooped over by the fireplace in his shirtsleeves. His normally rosy face was drawn and pale, his eyes shot with red. An empty glass sat on the mantelpiece. The half empty bottle on his desk.

"Sam," Andrew spoke as he went up to him, placing one hand on his friend's shoulder. "I am so sorry. I had no idea it was so bad."

Samuel paused, fighting for the strength to speak. "We were praying he would pull through. He always has before. I think we just didn't want to admit it to ourselves. Eddie just… just started struggling to breath yesterday evening. The doctor couldn't do anything."

"My poor chap," Andrew began, before falling silent. He had no children of his own, though he and Claire were hoping soon to start their own family. He could not imagine how his friend must have been feeling.

The second blow to the Penwood family came a week later, on the day of little Edward's funeral. It was a busy service. The Penwoods were well liked and many in the town wished to pay their respects. As Samuel and Claire arrived at the church Andrew was at the door, his daughters at his side, quietly greeting the mourners. Andrew took his hand and shook it firmly. His friend looked exhausted, as well he might. His clothes hung untidily from his large frame, and his shave that morning had been uneven. They took their seats. The tiny coffin sat at the altar, unnaturally small in the grand old building. They looked around, but there was no sign of either Joanna or her mother anywhere.

Throughout the sombre service and as the coffin was

carried out to the churchyard, Samuel looked like a man whose life had fallen apart. He didn't say a word. The two girls clung to his hands, lost and alarmed in a situation they could not quite understand.

After the burial, Andrew found himself speaking to Doctor Parsons, the local physician who had been unable to treat young Edward. He was known as a good man and Andrew did not believe for a moment that he would not have done all he possibly could to save the poor child. As they spoke, Andrew took the opportunity to ask the doctor if he knew of Joanna's whereabouts.

"Oh, did you not hear?" Parsons answered, "Terrible thing. Mr. Penwood's mother passed away last night."

"Good God!" exclaimed Claire. "Poor Samuel."

"Yes, yes," continued the doctor, "Terrible thing. She was old, of course. Not too much of a shock in itself, especially in times such as these. I believe the strain of young Edward's passing simply proved too much for her heart. They called me in the morning, but she had gone gracefully in her sleep."

"And Joanna?" asked Claire.

"Mrs. Penwood? I'm afraid she is quite insensible with grief. I believe the two of them were very close. I was forced to prescribe a strong sedative to calm her. For her own sake. Mr. Penwood wished her to be able to attend the funeral, of course, but I am afraid it was out of the question. She just would not have had the strength to cope."

"Poor Joanna," Claire breathed.

"I know. Who can imagine losing a parent and a child so close to each other?"

Andrew nodded. As they stood there in the afternoon sunshine he could only imagine the sudden and crushing grief his friend must have been feeling.

The service over, most of the guests had begun drifting away back to their own lives. Samuel was standing by the open grave, looking down at the tiny coffin. As Claire took charge of the two girls, taking their hands and leading them off, Andrew stood with Samuel for a few moments before ushering him away. He hadn't spoken throughout the entire service, as if in a trance. Or was it that his mind found it impossible to process the emotions he suffered.

Andrew did not make any attempt to speak. If his friend needed silence, then he would not intrude. But the lack of speech allowed his mind to dwell on his own thoughts, and alongside his grief he could feel a kernel of realisation forming a pit within his stomach. A possible answer to the problem with his æthergraphs.

He looked ahead at Claire, leading the girls from the churchyard and back home. No, this was not the time to contemplate such outlandish ideas as the creeping thought that grew inside him.

* * *

It was late evening before he and Claire returned home. They had stayed with Samuel and the girls throughout the day. The house was unnaturally quiet. A stillness smothered everything. Parsons had returned with them to check on Joanna, and reported that the poor woman seemed comfortable. He left them with instructions that she take the dose again in the morning if she woke in the same state of hysteria. Claire agreed to visit to ensure Joanna was taken care of.

Samuel himself seemed almost as lifeless as his wife. Andrew took him to the study and poured out a healthy measure of brandy, which Samuel drank slowly without saying a word. The feel of the house made Andrew uncomfortable, but he stayed for his friend's sake. When at last Samuel found the strength to speak they talked of mundane, everyday things. Andrew and Claire left after dinner. with a promise to return the following day.

By the time they finally arrived home Andrew was exhausted, but with that strange tiredness which left him wide awake. As Claire, his beautiful Claire, went to bed he made his way upstairs to his study. Pouring himself a drink, he sat down at his desk. He had not found the time to work on his æthergraphs since the night they had gone for dinner at the Penwood's the previous week. In fact he had hardly given them a thought until today. Until his conversation with Doctor Parsons had dislodged the pebble of thought that rolled and bounced around his mind until the strange and sickening idea had grown to an impending avalanche of realisation.

He removed the folder of bad æthergraphs from the drawer and set it upon the desk. As he opened it Claire's image stared up at him from the top of the pile, her smile hidden behind a mist of caramel discolouration. He slid it aside and came to the Penwood's portrait. The portrait he had been thinking about since he had spoken to Doctor Parsons at the graveside. There they were. The whole family stood posed in their living room. Samuel and Joanna mostly perfect, their surviving children unblemished, but Mrs. Penwood and young Edward all but obscured by the indelible black smears.

Those alive, in clear focus. Those marked, now dead.

Andrew stared at the paper, unsure how he could even consider such a ridiculous notion. The picture matched, but that had to be coincidence. Didn't it?

He stared, willing himself to believe he could be wrong. He was shaken by the events of the last few days, that was all, and allowing his imagination to run away on such childish and macabre notions. Yet he could not shake the idea. The æthergraph sat there; with only those two who had, unknowingly, been so close to death affected. Andrew shuffled through other the pictures in the folder. There was Mr. and Mrs. Billings, where Mr. Billings was distinctly more washed out than his wife, with faint speckles marring his face and chest. There was Captain Goddard in sharp focus, the red jacket of his sharp dress uniform so bright it hurt the eyes while his wife stood beside him, obscured.

Andrew stared down at the pictures. What were they telling him? What were they showing him?

His eyes shifted, and fell to rest on the portrait of himself and his wife. The portrait he could not fix, no matter how hard he tried.

His Claire. So beautiful. So special. So wonderful.

So distorted.

Her Soldier

1915

5th March, 1915

My dearest Olwen,

We have arrived. I cannot say much more than this. Careless talk and all that. Just know that we have all arrived safely and are ready to stick it to the Kaiser! The journey across was a bit rough, but we made it all in one piece. Jimmy got quite seasick, but not so much he's not glad he's over here. It's all jolly exciting. Anyway, I can't write for long. We've only just stopped, but the sergeant says we'll be moving again soon. I just wanted you to have the enclosed photo. There was a chap in port doing portraits. He was using this new æthergraph stuff, so the boys and I clubbed together and got a couple of pictures done. I wanted to you have this one of all of us. Look at the colour! Isn't this æther stuff a marvel?

I miss you, my darling. All the lads send their love.
Your man in uniform
Douglas.

Olwen Page had read and reread the letter several times now. It was the first she had received from overseas. Suddenly everything seemed so real. Finally she put it down and took up the æthergraph again. Six familiar soldiers looked back at her from the stiff paper, their cheesy grins smiling out in bright contrasting colour. Douglas was in the middle, looking so handsome in his neatly trimmed uniform. Peter was there as well, along with Jimmy, Cyril, Bertie and Matthew. But Olwen's eyes were all for Douglas. Her Douglas. Her brave soldier.

Olwen remembered how proud she had felt as she stood next to him in the chapel at Christmas. Mrs. Douglas Page. Peter, dear Peter, had managed to get leave at the same time, and had been Douglas's best-man of course. She looked over at the mantelpiece where her wedding photograph sat in pride of place. The three of them, with her and Douglas's parents, all looking so happy. That one was plain old black and white; there was nothing as fancy as æthergraphs in the little town of Caerbran, even for a wedding. She didn't care though. It was her wedding day. The picture may not have been in glaring colour, but it showed her on the arm of the finest man in the British Army.

It had been just a fortnight since Douglas and the boys had shipped out. Two whole weeks since she had stood and watched the train pull away from the station, carrying them to war. She missed all of them so much. The town was strangely quiet now that so many of the men had gone, their familiar faces missing from the background of her life. It almost didn't seem real any more. People she had grown up with, people she kept expecting to see in the street or at chapel; absent.

Getting up, she fetched the cigar box from the shelf. It had been a wedding present for Douglas from her father. The cigars themselves had either been smoked already or taken when he left for France, and now Olwen used the box to store his letters. She placed this latest missive with the others and then laid the æthergraph on top. She had considered displaying it, but did not want to risk it fading in the light. Instead she had decided to put it with his letters. That way she would see it each time Douglas wrote to her; a reminder of her boys and everything they were doing.

* * *

20th March, 1915

Dearest Olwen,

I miss you, my darling. I was thinking of you as we marched yesterday. Your face hovers before my eyes always, giving me the strength to carry on. If ever my body flags, I just think of you, and of everyone we are fighting to defend.

I do hope and pray that you are well. As much as we are all keen to be stuck in, I cannot help but miss the comforts of home. Thank you for your last letter. It keeps me warm to know I am in your heart as you are in mine.

I still cannot tell you much of what we have been about, my love. We've been told that soon we will be allowed to say more, but for now all I can say is that we are poised to reach the front. I am so glad the Pals have been able to stick together. The men in the regiment are a good bunch, but having the boys here is wonderful. We can sit around and tell stories of back home.

Thanks ever so for the parcel. The gloves are perfect. I shared out the cake with the boys. They all say they wish they'd snapped you up first, if you can bake that well.

We'll be moving soon, so I'll sign off for now. I shall write again tomorrow.

Your husband
Douglas

Olwen folded the letter. True to his word, Douglas had so far written to her with a steady regularity, his letters combining to bring a small insight into the life of her soldier. He could not say much, but just hearing that the six of them were safe and well was enough. Olwen, at her end, wrote at least one letter a day, as well as sending the occasional parcel. She knew it wasn't much, but she would do whatever she could to help keep their spirits up.

Opening the cigar-box, she took up the æthergraph to place the letter atop the others. How handsome they all looked. So keen. Six wide grins shone up at her, each filled with excitement and pride. Looking closer, Olwen frowned. They did not look so neat as she remembered.

She shook her head. A silly fancy, nothing more. They still looked the heroes she knew them to be. Without giving it another thought, she placed the picture lovingly atop the pile and shut the box.

* * *

2nd April, 1915

My Darling Olwen,

We are at last able to tell you our location. We are in Belgium! It pierces my heart to keep anything from you, my beloved, but it is for the safety of the Empire. I am sorry, but a man must obey regulations. I promise I shall never hold anything from you of my own will, my love. It is only my duty that forces me to do so now.

Yesterday we at last reached the front line! Your heroic husband and his pals are now officially engaged with the Hun! Exciting! It is very different to that which I was expecting. The trenches run and run the whole length of the land. It's impossible to truly imagine the feel and scope of them without being here. They say that in some places you are so close you can actually hear men talking German! Luckily for us, our billet is a lot safer than that! We have yet to see any real action, but we're ready and keen to go.

A few older lads have been moved into our lot, some of whom were lucky enough to be here from the off. They seem a quiet lot. We've asked them to tell us about life on the front line, but they don't seem keen to talk about it. They say we'll appreciate it later. Personally, I can't wait to get stuck in and make you proud.

All my love
Douglas

P.S. Peter sends his love. He asks whether you could speak to Winnie for him. He hasn't received any letters for a while, and wonders if they are getting lost.

Olwen shivered. Belgium. Knowing where they were, even in such vague terms, somehow made everything seem all the more real. She had been reading every newspaper that had any account of action at the front, scanning every published death list, imagining Douglas in every field of battle. She recalled reading of a battle in Neuve Chapelle recently. That was in northern France, wasn't it? If Douglas was in Belgium, did that then mean they were part of the force replacing those who died there? She felt faint. She tried to tell herself that if there had been a battle there recently, surely that meant there wouldn't be another one soon. Surely?

Olwen clutched the letter to her chest. How could one letter make her beloved Douglas seem so far, far away? The distance between them and the worlds in which they lived seemed incomprehensible.

Opening the cigar box, she slid the letter under her precious æthergraph. She had worried that moving it every day would damage it, and so to protect it had wrapped it in a piece of tissue paper. She wanted to see him. To hold him and feel his warmth in her arms again. To have him tell her everything was alright. She lifted it out and peeled away the tissue. There he was, as brave and heroic as ever. Just seeing him standing there with his five friends calmed her. She took a deep breath and tried to forget her worries.

Something seemed out of place. Olwen looked closer at the six men. Had they been carrying their rifles before? They clearly were now, the weapons held firmly in their hands. She could have been sure they hadn't been. They didn't look so happy as she remembered, either. Their smiles were forced and glassy; muted reflections of the open grins that she recalled.

Olwen shivered. The worry was causing her mind to play tricks. Rewrapping the picture, she dropped it inside and hurriedly shut the box.

* * *

15th April, 1915

My Dearest Olwen,

It has been quiet today. I have been rereading your letters. Please keep writing, they are what keeps me going, my love. When I falter, I recall you and everything we are here to fight for. The weather these last few days has been ghastly, but at least my platoon has been in the rest camps and able to find some shelter. With no Stand Tos and night watches, a man can finally rest. I feel for those poor blighters at the front in this weather, but then we will be back there ourselves soon, and who then will feel sorry for us?

It is hard to explain what life is like over here. All the training in the world cannot prepare you. The boys are all together, and that keeps things upbeat. The older lads still do not talk much. I can imagine that after a few months of this it could get pretty tiring. But we are here to do our part, and you won't find Douglas Page complaining.

We'll be heading back to the front in a few days. The respite has been welcome, but we came here for a reason. They say it's been fairly quiet around us recently, so nothing to fear, old girl. The lads are waving, and send their love. I will write again as soon as I get the chance.

All my love
Douglas

Olwen looked at the date of the letter. It was three days old. Douglas and the boys would be back at the front by now. She shivered. She hated thinking of him in danger. Of any of them in danger. The longer they were all away, the stronger the sense of fear that had settled on her these last few weeks had grown.

Holding the letter tightly, she walked over to the cigar box where it sat on the mantel. Next to it, Douglas and Peter grinned at her from her wedding photo. So handsome. So far away. She opened the lid and slid the folded paper under the tissue wrapped æthergraph. She had not been intending to look at it. The sight of all of them together would have been too much. But as she tilted it to slide the letter underneath the tissue fell to the side.

Peter's arm was bandaged.

Olwen stared. That had not been there before, she was certain this time. They had all been fresh and clean; six new Tommies going to war. The rest of them were as she remembered, in grubby uniforms bearing their forced grins, but Peter clearly had a white linen bandage wrapped around his forearm.

Alarmed, she snapped the lid shut and thrust the box back

onto the mantelpiece, backing away quickly. What was happening? Her mind was racing. She couldn't tell anyone, could she? Of course not. No one else had ever seen the picture, and if she tried to convince them that it had somehow changed they would think she had gone soft in the head. Mad with worry.

Oh, why did her Douglas have to be so far away?

* * *

25th April, 1915

My dearest Olwen,

I am so sorry that I have not written for so long, but life here has been hell these past few days. I cannot tell you how I am feeling, or answer the questions in your previous letters. I am sorry. It is too much to put it into words, and I do not wish to worry you overmuch.

I am sure that by now you have read of the events of the 22nd at Gravenstafel. Those poor French blighters. We were not on the line where the gas came over, thank God, but we could see it; a billowing green cloud rolling over no man's land, a physical manifestation of the death that hovers over the trenches and the evil we are fighting. I am not ashamed to say I was terrified. We all were. It was impossible to tell what was happening. All we could see were the French running, and the cloud drifting over no man's land. We were hit by an attack soon after. I had never been on the line for a full attack before. My darling, I hope that I can say I did my duty and made you proud, but we were in the end driven from our trenches by the German advance.

Cyril and Bertie are dead. I am sorry for putting it so bluntly, but I cannot fathom any way to soften this news. I cannot come to terms with it. My two school chums, gone. They both fell in the attack. Cyril was standing next to me on the step. It was terrible.

Jimmy, Matthew and I are fine, as is Peter who was in the hospital having taken a piece of shrapnel in the arm last week. Please do not worry for us. We are all uninjured.

It is raining now. We are digging new trenches while the boys in artillery are trying to pin down Fritz.

I will write again soon.

Douglas

Olwen wiped her eyes, sobbing into the handkerchief. Douglas's letter was clasped in her hands. She had already known about Cyril and Bertie. She had spent the whole of yesterday with Bertie's mother. The poor woman had been distraught. Olwen had done what she could, but the whole time all she had been able to think about was how she would have felt if it had been Douglas. She had managed to hold back the tears until now, but hearing it from Douglas' own hand had torn them from her. Her poor brave soldier. She prayed that he was alright. Bertie and Cyril had been his friends from childhood. She could only imagine how he and the others were coping so far from home.

She took the cigar box from the mantelpiece and sat down with it on her lap. Opening it, she took out the tissue wrapped æthergraph to look on the faces of those poor, brave boys who had fallen for their country.

They were not there.

Only four men stood in the picture. Douglas and Peter were in the middle, with Jimmy and Matthew either side, but Cyril and Bertie were gone.

Olwen froze. It was the same picture. There was no way it could have been swapped for another. The four of them stood in the same places they had stood before, but with empty spaces where Cyril and Bertie had once been. Olwen's mind tried to make sense of what she was seeing. Of course the picture had shown all six of them. Her memory was so clear. So what was this strange alteration?

She looked closely at the men in the picture, trying desperately to spot some indication that she was wrong. Any sign that all was not as impossible as it seemed. As the immediate shock wore off, she also saw other changes. Each of those remaining four were different than they had appeared before. Gone were the smiling, happy soldiers excited to go to war. No longer were they straight backed and eager. In their place stood four weary, frightened men. None of them smiled now, but stood grim faced, their rifles gripped tightly in their hands, their uniforms hanging ragged and dirty.

Olwen stared in horror at the picture in her hand, the handkerchief clasped to her mouth. Roughly rewrapping the paper around it to hide the impossible image, she dropped the æthergraph into the cigar box and slammed the lid closed. Standing and thrusting it back onto the highest shelf, she fell, sobbing, back into the chair.

* * *

29th April, 1915

My dearest Olwen,

Thank you for your last letter. Truly, I need your words of kind encouragement now more than ever. The fighting is still intense. The Germans seem desperate to break our line. They have been using gas again, but we are now more prepared, so do not fear. The French seem to be taking the brunt of it, but we are holding our own and filling the gaps they leave.

It is hell here, but this last week has shown just how much we need to defeat these monsters. This gas is a truly horrible thing, my love. I shall not describe its effects, as they are terrible to see. I do not wish you to worry, so please know that the lads are holding up, and all send you their love.

It has not been the same since we lost Cyril and Bertie. It's strange; so many men are dying around us, and still only those two seem real to me. Even the deaths of others from home have not affected me in the same way.

We've been hard pressed since then. I probably should not be saying this, but we have not been taken off the line since the first attack. Everything is strained, but none of us are willing to give in.

I wish I could write more, but things are stretched and I must take another watch.

All my love

Douglas

Olwen held the letter tight. She didn't want to think about how terrible things were across the Channel. Over the last couple of weeks, families all through the town had been receiving telegrams bearing that final, terrible notification from the front. As much as she felt their losses, Olwen's thoughts were only for her husband. She read every newspaper account. They were bare, leaving her imagination to fill in what details were omitted. She could not comprehend how her Douglas could survive such horrors.

She looked up at the cigar box. It was still on the shelf where she had left it. She had not touched it since the æthergraph had manifested its impossible alteration. Douglas' last couple of letters lay on the table beside her, waiting for her to summon the courage to add them to the rest.

This was foolish. She couldn't continue to allow a silly fancy to hold her hostage like this! Steeling herself, Olwen stood and walked over to the shelves, reached up and grabbed the box. Holding it firmly in both hands as if she didn't know what it might do, she placed it on the table next to the letters. Taking a deep breath, she opened the lid. There was the picture, still wrapped in its tissue paper. Had it changed again? Had it changed at all? Or was it all some symptom of a mind fractured with worry? It was right there. Her hand hovered over the box. All she had to do was move the paper aside and see once and for all the truth of what she remembered.

For a second her fingers rested on the tissue, but then pulled back as if shocked. For a long while she fought with herself, the battle between wanting to know and her fears of what it might show. At last she gave in and thrust the latest letter into the box, hiding the tissue paper from sight.

* * *

11th May, 1915

Dearest Olwen,

Peter is dead. I am so sorry to say this. I know you two were close, perhaps as close as he and I. No doubt Winnie has heard by now, but can you make sure she does. He would have wanted her to know he still loved her.

He hadn't been the same since he missed the first gas attack. He felt guilty that he had been away when the others bought it, and after the barrage which killed Jimmy he just seemed to be in a daze. There are several men like him now. Some cannot stop shaking, while others just stare into space. Peter was like that. He could perform any action he was instructed. He never shirked from his duty, like some. He just didn't seem to care any more.

The Hun were attacking all along the line. A morning attack. I don't think he had slept at all. None of us have much chance to sleep anyway, what with the constant noise, but he was having a harder time even than the rest of us. I think perhaps he could not have taken much more. We were counter attacking when it happened. I'm not sure exactly how, but Matthew was near him. I believe it must have machine gun fire. There was a so much of it.

I don't know how to feel. It seems all so detached. There's just Matthew and I remaining now. I can't quite shake the feeling that the lads will walk around the corner any minute. We're kept far too busy to worry, which is some small help. Fritz wants this town. We're not going to let them have it. Not if it costs a thousand lives! British men will never falter in the face of evil. All this death cannot be for nothing.

I shall write more when I can.

Love

Douglas

Olwen let the letter drop. She felt hollow. She couldn't even cry. It was impossible to process the words in the letter. Peter. She walked to the mantelpiece and picked up the black and white photograph that had stood there these last few months. There he was, smiling in his new uniform. So smart. So happy at seeing his two closest friends married. Poor, dear Peter. He had been like a brother to her for so long. He had been Douglas' best friend since they had started school. Douglas had told her once that he had been afraid that Peter had been secretly in love with her himself, but at their wedding Peter's joy had been as genuine and obvious as their own. On that day it had felt like nothing could blight their lives. Not the war. Not the Germans. Not anything.

Just five short months ago. Now he was gone. Dead. Fallen in some Belgian field with so many other poor souls.

She couldn't comprehend that he could be gone. She just stood there, the letter forgotten on the floor, her fingers resting on his face in the grainy black and white photograph.

* * *

* * *

Army Form B 104 – 82
  26th May, 1915
  Madam,
  It is my painful duty to inform you that a report has this day been received from the War Office notifying the death of…

Olwen could not read any further. She had tried several times since the telegram had arrived, but on each attempt her eyes filled with fresh tears and she had been unable to continue. She knew the words. She had read so many identical messages to grieving mothers and wives these last weeks. Her chest felt as if it were caught in a vice that grew tighter with every passing second. She could not accept it. Would not accept it!

She had not received any new letters from him in days, and when she had read about the fresh German offensive towards Ypres somehow she had known. With so many deaths coming in from France, how could her own, dear husband have been spared? She'd spent the days since then in a state of limbo, unable to process how she felt. Only the fact that she couldn't know for certain had kept her functioning. Now the cold, military words of the telegram had brought everything crashing down around her.

Olwen balled the telegram in her hands and clasped it to her face. Tears ran as she wept with all the sorrow within her. A sorrow that had been building from the day that he had left her waving on the station platform, leaving her barely a week after they had married. The day he had left her to go and die in some wretched foreign field.

When she finally managed to stop sobbing she had no idea how long she had been sat there. Her cheeks were wet and her throat sore, but inside she simply felt numb. She looked up, gazing sightlessly around the room, the room that one day he was supposed to have come back to. Her eyes fell on the old cigar box where it sat on the high shelf. She hadn't opened it in days. She had wanted to, if just to see if what she had feared was true, but had been too afraid. Whatever that cursed æthergraph might have been able to show her, she had not wanted to know.

A fierce determination struck her. She would see, now, once and for all. She rose from her chair and strode over. Grabbing the box, she fumbled it open, tipping it so that the collected sheets within cascaded down onto the floor, her poor Douglas' words mingled and fallen together like those brave boys in France. From amongst them the heavy card of the æthergraph fell like a stone. She dropped to her knees and brushed the letters aside to grasp it. It felt heavy in her hands, still wrapped in the soft, crumpled tissue paper. For a few moments Olwen just knelt there, staring at the littered letters. Everything felt unreal, as if Douglas had died on that train platform all those weeks ago and these letters were just the ghostly echoes that had now finally faded away to silence. Then softly, slowly, surrounded by Douglas' words, she removed the tissue and let it fall.

She stared. Stared at the picture before her in fear, grief, and disbelief. Stared at an æthergraph that showed nothing but an empty photographer's studio.

* * *

Olwen's mother arrived to find her sat on the floor, curled in on herself with silent tears tracking down her face. Discarded letters littered the floor by an empty cigar box. It didn't take a mother to guess what had happened. As she moved to take her daughter in her arms, Olwen held something out to her. It was a æthergraph. Six young soldiers stood in a line, smiling out at the camera.

"They're gone," sobbed Olwen, "They're all gone."

Guilt & Illumination

1924

It was in May of 1924 when it happened. That was when I visited Thornbirch.

I was working for the State at the time, as a consultant for serious criminal cases. Well, actually I worked as a doctor and psychologist at a facility down in Danville, right on the State line, but I had a sideline going as a consultant for the District Attorney's office. I was called in when a man, or a woman, needed a psychological evaluation before their trial.

You see, folk will kill for a number of reasons. Sometimes a man will have no choice. If they need to defend themselves or their family, for example. Others will kill to get something they want, persuading themselves they have no other choice. Some kill just for the pleasure of it. But whatever their reasons, good or bad, on the spur of the moment or premeditated, they'll come to the decision rationally same as you or I. But some folks, well they're just not right in the head. They don't know what they're doing, and should be locked away for their own safety as much as ours. And when a body's dead and punishment's got to be set out, the judge has got to know which folks are which. When the culprit might fry for what he's done, that final decision comes down to whether they knew what they were doing.

That's where I would be called in.

I can't recall exactly how the job came to me. Plenty of other doctors could have done it, but somewhere along the line I became the regular go-to-guy. I wasn't complaining. I got paid, same as any job, plus it was good for my career. See, a lot of folk'll try to plead insanity to avoid the chair. Some of them are good at it too. If they manage to get a lawyer who knows what he's about, and have a fair idea of how to come across, it ain't a judge's job to know the difference. It was down to me to whittle out who was faking from those who really were disturbed.

Them criminals might have been good, but I was better and I soon learnt to recognise all the signs that someone was putting it on. It became a game, a battle to discover the truth within the mind. With some it was easy. Those who thought being mad was simply a case of talking nonsense or yelling about the voices in their head. Others were smarter, or at least had a smarter lawyer who knew what to teach them. I had even written a paper on methods of recognising imitation over true mental disorder that was garnering significant notice.

And I was doing good, or so I thought. I was helping ensure justice got served. It never bothered me that I had such influence over these decisions of life and death. I was just giving a professional opinion. I never had a say on the judgements themselves. That my decision on the minds of these men might affect their sentence was no skin off my nose. It was the lawyer's job to deal with that. So what that if I judged one way a man might be carted to hospital for the rest of his life, and if I judged another he'd be dragged off to death row? It was nothing to rest on my own conscience.

Not until I visited Thornbirch.

* * *

Thornbirch wasn't one of my normal duties. I worked down in Danville at a private institution whose residents were mainly members of finer families who wanted expert and above all discreet care. However, by this time I had cultivated somewhat of a reputation in the assessment of criminal psychology. So, when I received the letter asking if I would travel to Thornbirch Penitentiary for a psychological evaluation of some of its patients, I saw no reason to refuse.

Thornbirch. One of the State's maximum security, long-term facilities. They call them "correctional facilities", but only the most naive believe that. These places are designed to incarcerate and separate from society. The men who had been sent here were those unsafe to be left amongst law-abiding folk. They were murderers, for the most part. Men who had chosen to kill but, through some twist or technicality of the law, had escaped just retribution.

And, over the last few months, each and every one of them had begun to go mad.

It took me a couple of days drive to get there from Danville, stopping over at local motels on the way. It sat some way off the main roads, down a long, narrow track obscured by a small patch of trees. I can still recall how it loomed over me in the early morning light as my car rattled down the uneven tarmac. It sat in the middle of a vast open field; a blank rectangle of thick, dirty white stone surrounded on all sides by high wire fences. Towers were spaced around the grounds at uneven intervals, each one manned by men darkly silhouetted against the sky. It was a truly dispiriting sight, and you could only imagine that if they had been seeking to generate an image to erode the hopes of those poor folk sent here they could not have done a better job.

I pulled up to the gate and stopped. A surly faced guard stepped out of the hut that stood to the side. I wound down my window and showed him the letter as I introduced myself. Without saying a word he walked back to the hut and the gate slid open. As I drove through into the interior I could see his gaze did not leave my car, his open distaste obvious in my rear view mirrors. Following the road I arrived at what must have been a visitors' car park. I shivered as I stepped out of the car, though the weather was fine. There was something about this place that sapped warmth from the air. I could only imagine what it must have felt like to those coming here for the first time knowing they would likely never leave.

Standing at the entrance was the warden himself; an unusually tall man in a neat, dark grey suit. He had an undernourished cast, with sharp features and sallow cheeks, and his pale blond hair, slicked back against his scalp with wax, gave him an almost skeletal appearance. He towered over me, peering down as I introduced myself. He seemed distant, as if his attention was only partly on our meeting.

Satisfied that I was who he had expected, he turned and led me into the building with a brisk pace that forced me to trot to keep up. As we walked he began to fill me in on the details of their situation. Over the last month, the inmates - or 'those under my care' as he phrased it - had begun developing signs of some shared mania. At first the doctors had ignored the problem. It would not have been the first time an inmate had faked an illness to gain a few days in the relative comfort of the infirmary. But more and more men began displaying the same symptoms until not one of them seemed to be any longer in their right mind. The building had been inspected for any kind of chemical or environmental contaminant, but nothing had been found. Also the guards, who each spent almost as much time in and around the cell block, showed none of the same symptoms. At last, the facility's doctors had been forced to seek outside help. Namely, me.

As the tall warden spoke, he led me through Thornbirch's heartless interior. The buildings were fairly modern, the prison having been established towards the end of the last century. The administration buildings seemed comfortable enough, but as we passed through into the cell block all pretence of comfort ended. This was a place of cold, modern utility. The corridors were plain and unadorned. Along the ceiling were strung recently fitted ætherbulbs, filling the rooms with their soft, white-blue light. I commented on this as I had not seen many institutions fitted with full æther power, although many folk argued its benefits over electricity. Even the institute where I was employed, not a poor place by any man's standards, had not yet moved to make the switch. The warden curtly informed me that Thornbirch had gone through renovations the year before, and the State had chosen to fit ætherlights to test the supposed cost benefits. If he personally felt there were any benefits to this modernisation of his prison, he did not show it in his voice.

A feeling of strange unease had settled upon me by this time. Each time we entered a new room or passed through a gateway I would see a flicker in the corner of my eye, as if someone were waiting just out of sight. Barely noticeable at first, as the effect continued it became harder and harder to ignore. I began to wonder if the man who had designed this building had been a genius or a madman. Either way, the effect of the imposing exterior and stark corridors seemed to combine to cause no small amount of mental distress.

Eventually we came to the cell block. A large pair of doors opened into a long courtyard containing three floors of cells. Winding metal stairways ran up the walls at regular intervals, connecting the walkways. Guards prowled along the metal framework, staring with open hostility into the closed cells. They all shared the same harsh expression as the man on the gate, a distaste that was only just on this side of aggression. I wondered if there had been some trouble recently that might have caused this, perhaps some act of violence upon one of their colleagues, but nothing of the sort had been mentioned. Something about their attitudes made me feel unwilling to ask the warden in their presence.

As we entered the cell block, the tall warden told me that they had begun keeping the inmates isolated in their cells several days ago. As more and more of the prisoners showed the symptoms, fighting had grown out of control. I gazed around. The faces staring out from between bars did not have the look of men on the brink of violence. They looked more nervous than anything. Men teetering on the edge of some terrifying precipice. Something that also struck me was the unusual quiet. Prisoners in any jail are not normally the retiring or reticent type. I would have at least expected my appearance to illicit some response. Instead there were whispered mutterings and low-pitched moans which only underlined the silence.

The warden did not seem to find this unusual at all, and spoke loud enough so that his words echoed unnaturally in the open, cold room. He stepped to one of the cells, gesturing for me to look inside. I peered through the bars. Sitting on the narrow bed was a thick-set negro in ragged prison overalls. He appeared agitated, leaning forward and holding his head in his large hands. The warden told me his name was Theodore Archer, imprisoned for killing another man in a fight over a farm boundary line. The man never once acknowledged my regard or the warden discussing him. He simply sat there, his hands clasped over his face.

We moved to the next cell. This one seemed more aware of

his surroundings and looked at us as we stepped up to the bars. He was an elderly white man with a thick growth of stubble across his face almost to the point of being called a beard. He said nothing as the warden recounted how he had attacked and killed a young girl, but had managed to cut a deal to avoid the death penalty. As the warden spoke, the prisoner looked away and began to mumble something under his breath. I leant in but his words were too soft for me to make out. He flinched as the deal was mentioned, and for all the world, I was left with the impression that here was a man who regretted making that arrangement.

The warden showed me a few more cells, enough to show me that the apparent symptoms were indeed fairly uniform across each prisoner. The men were all under some form of mental stress, that much was clear. Some were more agitated, and seemed to have less awareness of their surroundings, while others had the haunted look of men who saw no hope in their future. Understandable, in the circumstances, yet this did seem something more than the broken morale of an incarcerated man.

Looking to gain a more detailed understanding, I asked to be taken to the penitentiary's medical rooms where I might interview a few selected inmates. My profession is one of details. While many folk still labour under the delusion that the symptoms of the mind can be categorised with broad, easily applied strokes, I did and still do believe that detailed diagnosis must be made individually before labels can be applied. Often a condition may come about from different reasons, and though two men might suffer from the same symptoms their treatment might be as different as these causes. Despite what I had seen I did not yet believe for one second that there could be a singular source for each man's madness, if indeed madness it truly was.

I was led away from the imposing wall of cells and

through yet another long corridor. Again, each time I passed through a doorway I would be distracted by flickering figures haunting the corner of my vision. It was quite disorienting, and soon I found myself shutting my eyes before stepping through each portal for the sake of my equilibrium.

The medical rooms were just as I expected in such a place; stark white walls lined with the harsh silver of cold equipment. Clean, hard surfaces and neat cupboards ran the length of the walls. Two examination tables, each with heavy leather restraints, sat in the middle. I shivered. I was used to working in places of medicine designed to comfort and reassure my patients. This was a place designed for the most basic necessities of treatment only, with nothing to encourage lingering or desire to visit.

I was introduced to the facility's doctor; a man by the name of Jefferson, with a small frame and stern, pointed features that gave him an unpleasant, rodent-like appearance. I did not know him, either by name or reputation, but he seemed exactly the type you might expect in a place such as Thornbirch. A man of the past, favouring harsh brutality for his charges rather than accepting more modern advances. I had an immediate dislike of him. Prison doctors do not have much training in my field. Who would assign money and resources to the mental wellbeing of a murderer? I could only imagine that any psychosis or delirium presented to him would be treated with the kind of strict discipline that would make the matter worse. My request for a private room to conduct interviews with the inmates brought a sneer to the man's narrow mouth, but he led me over to a side room that was more than adequate to my needs.

The first man was escorted into the room, a sullen looking guard leading him with a hand on one arm. I noticed him visibly flinch as he was pushed through the doorway, his head whipping left and right as if expecting someone to leap out at him. The guard pushed him into the chair and tied his wrists in place as I read over the notes I had been given. Henry McCarthay; a farmer who had been involved in a spate of lynchings several years ago. He was a wiry old man; white, but deeply tanned from a lifetime working in the fields. He had the appearance of having once been thick and muscular, but that strength had been allowed to waste away. He looked as if he had not slept in days; his eyes were red and his skin sunken and pale. He seemed agitated throughout our interview, not once managing to keep still for more than a moment. He had been in Thornbirch for fifteen years, and was one of the first to show symptoms of this madness. I attempted to speak with him, but all he would offer were wild mutterings. I noted down what I could of these, and found a repetition of the words "light", "edge", "haunt" and the unfortunate usage of the distasteful phrase "them niggers be followin' me."

His entire appearance and demeanour unsettled me in a way I had never before felt from any patient. In the course of my career I had, of course, dealt with folk suffering from deep psychoses and mental troubles; both those treatable and also those ingrained into the mind so deeply there is nothing that can be done. In my time I have seen all varieties of mental sickness, and often looked into the eyes of men who had killed and were prepared to kill again. What I saw in this face was something else. Something new and unsettling that I could not place.

He gave me no immediate indicators of any obvious syndrome, but I noted his most prominent characteristics in the hope that they would be a starting point to my diagnosis. Having gotten all I could from McCarthay, I requested the guards next bring me one of the least affected men.

Herbert Cowley had been convicted two years ago of murdering his wife and her lover after discovering them together in his home. Upon his arrival I could clearly see his mind was in a far better state than McCarthay, though he held the same haunted look in his eyes. He also flinched as he entered the room, though not to such a degree. His distraction was obvious and he refused to look me in the eyes. I was required to repeat myself several times before he would answer my questions, although I could not be sure if this were due to a stubborn refusal or simply a lack of attention. He seemed obsessed with the lights. Half way through our interview he looked up and began mumbling to himself, and when I asked him to speak up he flared into a wild desperation and begged me not to switch them off. From this point on his agitation continued to grow until I could get nothing further from him.

I interviewed four more men over the course of that day and saw that they did indeed all seem to be suffering, to various degrees, the same form of mania. At best they were only half aware of the world around them, buried deep in their own thoughts.

Each of them had the same haunted, withdrawn cast to them. The closest thing I could relate it to was one patient I had back at the institute; a man who had served in the war in France, and had come back a simpleton. He hardly spoke, but would look at you with the lost and withdrawn sight of a man who had seen and done things he could not forget. But not one of the men I had seen today had been involved in the war, so I could not figure it to be for the same reason.

By the time I had concluded the interviews for that day I found myself forced to consider that the men might indeed be sharing one overarching condition. As unlikely as I knew this situation to be, the folk here appeared to all share symptoms too similar to be a coincidence. Also, none of those I had met struck me as the type of man capable of such acting ability, or ability to work together to fool so many. I spent some time reading through the files of the men I had spoken with, seeking out a link or common aspect in their crimes or personal histories that might offer an unseen connection. Each of the six I interviewed had widely disparate backstories. They came from different backgrounds and while all were murders each had been driven by separate motives.

My next steps, I decided, were to document these symptoms and look for the unifying characteristics. Only then could I begin to delve into a possible cause. Despite the warden's insistence that the structure had been thoroughly checked I did not rule out an environmental cause as the most probable outcome. One obvious symptom all the men had shown was sleep deprivation. I could not say if this might have been deliberate, but it would not be the first prison where the guards felt it within their rights to torment the folk under their care. All the guards I had seen so far in my visit had been quiet, filled with tightly controlled rage. Could they be concerned that I might uncover something? Or could it be the building itself? I had felt firsthand the effects that the corridors of Thornbirch could have on the mind. Could the layout and design contain some optical effect able to cause this mania? I was no expert on documented cases of mass hysteria, but I knew enough not to dismiss the idea out of hand. But then would the effect have not manifested sooner? The building was some fifty years old. Perhaps some alteration had taken place during the renovations? I determined to ask the warden for a full breakdown on the work undertaken.

As I made my notes, I found myself thinking on the two obvious connections that had immediately linked all six men. The first had been how each reacted on entering and leaving the room. To a man they had flinched, looking to the side as if expecting some horror to greet them. I could not help but think on the strange feelings I had experienced myself as I had been led through the rooms and hallways. I had not seen any of the guards so affected, as hostile as they seemed, nor the warden. Curious, I walked to the door and stepped through. Once more I saw the same flicker in the corner of my eye, as if someone stood there. The closest approximation I can give is the feeling when someone approaches you from behind in the street, the disconcerting knowledge of proximity. I turned quickly, stepping back through the doorway. Again the feeling came to me, just as I stood on the cusp of entering. Even though I knew no one stood behind me, or could have possibly come up unseen in the time since I had turned around, I felt as if someone were there.

The other was the fascination they had with the lights. Why would something so simple as turning the lights in a room drive a man to such passion? In every case, as soon as I questioned them they had gone silent, refusing to answer any more questions, other than begging me to leave the lights as they were. This was interesting. Photophobia could be a symptom of a number of possible disorders. Even heliophobia. But I had never encountered this fear of the physical act of lights being switched off.

Curious, I reached over and flicked off the light switch. Above me, the large ætherbulb winked out and left the room dark. In that instant, in the moment between light and darkness, I saw a group of people standing before me. Only for a second did this apparition last but in that second each and every face was as clear to me as yours is now. Startled, I cried out, but by the time it had left my lips the vision had passed and the room was empty. No evidence remained, other than my own memory.

On seeing such a unnatural vision, I panicked and immediately turned the lights back on. In the brief fragment of time between the light flaring into life and the illumination filling the room I once again saw the figures crowding the room before me. Some young, some old, their faces illuminated by the ghost of the extinguished light and filled with hatred and recrimination. None of them had moved. This time I felt certain that I knew them. Their names hung on the edge of memory.

Shaken, my pulse racing, I grabbed my briefcase from the table and fled the room. I did not dare touch the switch again, leaving the lights on behind me. As I stepped through the door I once more felt that sensation of someone coming up behind me, but I forced myself through without looking back for fear of what I might see.

In the corridor I saw the rat-like Jefferson coming from the infirmary. He sneered at my appearance. I must have looked rattled, and he believed it caused by my interviews. No doubt he saw me as some bleeding heart psychologist unable to handle close interaction with honest-to-God criminals. He told me the warden had come to escort me out. It was close to lights-out in the cells, and as a visitor I was required to have left the building by this time.

The warden stood waiting in the infirmary's main room, his sharp, grey figure standing out in the cold white room. As he gestured for me to follow him I suddenly found myself asking if I could be present when the lights were shut down in the cell block. He looked at me with the closest thing to emotion I had so far seen from him. Realising how strange this request seemed I told him about the reaction each of the men had shown to the idea of the lights being turned off, and that I wished to witness this en masse. In truth I believe that I wanted to convince myself my experience had all been in my head. A symptom of my long drive and the unpleasant atmosphere of Thornbirch. I could have left, driven away and never come back, but I needed to know for certain. Years of study and analytical research drove me forward in unavoidable habit. In those last moments in the small office I believed I had stumbled upon exactly why the inmates of Thornbirch were being driven mad. I couldn't ignore the chance to prove, or perhaps I rather hoped to disprove, this new hypothesis.

How I wish now that I had not allowed my curiosity to drive me to do such a thing.

The warden regarded me for a moment, then nodded once before turning and leading me out. Again I was forced to jog to keep up with his long stride. If the hallways had made me feel uneasy before, the effect was now magnified. The stone seemed to have leached the heat from the air. I shut my eyes at each gate we passed through, fighting to ignore that sense of threat that hung on every threshold.

Soon enough, we were back at the cells. The sky beyond the windows showed the twilight darkness that follows sunset. The lightbowls hanging above cast long shadows across the courtyard. Guards stood at their posts, glaring into the cells with open hostility. Everything was quiet aside from the odd shouted instruction. The sense of terrified apprehension was palpable. I stood, nervously peering up at the lights above me. The warden said nothing as we waited. I might as well have been stood with a statue. Then as the guards began to file out I could hear the muttering of the inmates grow. A lone voice called out, followed by others as the broken silence allowed them to sound their own fear. Some began to beg, while others merely keened, their broken thoughts far beyond words. I looked at the guards as the noise began to echo around the empty space. None of them seemed even vaguely affected by the cacophony. Was this a usual occurrence? Were they used to this, or did they simply not care?

My palms felt clammy. I feared what was coming yet still had enough strength to tell myself that it was all a fancy, and that nothing would happen. Then came the final call. Lights out! The words echoed around, mingling with the outburst horror from the inmates. The room quickly filled with the sounds of begging and pleading, desperate entreaties for the guards to leave the lights on, but the switch was thrown and all sounds ceased as the great lightbowls hanging above were extinguished and the room plunged into blackness.

That moment has haunted my mind ever since that day. In that second, in that brief instant between light and dark I know each man stared into their own private hell; the faces which haunted their dreams, their nightmares, and their waking hours. Faces of the men and woman they had killed.

I know you likely do not believe me, but in that moment I once again saw the figures I had seen before. And I recognised them. I had met each of them only once, and only for as long as it had taken me to assess their mental state for the purpose of the court. Yet I remembered them. They had each gone to the chair. I had not convicted them, or sentenced them, or pulled the switch myself, but in their eyes I could at last see the truth.

Each of the figures before me had died because I had judged them sane.

All noise had ceased at the moment the light had fled, but the silence did not last long, for as darkness claimed the room completely the sobbing and moaning of those forever plagued by the spectres of their guilt rose to fill it. Did every man in Thornbirch see the faces of their own demons each night and every morning? Staring? Accusing? Unforgiving? Undeniable?

* * *

I never returned to Thornbirch. Nor did I write any report as I had been asked. I ignored that obligation, refusing to return their calls or letters. I never worked in the penal system again. Even if I had wanted to, I believe that news of my behaviour in this case spread and I found myself called upon for my professional services less and less. Combined with my refusal to answer any queries on the matter, that side of my career died. I soon found I could not continue working in Danville either. Everything I had done while working there haunted me. I moved north, and began my private practice. Seeking to help people. To heal and keep them safe.

I do not know why I'm telling you this now. I cannot imagine that you believe half of it. Most folks wouldn't. But occasionally, I still see figures in the corner of my eye as I enter a room. And sometimes, sometimes I cannot bring myself to switch off the lights, for fear of what I might see waiting for me as the brightness flees and the night rushes in.

Force of Habit

1933

The wind gusted through the stark, dull blue sky, cutting through the thick wool of Lori's overcoat. She shivered, pulling it tighter around herself. Breath misted around her lips as she hissed at the sharp cold. Despite it being well past mid-morning the weather showed no indication of letting up. It was one of those harsh, late-winter days that seemed to take joy in suppressing all the life around it, revelling in the fact that summer was long dead and spring merely a distant hope.

Lori couldn't think of a more appropriate day to bury the miserable old sod.

She held tightly to Hank's arm as they stood together at the graveside. While she knew her husband had shared her opinions about Harry Senior, the old man had still been his father. Even a lifetime of indifference could not erode that bond, and while the old man had probably never once shown a single moment of affection towards his only child, no human being with a heart could fail to feel the acute loss of a parent's passing.

But Lori had no such familial connections, and all she felt was relief. Relief that her home was finally her own again. Relief that she no longer had to live her life to someone else's schedule. Relief that the grumpy, irritable spectre that had haunted their lives these last two years was finally gone forever.

* * *

Harry Lewis Senior had been a hard man when she met him, and the passing of time had done nothing but calcify him further. Back when she had first met Hank she could remember him telling her about his father. Warning her, more like.

An old-school military man, Harry Senior had lived most of his life in regret that he had left the army. Brought up in a deeply religious household, he had enlisted at the start of the war despite his family's objections. At twenty-nine he had been old for a soldier, but that hadn't dampened his belief that it was his duty to fight for his country. He served in France as a medic, and discovered that, in spite of any moral misgivings that may have lingered from his religious upbringing, the military life suited him perfectly. He had been exactly the sort of person to whom the world of strict discipline and certain purpose made perfect sense. He made it through most of the war, until finally getting gassed back home in the final months of 1918. He survived the attack, but his chest would be weak for the rest of his life. On leaving hospital he was discharged and returned home to his wife, his son, and a world that would never match the sense of belonging he had experienced throughout the previous four years. He joined the police force, but it had always been a pale imitation of military life. The peacetime world moved on, and in the eyes of men like Harry Senior it would never earn the sacrifice that had been given for it.

Lori had first met Harry Senior when Hank had arranged a visit to introduce his new fiancée to his father. His mother had passed away a few years earlier, leaving his father the only family he had left. She had been nervous but excited, certain the old man could not be as bad as Hank had described. She had pictured a stern old military gentleman, strict and firm but with a secret heart of gold that would shine through for those who got close enough. Someone who would ensure their grandchildren would grow up with a sense of tradition threading through their modern lifestyle.

That illusion didn't even make it through the front door, which had opened to the thin, slate grey man who stood looking down at her with such a look of distaste that she had thought he was going to slam it in their faces.

The rest of the evening had been no better. Once they had been allowed inside there had followed one of the most awkward and uncomfortable evenings of Lori's life. Desperate to ingratiate herself with her future father-in-law she tried to find some topic of conversation to engage Harry Senior. She might as well have saved her breath. Other than few muttered comments about her name - apparently too 'modern' and 'American' for his liking - Harry Senior barely spoke a word throughout the entire meal, and none of them to her. Other than to make it clear that there would be no 'Hank' at his table. His son's name was Harry Junior, or just Harry. Like that wouldn't have been confusing. If it hadn't been for Hank's - sorry, Harry Junior's - forced jollity she was sure the old man would have had them sit in silence the entire time. When they had left at the end of the night she had burst into tears, feeling small and useless at her failure to impress the old man. It had taken Hank some time to convince her she had done nothing wrong. Harry Senior simply wasn't someone who let people in.

By the time they were married, Harry Junior had already followed in his father's footsteps and joined the police force. Lori had never understood exactly why. He was such a likeable man, so unlike his father, and while his personable nature made him a popular figure in the town she could never say that he was a figure of natural authority. She was certain that the only reason he had become a policeman was a last vain attempt to get some kind of praise from his distant and discouraging father, but as far as she was aware he never achieved his goal. For Harry Senior the police force would always be a poor substitute to the military life, and as his son had never shown even the slightest inclination towards a career in the army, he would never be, in his father's eyes, deserving of that longed for approval.

Lori soon came to believe that Harry Senior had just long ago decided that nothing in the world would ever be good enough. No matter what he experienced, no matter what lengths anyone went to for him, it would never reach his exacting standards. There was barely satisfactory, and there was disappointing. The greatest commendation anyone could possibly hope for from the stony old man was a grunt; an almost inaudible verbal shrug to acknowledge something you had said or done was considered acceptable. She wished she could have met Hank's mother. She couldn't understand how her happy, personable husband, always ready with a smile and the ability to see the best in anyone, could be the son of such a miserable, misanthropic scarecrow. The few photos there were of her showed a happy, motherly woman with a warm smile and a short, plump figure that starkly contrasted with her husband's rake-like physique. But if she had been the sort of woman who could love a man like Harry Senior, those photographs should have showed an actual halo.

⁂

* * *

The wind gusted again, jolting Hank from his reverie. He turned away from the grave and Lori gave his arm an affectionate squeeze. Wan and sad as he might have been, he was able to manage a smile for her even now. She felt a stab of emotion cut through her. No matter what baggage Hank might have come with, she still loved him more than ever.

The other guests had given them some space while he had been saying his final farewell at the graveside, but now they turned back to join them. The funeral had been better attended than she had expected. Harry Senior hadn't come from a large family and had never been one to keep in touch with any of his more distant relatives. He had certainly not had any friends. However the numbers had been made up by a contingent of old soldiers who still felt enough camaraderie to attend the funeral of a man they had fought beside through Europe, even if they hadn't seen him in years. There had even been a few younger men, sent officially or unofficially, she wasn't sure, to represent the regiment, but they had left straight after the service. There were also a few old coppers in the crowd. Lori suspected that Hank might have sent out some letters to ask people to attend. It was the sort of thing he'd do. She couldn't imagine for one second that Harry Senior had kept in touch with any of them himself, or would have cared either way had no one attended the funeral at all. The old man hadn't had an ounce of sentimentality in him. He would have poured scorn on the idea of people coming out for his funeral, wasting time and money for someone they hadn't seen in years. But his son would have wanted people to be there to remember him.

Lori stood with Hank as he made small talk with old men he had never met, sharing half-remembered stories of a man they hadn't seen in almost twenty years. She felt an acute sadness, but only for her husband's grief. For Harry Senior she felt nothing, other than perhaps guilt at that lack of feeling. She knew it was wrong to speak ill of the dead, especially so soon, but the overwhelming sensation she felt was relief that she was finally rid of the curmudgeonly old goat. The burden she had endured for the last two years, almost the whole of her married life, was finally gone.

As they left the churchyard to gather with the remaining guests at the local pub and raise one last drink to Harry Senior - the old man would have scoffed at the idea of spending money on a proper wake, even if Lori wouldn't have absolutely refused to hold one anyway - she could feel only elation for the freedom that her future held.

* * *

They had only been married a year when Hank had invited his father to live with them. The old man's weak chest had forced him into early retirement, and Hank didn't want him living alone. It was the first time she could remember ever being truly angry with her husband. More than that. Furious. In the year since their wedding her father-in-law had not once made any effort to get to know her or her family. The rare weekends they had visited, at Hank's insistence rather than Harry Senior caring one way or the other, he had either ignored her or expected her to wait on him hand and foot; the meek wife and servant of some ridiculous Victorian fantasy. The idea of living with that every single day was horrific, but Hank had been insistent. He didn't want his father living alone and unwell in some flat or care home. Family was family, he argued, and his father was going to live with them whether either of them liked it or not.

And so for the next two years she had endured a life with the miserable sod firmly entrenched in her home, watching heart-broken as her beloved Hank tried desperately to earn some acknowledgement for the invitation, any sign of love or gratitude from a father who had no heart.

What was most upsetting to Lori was how their routine had so quickly been reshaped to the old man's design. He woke everyday at six thirty and would take himself out for a walk around the town, whatever the weather. His son had tried to persuade him that he should stop for the sake of his health, but Harry Senior wasn't going to break his invariable schedule for something as unimportant as concern for his health or his only son's feelings. Lori didn't mind, as it meant that she had the house to herself for a few hours every day. He would return around mid-morning with his newspaper and settle in the living room, her living room, to read by the light of his old fashioned æther stand-lamp until twelve thirty sharp when lunch was to be served. Then he would return to his chair and read, do the crossword, or just sit silently for the rest of the afternoon until dinner at five thirty. Again, this meal had to be prompt to allow him time to be ready to listen to the news at six o'clock. Silence was expected during the broadcast, and only then would he allow them to turn to their own choice of station or put on a record, as long as it was not something that he considered too "frivolous" or "childish". Once he went up to bed at nine, silence was expected through the house. The only day this routine varied in any way was Sundays, when he would march the two of them to church for both the morning and evening service.

This had been Lori's life for the past two years. Whatever her or her Hank's plans might have been, whatever habits they had maintained before old Harry had arrived, once he was living with them everyone in the house was expected to keep to his routine and may-you-be-forgiven if it were disturbed.

At first she had rebelled against the old tyrant on principle. This was her house, hers and Hank's, and she wasn't going to be dictated to by a crotchety old man she had never wanted there in the first place. She had tried to be rational. She had not expected him to be friendly, but had at least thought he would accept that he was now living in someone else's home. But it soon became apparent old Harry fully expected that his routine would supersede whatever had come before. In these first few weeks the arguments had been heated, and old Harry's military background and antique attitudes towards women quickly came to the fore each time Lori dared try to assert herself. In the end it came down to each of them attempting to force their routine on the other, but in a battle of wills hers was no much for the entrenched stubbornness of Harry Lewis Senior.

It wouldn't have been quite so bad if Hank had backed her up. She had fully expected him to take her side in these arguments. This was his home, his and Lori's, and his father had been invited as a guest and would have to accept that he was no longer the master of his own castle. But always it would be Harry Junior, not Senior, who backed down. With barely an argument he would give in to each and every demand, calming his father's argumentative nature with promises that he would "have a word" with Lori about her attitude.

Oh! Oh, her reaction when he first used that phrase in her hearing. By this point feeling anger at her husband was no longer a strange occurrence. The conflict in his eyes was painful to see but Lori made damn well sure he was aware it would be a long time before she would forgive him for speaking about her like that. She might not have been able to do anything about her invasive father-in-law but she was damned if she was going to let his archaic attitudes bleed into his son. She didn't care how desperate he might be for the old man's approval. No. She made him painfully aware that she was not prepared to take second place. Harry Senior may have been his father, but she was his wife. She had only agreed to marry one of them and at no point had that arrangement ever included being a servant to the other. He had looked honestly hurt at her being so upset about the situation, but still he would not budge. On any point of contention, Harry Senior got what he wanted.

The fact was, Lori had underestimated the sheer force of will that her father-in-law exerted. She soon learned that, argue or rage against it as she might, the simple fact was Harry Senior set his schedule and stuck to it and as far as he was concerned that was the end of the matter. Her only option was to arrange her life as well she could to just avoid him, an arrangement that suited them both. She wanted to avoid him completely and he wanted to be left alone. But despite it all he still expected her to wait on him and keep his house, and while she hated herself for it the truth of it was that it was simply easier just to get it done. It was depressing how quickly her resolve eroded against the force of the craggy old man's nature. As time passed the arguments had become fewer and further between. Hank had tried to portray this as the three of them learning to live harmoniously, but Lori knew full well that through sheer stubborn pig-headedness Harry Senior had completely overridden their own life and asserted his own in its place.

But now he was gone. It may have taken twenty years for the German gas to prise him from his stubborn grip on life, but finally it had done its work. No longer did she have to arrange her life to the whims of that miserable excuse for a father. She could do the housework whenever was convenient. They could curl up on the sofa again without the irritated chuck that had been Harry Senior's sign he thought they were being too affectionate in public. She didn't have to watch her husband bend and scrape for the approval of a father who simply did not care one way or the other about him.

No more old Harry Senior.

* * *

On the day after the funeral, it wasn't until she had completed all of her morning housework and settled into the kitchen with the radio on quietly and a pot of tea brewing that Lori realised she was waiting for the sound of Harry Senior coming in from his walk. When Hank had left for work she had unthinkingly set about her usual routine. Realising what she had done actually caused her to laugh out loud, clapping her hand to her mouth as a stab of guilt immediately followed. All her morning work done already and she hadn't even needed to do it. There was no old man due back to stomp through her house, expecting her to have lived up to his nineteenth century ideals. Nothing but force of habit.

She felt a little bad at how she had laughed, but not much. She felt a real sense of contentment that she hadn't experienced in years. But despite this hidden elation - she couldn't possibly let Hank realise how happy his father's death had made her - it did feel strange knowing the old man wasn't about. His presence had haunted her like a spectre of disapproval, hovering at her shoulder. Even now she could still feel it, or she would not have gone the entire morning expecting him to return. For the last two years she had been woken by the sound of his slamming the door shut on his way out for his walk. She was convinced he closed it so hard to purposefully wake her and ensure she had enough time to get her chores done before he returned. It had become so ingrained that this morning she had woken at the usual time without any outside influence. She wondered how long that habit would last.

Leaving her tea to brew, Lori walked into the living room. Turning on the wireless she settled into one of the armchairs and sighed. The room was hers again. It felt strange having it on this loud. This room had been Harry Senior's realm, with her relegated to the kitchen or garden. Even now she felt like an intruder. His chair sat empty in the corner, the tall æther-lamp standing behind like a sentinel remaining to guard Harry Senior's place. The usual small pile of newspapers neatly set to one side waiting to be thrown away at the end of the week. His pipe had been buried with him - Hank had said he couldn't picture his father without it - but the ashtray sat empty in its usual spot on the arm of the chair, with an almost empty packet of tobacco resting on the small wooden table beside it.

Lori stood. She should probably clear those things away. Neither she nor Hank smoked, and the newspapers could easily be thrown out today rather than at the end of the week. But something held her back. They were Harry Senior's. More than anywhere else, that armchair had been his. The one spot where his presence was the most indelible. She was aching to sweep away the remnants of his investiture, but now she had the chance it just didn't seem right.

Maybe it was too soon. It had only been a day since the funeral. Hank would probably need a little while at least to get over it.

* * *

Two weeks had passed now since Harry Senior's funeral but still Lori did not feel comfortable in her own home.

Hank had been quiet for the first few days but then pulled through far sooner than she had expected. As much as he was sad for the death of his father, even he couldn't argue that their lives were better with him gone. They had their house back at last and had already begun discussing the changes they were going to make. As it turned out, they had ample opportunity to realise their ambitions. It had come as a genuine shock to both of them to discover that Harry Senior actually had a significant amount of money in his savings when he died, and an even greater one to learn that he had left almost all of it to his son. Lori had always assumed that the old man's frugality had been down to poverty, but it seemed that it was just another part of his miserable nature. Some of the money had been bequeathed to a selection of charities but the remainder, a not insubstantial amount, had been left to his son to dispose of as he wished. There could be no doubt that he had expected them to do something sensible with it - such as ferret it away just as he had done so that they would have an equally large sum sitting unused to pass onto their children - but instead they were planning on spoiling themselves.

Lori had harboured one secret fear since the funeral; that Hank would somehow be unable to move on after his father's death. She had worried that some familial loyalty would kick in and she would have to fight him at every step to move on and let them live their lives. But in fact, after a short period of mourning he had thrown himself fully into planning for the future, ridding the house of his father's memory and starting a life of their own. As far as he was concerned he had done his duty to his father. He had taken him in and endured his controlling influence over their lives, and in doing so had satisfied any unbreakable obligations of family that he believed necessary. With the old man's death those obligations were fulfilled.

As it turned out, it was Lori who was finding it hard to shift her old habits. She still woke up at six thirty on the dot every morning, and try as she might was totally unable to remain in bed. She could not get comfortable until she was up and working, like an itch she couldn't scratch.

If lunch wasn't ready at the usual time she found herself getting ravenously hungry. If she left the radio on while working she found it impossible to concentrate, preferring instead the same quiet that old Harry had insisted upon. Housework that wasn't finished before lunch gnawed at her mind, burrowing at her concentration until she inevitably gave in and fixed the issue to what she could only describe as old Harry's satisfaction.

It was the same in the evenings. She and Hank had taken to curling up and listening to their records each evening before bed, just as they had when they were first married. They never listened to the news programmes anymore. In fact her husband seemed to be taking an almost perverse delight in living differently to his father. With the risk of discovery and censure removed he was finally letting himself feel the heady joy of living his own life to his own wishes.

Originally, Lori had felt the same way. It was as if they were newly-weds again; a young couple experiencing life together for the first time. But after a few days had passed she had begun to feel more and more uncomfortable with anything that deviated from their previous lifestyle. She worried about the radio being too loud. About food being served late. Any time Hank wanted to be affectionate she would get a sudden fear that someone might walk in on them.

Hank had only laughed off her worries. He joked that she was acting like a crotchety old maid, aged before her time and worrying over nothing. Lori knew he was right. It was ridiculous. If Hank could move on, then why not her?

Was it guilt? Did the fact that she had felt nothing but relief at the old man's death mean that she was suffering from some kind of delayed mourning? Hank had mourned properly, as was correct for the deceased's son even if the deceased had been utterly disinterested in that son. Was that why he was finding it so easy to move on while she could not?

She hoped that it was simply an emotional problem she would eventually pass through. Because she had begun to fear that some part of Harry Senior still remained, haunting the house that had been his domain for two years. Could it be possible that even death might not have been enough to counteract that old man's stubborn, iron-solid will?

* * *

It had been two months now since the funeral and in that time Hank had become a new man. Free at last from his barely subconscious need to please and placate his father, he seemed freer and more alive than she could remember since before they were married.

Lori, on the other hand, was growing more miserable by the day. If things weren't done the way Harry Senior would have wanted, she would be haunted by the creeping fear that at any moment his key would sound in the door and she would have to face him. It was ridiculous, but now it almost felt worse. This was no longer the fear of having to face an impending argument. It actually felt as if there were a threat lingering over her. Leaving a job undone, at least by Harry Senior's standards, triggered something primal within her that she could not fight.

The house looked so different now. A new wireless and record player had been joined by a whole range of items and accessories they had bought with their inheritance, the entire aspect of the place had altered. Hank had wasted no time disposing of the furniture and family heirlooms they had put up with for two years. The terrible portraits of family members long dead. The kitchenware that Lori had felt so embarrassed about using. All gone. But where once these things had seemed like intruders in her home, now the places they had sat seemed empty, their modern replacements gaudy and vile. All the changes, changes that she had been longing to make for so long, now made her more uncomfortable than she ever had ever felt before.

What was causing her to feel this way. They had regained free rein of their own lives and home. She loved having new things in the house. It had transformed the place. The look on her Hank's face when he got home melted her heart. Yet every so often she would look over and feel a deep stab of anger at how much he had spent on something they didn't really need, or a stab of fear that they had foolishly squandered money that they should have saved. What if some disaster struck and they were unable to pay their own way? He would try and curl up with her on the sofa, something she had more than encouraged when they had first been married, but now it irritated her. It was their house, and their business, but all she could think was that it wouldn't be appropriate to be affectionate like that in front of people.

One thing that still remained was Harry's old ashtray and the ætherlamp that still stood vigil in the corner of the room. The ashtray was no longer in its accustomed place on the worn fabric of the arm-rest of Harry Senior's chair. The chair was long ago disposed of and now the glass bowl sat cold and unused on the coffee table. Neither of them smoked, and at least once a day Lori would pick it up to throw it out, or at least tuck it away in a cupboard somewhere until they had guests who might use it, but every time she ended up putting it back. Once she had got as far as throwing it in the bin, but for the rest of the day all she had been able to think about had been the gap where it should have been. She could almost hear the irritated chuck, Harry Senior's sign that something was out of place. If she turned around she was certain he would be right behind her, his face set in the look he would give her as a warning to fix the issue before he would be forced to "have words". The man was dead, but somehow his disapproval lived on. They may have been allowed to do what they liked with the rest of the house, but this last item was the limit. After a few hours she had broken and run back to the kitchen to retrieve the ashtray and return it to the room. She could have sworn she had almost heard old Harry's satisfied grunt. The one he would make when a mistake had been sorted to his satisfaction. The closest he would ever come to a "thank you".

The lamp also played on her mind. They had not replaced it as it was still perfectly serviceable and actually one of the less offensive pieces Harry Senior had brought with him. They had replaced the lampshade and let it stand in the corner of the room where its soft blue glow illuminated more than just the single chair.

It had taken Lori some time to realise that something was not right with the lamp. She hadn't noticed anything at first, until a few days ago when Hank had asked her why she was always turning it off halfway through the evening even if they were still up, and on in the middle of the day. She hadn't even realised she was doing it, but now she saw that it had been one of her habits for weeks.

She had laughed it off at the time, but lain awake that night wondering. How long had she been doing this? Why had she been doing this? Why on earth did she end her morning routine by switching on a lamp she didn't need, and then instinctually turn it off at the same time every evening?

The next day she found her mind still dwelling on this as she worked. She had hoped that knowing about this would allow her break the habit, but once she was done she found herself with her fingers on the switch. Then it hit her. Every single day while Harry Senior had lived here this lamp had been switched on when he came in from his walk, and then switched off again at nine when he went to bed. On in the morning, and off at nine. Every day for two years. Without even realising, Lori had been keeping the lamp lit in tune with her dead father-in-law's daily schedule. Even now, realising what she was doing, she could not stop herself pressing the switch and letting the soft blue light spill out over the room. She tried, but as she pulled back her hand she felt the familiar sensation of nervous expectation overcome her and she was helpless to resist the silent demand that the routine be accepted and maintained.

It wasn't her house any more. These weren't her thoughts. While he had still been alive she had always thought of Harry Senior as an interloper. A stranger invited into her house against her will. But now he was gone, what excuse did she have? What reason was there for following his routine? For resenting replacing his belongings, or for feeling uncomfortable when she made noises in her own home?

They say old habits die hard, but this was something more. For years they had been living their lives on the track Harry Senior had set in place. Arguing with him was as useless as arguing with a train. It would always follow the rails, no matter how much it inconvenienced anyone else. His was the kind of personality that did not simply fade away, and even the echoes were impossible to ignore. In the same way people follow the same worn pathway through a field, even though there is nothing to stop them straying out onto the grass, Lori's habits followed the well worn ruts. She wasn't living her own life any more. She was living Harry Senior's.

A sudden burst of fear and anger caused Lori to grab the lamp and drag it from its place in the corner, where it had stood since they had rearranged the room. She gasped at the sense of wrongness moving it gave her. As it fell to the floor she dropped to her knees and scrabbled with the lampshade, throwing it aside. She grabbed the ætherbulb to pull it from its place. It was searing hot. Ætherbulbs didn't heat up like electric bulbs, but she yelped as her fingers burned on the glass. Panting and sobbing at the pain she managed to unscrew the bulb and flung it to one side.

She sat back, the breath heavy in her chest. She looked at what she'd done. Emotional memories flooded through her. The feeling of helplessness of a child caught having broken the rules. The powerlessness felt as a parent or teacher stood looking over you at the point of discovery. The dreaded anticipation of what was to come. The knowledge that everyone will know what you did. It didn't matter why. All that mattered in those moments was the certainty of the oncoming, inevitable punishment. The moment of uncertainty far worse than the act itself. And the knowledge that there was nothing that could be done to avoid it or escape.

Slowly, tears running down her face, Lori righted the lamp and picked up the ætherbulb. She touched it cautiously. The glass was cold, but her burned fingers were proof of what she had felt just moments ago. Carefully she screwed it back into the stand, positioned it back in the corner and pressed the switch.

Then, as the cold blue light of the lamp that had sat at Harry Senior's shoulder for so long washed over the living room, Lori fled.

* * *

Carefully wrapping the last of the picture-frames in a scrap of newspaper, Lori placed it in the cardboard box. It tucked in with the other knickknacks and ornaments, neatly taking up the last of the space. Closing the flaps carefully, she stood and carried it out to the others in the hallway.

She had done most of the packing herself. Hank hadn't said it outright, but she knew that he was leaving her to arrange as much of this move as possible on her own, and handle any of the packing that could be done by one person alone. After all, it was her who had insisted that they move. He didn't want to, and he didn't understand why she did. He loved the house. They had moved in together straight after they had been married. It was perfectly located for both of them, and had more than enough space for children now the spare room was free. He couldn't understand why, after waiting so long to be free of Harry Senior, delaying all their plans, she suddenly now wanted to move.

It had taken her two months to persuade him. She told him she wanted a new start, insisting that this place would never truly be theirs again. She had tried to be honest. Tried to explain how Harry Senior's presence still hovered over her shoulder, that she could not shake the feeling he was still on the verge of walking in on them. He had just laughed, dismissing the idea. He hadn't said anything to her face but she knew he felt she was being childish. He had never been under any illusions about how people had felt about his father, or ever suggested that those feelings weren't justified. He couldn't understand why she was unable to move on. He had, so why couldn't she?

Lori hadn't mentioned the incident with the lamp. What would she say? What *could* she say without sounding like a half-crazed fantasist? But still she was compelled to switch it on and off at the same times each day. He had commented at first, but after she had snapped, hissing at him to leave her alone and storming upstairs to bed, he left her to it. Whatever he believed made her do it, Lori considered, it couldn't be worse than the truth.

Still, she had insisted, and eventually, after accepting just how unhappy living here was making her, Hank had reluctantly agreed.

It hadn't taken them too long to find themselves a new place on the other side of town. It was a little bigger, which was the reason they were giving their friends for the move, but not as well located. Most of the house was packed now. All the crockery that they wouldn't need to eat a last few simple meals was packed, and all their spare clothing and bedding wrapped up in bundles. Most of the shelves were empty, their contents filling the boxes that lined the hallway. There wasn't much left to do now that could be done before the final moving day.

Even now she still always managed to get far more done in the morning than the afternoon. It was so easy to concentrate, but as soon as twelve o'clock came around she would have to stop, turn on the lamp and go to prepare lunch. The same compulsion still keeping its hold on her. She knew she would never escape it as long as she remained in this house.

Lori hugged herself and looked around the living room. It felt cold. With most of the decorations and items they had bought since his death packed away the house once against had the stark, unloved feel of old Harry's time. The walls were bare, the tables littered only with those bare essentials needed to live. Nothing warm. Nothing homely.

It scared her how comfortable she found it. That they didn't need any of these superfluous knick-knacks that cluttered up the place. Simple, clean, utilitarian. They were better off saving money for an emergency, not flittering it away on such nonsense.

No. No, it was their house. They could spend their money as they saw fit.

But this wasn't their house any more. That was why she had to get out. To run and start anew. She did not know how, but old Harry still claimed this place, his will superseding her own. She had to accept the inevitable.

But now it was coming up to lunchtime. It was a good job she had finished that last box. She turned to the kitchen, but stopped herself and turned back. She was forgetting something.

Walking to the corner of the room, a tear running down her cheek, Lori reached out and turned on the lamp.

The Call

1934

Damn the woman. Phillip gave up trying to read his newspaper, folding it roughly and letting it fall into his lap. *Damn her to hell!*

The train was speeding down the line, the regular clack of the carriage wheels on the rails sounding over and over again. Phillip's body jogged with each movement, bobbing and leaning in unison with the two strangers who shared his compartment as it rushed through the English countryside. He had been attempting to read the broadsheet on and off for the entire journey, but as always the motion of travel made him nauseous. He sighed. He had hoped that he would at least be able to use the time during this annoyance of a journey to keep up with the news from abroad. The Secretary of State had made it clear that this visit was to be treated as personal time, and therefore had not allowed Phillip to bring any official papers along with him. He was forced to rely on the newspapers, and they were so irritatingly vague. The forced inaction burned away at his patience.

With nothing better to do, he pulled the letter from his

inside jacket pocket. He couldn't read it without feeling sick, but taking it out and looking at it was at least a break in the monotony. He knew everything it said anyway, and could condense its contents into a far simpler form than the writer had used.

The whole situation was intolerable. There was simply too much going on to be away from Whitehall. India was playing up again, and since the markets had crashed nothing about the economy had been stable.

Phillip Anderfold held a position within the Ministry that many men his age would envy, and his prospects depended on his keeping abreast of the global situation. Being away from the city for any length of time was unacceptable. But now his mother had contracted the influenza, of all things, and with her typical hysteria he was recalled from London with all haste to attend her. The letter, written in his sister's hand but surely using his mother's words, did, in his opinion, completely overblow the situation. He was certain he would arrive at the house to find her sitting by the fire with a blanket around her knees, suffering from nothing more than a common cold.

This would not be the first time he had been forced to endure one of her panics. Phillip's mother was notoriously paranoid concerning any kind of illness. Her own parents had perished in the great Spanish Flu outbreak of 1918 and since then her fear of sickness and infection had been ingrained and insurmountable. Phillip recalled a childhood growing up in a home where the sharp scent of disinfectant coated every surface, and where the slightest winter sneeze or running nose would have him immediately taken from school and placed in a quarantine of blankets, heartening soups, and unpalatable medicines. All activities that might weaken or excite him would be forbidden. Even reading would be judged too dangerous, lest it strain his mind and bring about a fever.

For such a studious boy as Phillip, the days spent lying inactive with nothing to occupy him had been pure torture. In that desperate boredom, the young Phillip would appeal to his father. Great and stern, Mr. Anderfold had been a serious man with little time for frivolities, but when it came to the raising of children not once in his life had he questioned his wife's judgement. He was a traditionalist and would no more have given an opinion on childrearing than he would have accepted a woman's advice on his business affairs.

Crumpling the letter, Phillip thrust it back into his pocket and sat staring irritably out of the window. For the remaining hour of his journey he watched as the train sped through towns and village stations, the countryside becoming progressively familiar.

He rarely visited his family home. Since his father's death only his mother and sister remained, and he found small pleasure in either of their company. His sister, Mary, had the same temperament as their mother; skittish and overwrought, and liable to the most enraging flights of girlish fantasy. What letters did pass between them rarely contained anything of real interest. There was little about his business that she would understand, and her missives consisted of nothing but witterings regarding goings on in the village. Rational and ordered thought were what Phillip Anderfold believed in, not the petty frivolities of women.

Eventually, the train arrived at Phillip's destination. As it began to slow, Phillip stood to gather his luggage. The locomotive hissed and steamed as it pulled into the station, jolting the passengers and nearly throwing Phillip off balance and into the lap of the man seated next to him. Grumbling an apology, Phillip manhandled his suitcases out of the compartment, around an elderly man who seemed to be wandering the corridor aimlessly, and pushed his way out onto the platform.

He looked around. Not much had changed in the years since his last visit. The stairs seemed to have recently had a fresh coat of paint, but that just made the drab, peeling decoration of the rest of the station stand out in relief. A couple of other passengers had also disembarked here and were now making their way out onto the road. Soon they were gone, and the train pulled away to leave Phillip alone on the platform.

He looked around, annoyed. He had replied to the letter, informing them when he was due to arrive. Mary should have met him here with the car, or at least have sent Fawles. Snarling, he made his way out of the station and into the street. No one was waiting for him there either. This was unforgivable! Here he was, dragged away from London by his hypochondriac mother, away from his very important work, and they had not even the courtesy to be here on time. It was outrageous!

He turned back into the station and sought out the Stationmaster. The bewildered looking lad at the ticket window was soon made to understand the situation, and within a few moments the Stationmaster was summoned. He was an old man, sporting a hunch in his right shoulder which caused him to look up at Phillip at a particularly disconcerting angle. His thinning hair was slicked back, and a tiny black moustache sat neatly trimmed and waxed on his upper lip.

"Yes sir, what can I do for you?" he politely enquired.

"I wish to use your telephone," said Phillip. "A car was supposed to be here waiting for me. This does not appear to be the case, and so I need to call ahead and see what the problem is."

The old man absently scratched his nose. "Whereabouts is you heading, sir? Might be someone can help you out?"

"Oakwood House. And a car will be sent once I have contacted them. I shall not require your assistance any further than that."

"Oakwood?" The old man regarded Phillip impudently for a moment. "I thought I recognised your look. You're the young Anderfold boy, ain't you? Old Sir Anderfold's lad?"

Phillip bristled at being addressed so. Having boarded at school and spent his holidays studying at home, he had no friendships and few connections remaining in the town that he wished to cultivate, and cared little for being recognised by this elderly Stationmaster.

"Yes, I am Phillip Anderfold. Now if you would be so kind as to direct me to your telephone I will make my call and be on my way."

The Stationmaster continued to look up at him, roughly scratching at a patch of flaky skin on his neck. "Well sir, there's where we have a slight issue. All the lines is down you see. Some problem at the exchange, apparently. Don't rightly know when they'll be up again."

Phillip hissed. Was this entire trip to be nothing but hindrance and irritation? He had no desire to make the walk to his mother's house himself. With good boots and fair weather the journey could be done in less than an hour, but he was tired and had no wish to go to such effort when he had made pains to arrange alternate transport.

"So, there is no way for me to contact Oakwood?"

"Well, I didn't say that, sir. We do have one of them Ashphones. I recall hearing that old Sir Anderfold was having one of them up at his house. Might be you could use that?"

Phillip thought for a moment. His father had indeed installed one of those damned æther powered telephones in the house. But as much as Phillip was for modern technology in its place, he had a deep mistrust of the Ashphones, as they were known. Tapping the æther-cloud for communications, they did not require the wires or connections that their electric counterparts did. If one had an Ashphone, then, with the correct connection code, one could theoretically speak to any other, anywhere on the globe. They were also clearer and cheaper to use, once the initial cost was made up. It was that cost, prohibitive to most individuals, that kept Ashphones in the realm of business and government.

They were a staple of life in Whitehall, of course. Phillip used them often when speaking to overseas offices. And there was indeed one at Oakwood. Phillip's father had borne the expense of purchasing one to allow him to speak to his business interests while at home. Phillip had, however, developed a sharp dislike for the technology. While most people lauded and praised æther communication for the clarity and convenience it offered, all too often Phillip found Ashphones would exhibit unusual and irritating flaws. Ashphones he used would often fail to connect, or calls would be cut off at random. Sometimes he could hear the echo of other voices on the line, though the technicians he spoke to assured him this should be impossible. On the most frustrating occasions it would transpire that words he had clearly spoken at his end were not those heard at the other. No one else seemed to suffer in the same way, but Phillip wasn't sure if those lacking his own standards simply didn't bother to report such things. All in all, compared to electric telephones, Ashphones were far more trouble than they were worth.

The problem was in the technology. The first of these devices had gone into production a little under a decade ago but, as far as Phillip knew, no one could fully explain how they worked. He had spoken to a number of scientifically minded folk about the inner workings of the machines, but other than vague thoughts on the so called æther-cloud and tapping into some hogwash called the Flow, they could never explain the technology to Phillip's satisfaction.

It made sense that the station would have one, even a country branchline such as this. The government had designated local stations as "Community Communication Hubs", and over the last few years a vast amount of money had been wasted, in Phillip's opinion, on ensuring as many as possible were fitted with both electric and æther telephones for public use. While most people wouldn't think of using an Ashphone for such a local call as Phillip intended, there really was no reason why they could not.

Sighing, Phillip indicated for the Stationmaster to lead him on to the damn thing. If he must, he must. The hunched old man smiled and led him around to a small room just off the platform. Inside were two privacy cubicles, each with a wooden door and a small window. Inside one was the electric telephone, with a hand written sign pinned to the door showing the room as "Out of Order". In the other was the Ashphone.

Much the same in appearance to its electric cousin, its body was a significant proportion larger. It was round, about a foot across, and had a hard wooden casing that covered the glass ætherbowl that was the basis for the science behind it. A thick rubber tube snaked out of the bottom of the case and connected to the handpiece. The dial and operation switch were on the front. It was a cheap unit, clumsy and unattractive. The ones Phillip was accustomed to in Whitehall were elegantly decorated, but clearly here that expense had been spared.

Phillip entered the cubicle and shut the door behind him. Looking back, he waited for the old Stationmaster to shuffle out of the room before turning to the machine. Taking the receiver in one hand, he flicked on the switch and waited for the Bowl to warm up. After a couple of moments a light blue glow came from a cutaway section of the wood, indicating that the machinery within was ready for use. Tapping in the code for his mother's Ashphone, he sat back on the stool provided and waited.

The speaker whispered quietly in his ear. There was no dialling tone with Ashphones. Instead, once the number was entered in full, it sounded as if a long tube had been opened. It was akin to the sound made when a child places a seashell to their ear, but with a much greater sense of depth.

After a good few moments Phillip at last heard his mother's voice at the other end.

"Hello? Who's this then? Hello?"

Phillip was surprised that she had answered the phone herself. She was loath to touch anything that could possibly be avoided even when she was well, let alone during one of her supposed sicknesses. He had expected Mary to answer. This was just another sign that this entire trip was a waste of his time.

"Hello, mother?"

"Who's that?" she continued? "Sebastian? Is that you?"

Phillip sighed irritably. Whatever ailment she might or might not be suffering from, it appeared that her mind, at least, was going. He knew that he did indeed take after his father in both voice and physical appearance, but his father had been dead now three years. There really was no excuse for her to mistake him.

"No, mother. It's Phillip. I've come up from London. You sent me a letter."

"Oh, that."

"Yes, mother. Look, I'm at the station and there is no one here with the car. I can't be expected to trudge my way up to the house. Is Mary there? Or Fawles?"

"Oh, you know," continued his mother's wavering voice. "They're around here somewhere. Mary's making a bit of a fuss. I think she may be coming down with something, but she won't listen to me today."

Phillip frowned. "Mother, the letter said you were unwell, not Mary. Look, I've had to take time of work at considerable inconvenience to come up here."

"Oh, you don't need to make such a fuss. It's not like it can get any worse, is it? We'll all have to make do."

"Mother, what are you talking about? I need to get to the house. Is Mary on her way?"

"The house? Oh it's pretty much as it always has been. I can't be doing with changing anything at my age."

"Mother, will you please talk sense," growled Phillip. "I'm not in the mood to wait around while you discuss this nonsense. Where is the car?"

There was a pause for a few moments. Phillip ground his teeth in frustration. This whole business was reminding him why he returned home as little as possible.

"Mother..."

"Yes, yes," she finally replied. "You'll do your own thing, I'm sure. It's always nice when you visit, Phillip. You never visited often enough."

"Yes, but I won't until the car..."

"This is rather all new to me, I'll admit. Although it is rather exciting. I haven't felt this good in years."

Good? If his mother had dragged him away from Whitehall for absolutely nothing there would be hell to pay.

"What? Look, is Mary there?" Phillip raised his voice, "Mother, can I speak to Mary?"

"Oh, she'll be alright. You'll deal with things in your own way, you always have. So much like your father, and it's not like I can do much about it."

"Mother!" Phillip was yelling now. Whatever was going on, he had no patience for it.

There was no response.

"Mother?"

Again, nothing. Just the sound of waiting air. Phillip gave up and slammed the handpiece back into place. *Damn Ashphones!* This was why he didn't use them. Always cutting out. And what the hell was going on at the house? Was the car on its way or not?

Picking up his luggage, Phillip slammed the cubicle door open and marched out along the empty platform and outside the station. Stalking over to a nearby bench he sat himself down, pulled out his newspaper and waited. When they finally arrived, Phillips was going to have a serious talk about punctuality.

After an hour, he gave up.

Growling to himself about the ineptitude of others, Phillip took up his suitcases and began the long walk from the railway station to the house. There was no point in trying to find alternative transport. By this point he just wanted to get on with it. Clearly he would be able to rely on nobody but himself.

It was a cool day, but Phillip was soon uncomfortably warm. He followed the road for half an hour before coming to a stile in the fence. Here he left the road and cut across the low fields that were just beginning to sprout the first growth of spring. He hadn't made this journey on foot since he was a child, but he remembered it well enough and after ten minutes or so he was starting along the path up Hestings Hill.

Once at the top, the familiar countryside lay out around him. To the west, at the end of the road that curled around the base of the hill, he could make out Oakwood sitting on the edge of the farmland. Biting back a fresh stab of irritation, Phillip began the last leg of his journey. This was why he hated the countryside. Within the confines of the civilised city a journey of this distance would have taken just a few minutes, and would not have consisted of this interminable trudging through damp grass and uneven ground. His shoes were muddy and the bottoms of his trouser legs wet.

Eventually he arrived at the heavy wooden gate. The afternoon was coming on now, and Phillip was both tired and hungry. His anger flared again when he saw the car sitting unattended at the side of the house. Clearly no one had been sent to collect him. Another automobile sat outside the gate on the road, one that Phillip did not recognise. It seemed that his mother had visitors. Visitors apparently more important than her own son.

Phillip pushed open the gate, marched up the path and hammered on the door. How dare they keep him waiting like this? He was going to have to have serious words about the conduct within this house whilst he was residing there. His father would have been appalled at such treatment.

After a moment or two his hammering was answered. As the door opened, Phillip found himself facing a man he did not recognise, with thick white hair with just a few strands of dark brown remaining. He had a gruff look, but was well dressed in a dark suit and appeared respectable.

"Good afternoon?" the stranger enquired.

"Who the hell are you?" Phillip demanded, looking the stranger up and down.

"Phillip!"

The new voice came from behind the greeter, who stepped aside as Phillip's sister ran past him. To Phillip's dismay, Mary flung her arms around his neck there and then, right in view of everyone.

"Oh Phillip, thank God you're here."

Embarrassed, Phillip tried to push Mary away, but she was now sobbing uncontrollably into his shoulder. "Mary! Get a hold of yourself. What is the meaning of all this?"

The stranger who had greeted him at the door took Mary

by the shoulders, pulling her away from her unabashed embrace then gestured at Phillip. "Perhaps you should come in and sit down, sir. I assume that you are Mrs. Anderfold's son? Phillip? Mary told me that you would be arriving, but not when."

"When I arrived was over two hours ago, as well Mary knew," growled Phillip, his anger and confusion at this whole situation still simmering, "Now who are you? And what the devil's going on?"

"My name is Doctor Farlane, sir. I'm the doctor for the town."

"What happened to MacDonough?"

"He retired last winter, sir. I've been seeing to your mother since then."

"Oh, Phillip," Mary wailed once again, sobbing dramatically. "Mother's died."

"What?" The statement was preposterous. "Dead? From a cold? Nonsense."

While Mary cried, Doctor Farlane nodded sadly. Behind them Phillip saw Fawles enter the hallway from the kitchen. He walked over and took Mary, who turned and huddled against the gardener who, in Phillip's opinion, held her in a far too familiar fashion. He would have to have words with both of them. Whatever the devil was going on here there was no excuse for such improprieties.

"I am afraid it was a little more serious than that sir," said Farlane. The doctor ushered all three of them into the parlour. They all sat, and to Phillip's annoyance Fawles sat with his sister, clasping her hands in his.

"I'm afraid your mother contracted a bad strain of influenza, Mr. Anderfold," Farlane continued, "I've been treating her for the past two weeks, but she was weakening quickly. Last night it seems that she at last succumbed."

Phillip looked up. "Last night? Nonsense. I was speaking

to her not two hours ago."

'I'm sorry sir, but it's the truth. We thought it best not to mention the severity of her condition in your sister's letter, so as not to worry you. We had hoped that she would hold on until your return, when I could explain the situation in person."

His mother dead? What a ridiculous idea. But with this stranger speaking to him like this in his own home, and his sister blubbering away in the gardener's arms, it was hard to make sense of anything.

"Look," said Phillip, trying to take control of this absurd conversation, "I spoke to Mother not two hours ago from the station. When the car didn't arrive I telephoned and she answered."

"I'm afraid that the lines have all been down, sir. No calls could come through."

"I know that! That's why I used the bloody Ashphone."

"I'm afraid there have been no callers today sir. Not whilst I have been here. Miss Anderfold?

Mary sniffled into her kerchief and mumbled a negative response. *Useless woman,* Phillip thought, *Must she always fall apart at any crisis?*

"Look," he said, "I wish to see my mother."

"Of course, sir," Farlane stood. "She is in her room. If you will follow me."

Phillip bit back a churlish comment about knowing the way around his own house, and stood to follow the doctor upstairs. In truth he was happy just to be out of the presence of his blubbering sister and the over familiar gardener. He had no idea what sort of game they were all playing, but he was going to get to the bottom of it.

They quickly arrived at his mother's bedroom. Doctor Farlane opened the door and stood aside. Phillip stepped in and looked straight ahead into the dim room. There before him, unmistakeable, was his mother. She looked old. Older than he remembered her. Phillip stepped closer. Signs of the illness that had taken her were clear on her face. Her skin was pale, far too pale. Her cheeks were sunken and waxy. There was no movement. No rising of her chest or flutter of her eyelids. The entire room seemed unnaturally still and airless. Walking up to the side of the bed, Phillip reached out and took her hand. It was cold. Lifeless. He let it go immediately and it dropped heavily onto the blankets.

Phillip felt his legs weaken and he fell back onto the chair that sat by her bed. He stared at the body, his thoughts reeling. He was not a man with any deep knowledge of medicine, but even he could see, as much as his rational mind tried to deny it, that the body before him had to have been dead for much longer than a couple of hours.

A hand fell on his shoulder. Phillip realised that he was shaking. It wasn't the sight of his mother that affected him so. He had borne the death of his father stoically and solidly, and now that this illness had taken his mother his feeling towards her were little changed. Phillip Anderfold was not a sentimental man. He trusted to facts. The world consisted of things to be put in order. Rational thought was what Phillip Anderfold believed in.

And he knew his mother's voice. He was shaking, for he knew that not two hours before he had spoken to a dead woman.

Echoes

14th September, 1923

As he turned out of Parliament Square and made his way down Whitehall, Bernard Galbraith looked around at the imposing buildings that surrounded him. After his five years at university, he was used to impressive, beautiful architecture, but these buildings had something the colleges lacked. They housed the government of the most powerful empire on Earth, with an air of authority that matched or even surpassed the history that imbued the walls of Cambridge.

Locating the address he had been given, Bernard knocked and waited. After a few moments the door opened and he found himself faced by a smartly dressed young man. His clothing wasn't fancy, but had the unmistakable air of quality and expense. Bernard suddenly felt very out of place in his own, rather worn, suit. Introducing himself, he handed his letters over to the other man, who read them closely before silently indicating for Bernard to follow him.

Once through the doorway, Bernard found himself in a long, high ceilinged corridor flanked by grand portraits of sombre men in formal robes, each sharing the same glare of authority and disdain. His guide led him up a set of stairs and along another corridor to a small waiting area where he was instructed to sit. The young man knocked heavily on a nearby door then turned and left without a word.

Bernard sat there for a few moments before the door opened and through it stepped a little man in a tatty, charcoal grey suit. He had a neat moustache, spectacles, and wild brown hair that stuck out untidily from his head at all angles.

"Ah! Mr. Galbraith?" the little man asked, walking over.

"Yes, sir," Bernard stood and offered his hand, which the little man took and shook enthusiastically.

"Welcome, young man, welcome. Please, call me Carter," the little man pulled Bernard through the door, still enthusiastically shaking his hand, "Glad to have you, glad to have you. Did you find the place alright?"

"Whitehall, Mr. Carter? No, no problems. Any policeman knows the way," Bernard joked.

If Carter noticed the weak attempt at humour, he did not show it. "Good good. Now, let's get you settled in and we can make a start. You were a military man, weren't you?"

"Yes sir. Joined up in '18. I was in France for the last few months of the war."

"Good man, good man. Had to sit it out myself. Terrible asthma. Terrible. Can barely run a few feet. Was able to do my bit, though. Research and development, and all that. R&D, that's where I ended up. Terribly hush hush at the time, of course. Couldn't tell a soul. I used to get terrible letters from my sister about 'not doing my duty', and all that."

Carter's stream of friendly chatter continued as he ushered Bernard into a small, wood panelled office. His desk, Bernard saw, was strewn with the detritus of the careless academic. A few books sat in untidy stacks where they had been placed for later reference, perhaps. Sheets of paper, both typed and handwritten, covered everything so Bernard could barely see the surface, with pens, pencils, rulers and other stationary strewn at random across everything. Bernard had seen hundreds of desks like this throughout his studies. Never his own though. He preferred to keep his own workspaces as clear and uncluttered as possible.

Carter sat down in the chair behind the desk, then indicated to Bernard that he should take one across from him. As he did so, Carter began rummaging around the mess on the desk, muttering to himself until he eventually found the paperwork he was searching for.

"So, you're our latest bod from Cambridge. Let's see. Yes. Very good reports, very good. You started your degree right after the war?"

"Yes, sir," answered Bernard, "I was offered a place out of school, but deferred it so that I could join up. I started my degree right after I was demobbed."

"Excellent, excellent," Carter muttered, still reading down the page. After a moment he finally reached the bottom of the report and let it drop to the desk. He looked at Bernard over his thick spectacles, "So, Mr. Galbraith, did you ever, in your days in the trenches, utilise any æther powered communications?"

"No, sir. By the time I joined up, æther-units were no longer being issued. They were deemed too unreliable."

"That's right, that's right. But after having studied the things as you have, I'm sure you know all about this little problem we faced."

"That all the promised æther devices the army tried to use throughout the war kept failing in the field, Mr. Carter?"

"Yes, yes!" Carter exclaimed, clearly pleased that Bernard knew the answer.

Bernard was a bit surprised by his enthusiasm for such a piece of trivia; everyone who had been in France knew how æther-tech had been useless in the field. Both sides had suffered the same problem. It had never been a secret. Just one more new technology too unreliable to be useful.

"And that's why you're here, young man," Carter continued, "We need to fix it!"

"Fix it, Mr. Carter?"

"Yes, yes, my lad. That is the role to which your brilliant young mind shall be put. We are a small team, at present, but it is our job to see that the British Army has access to the most advanced equipment science has to offer. It is science that wins wars, Mr. Galbraith, just as much as men. If not more. Tactics and strategy play their part, of course, but the side with the most advanced technology shall always hold the upper hand. There are men in the Government and the War Office who are quite adamant that had all the æther-radios worked as promised, it would have taken years off the war."

"Years?"

"That's right, that's right. Years! Now, the technology has improved some since the war's end, but it's still not enough. The units we have now are little better than those we had ten years ago. Our job here, and yours now of course, is to make sure they get better. That if, God forbid, Britain ever goes back to war in Europe her soldiers have access to clear, effective communication. No more of this grubbing around with wires nonsense. Come, let me show you around."

Carter stood and gestured for Bernard to follow him. Bernard jumped up, grabbing his briefcase from the floor as the older man ushered him out. He'd been expecting a lengthy interview, and the speed of this introduction and the informal nature of Carter's conversions had completely flustered him. Clutching his briefcase to his chest, Bernard was led out of the office and ushered along the corridor, through another set of doors, and then guided into another wood panelled room. This one was far larger, with four desks arranged in the middle. Two were clearly occupied, while the other two remained empty. A number of blackboards stood around the sides of the room, all covered in mathematical formulae. Two men were stood by one of the boards in their shirt sleeves. They turned as Bernard and Carter entered.

"Here we are, here we are," Carter gestured at the men as he made the introductions, "Bernard, this is Charles Doyle," he indicated the younger of the two, a middle aged man with an impressive black beard, "And I'm sure you know of Frank Spilling? Frank, Charles, this is Bernard Galbraith, our new boy."

Bernard stepped forward and eagerly shook hands with both. Throughout his studies he had read work by both men, but Frank Spilling was a legend. Along with the Goldfarns and Terrance Farning, Spilling was one of the four men universally recognised as the founders of the science of æther. He looked frail, with thin white hair and a pronounced stoop. Bernard hadn't known he was still working, yet here he was, shaking his hand.

"It's an honour to meet you, sir. Both of you," he stammered, looking back and forth between the two men.

Once the introductions had been made, Carter indicated one of the two empty desks. "This one is yours, Bernard. It's just us four at the moment; you three here, with me across the hall. But as you can guess, we'll have someone else in as soon as we select them."

Bernard flushed. It struck him that he had been selected straight out of university to work with none other than Frank Spilling! How could anyone consider him knowledgeable enough to work alongside Frank Spilling? His palms felt damp. He hoped the two men hadn't noticed when they'd shaken his hand.

"Anyway," Carter continued, seemingly completely unaware of the effect his introduction had had on the younger man, "We're working here for now, although I imagine at some point we'll be moved somewhere more convenient and get a few more people in. For now, we've got to start banging those numbers around, see if we can't work out what went wrong in the trenches. Are you ready to get started, Mr. Galbraith?"

"Yes, Mr. Carter," Bernard stammered, "Of course."

"Well then, gentlemen," Carter turned to the others, "Why don't you bring our new recruit up to speed?"

* * *

Seventeen years later

9th June, 1940

"Welcome to Ganley House, Mr. Daniels."

Bernard leant forward and took the youth's hand in a warm handshake. Just for a moment, he was taken back to that day, almost twenty years ago, when it had been him in this young man's position, and Ron Carter had welcomed him into that small office in Whitehall. He imagined the young man before him now must be feeling much the same way Bernard had back then; fresh out of university, nervous at being hand-selected to join a team he knew nothing about. At least when Bernard had been brought in, the country hadn't been at war.

"So tell me," Bernard sat back at his desk and indicated for the young man to take his seat, "What do you know about Project Forebridge?"

"Um, nothing sir," the young man answered, as if worried that his lack of knowledge would be seen as a failing of some sort. Bernard smiled. He knew he shouldn't wind up the new recruits, but he never could help himself.

"Don't worry, lad. If you did know anything about it then something would have been very wrong. Let me start from the beginning. Would you like a cup of tea?"

"No thank you," The boy looked too scared to drink. Bernard chided himself for teasing. When Ron Carter had retired, he had warned Bernard that sometimes his sense of humour was not the most reassuring. He had to try to remember. He was the man in charge now. Just because he may not have been used to the idea yet didn't mean he didn't have to act like he was.

"Very well. What we're going to be doing here has its origins back in the last war. When we were still picking up the pieces from that one, the Brass Hats were all fuming about how unreliable new technology had been in the trenches. Especially æther-tech. Believe me, back then it was terribly primitive stuff. It was hard enough to keep anything functional in the trenches, and æther-tech was worse than most. By the end of the war, no one was bothering to use æther-radio at all. It was woefully inefficient. I'm not sure of it ever once functioning correctly in the field. So, once things were over, the War Office set up our little department to lead fresh R&D. They wanted the army to have the best equipment possible should war break out again in Europe. Æther-technology was promising marvellous things, but at the time it was unable to deliver on that promise."

"Yes sir," Daniels chimed in, "I've read several of your papers on the subject. It was the basis of most of my degree."

"You flatter me, Mr. Daniels," Bernard smiled. Flattery or not, he knew the work he had done over the last two decades was significant in scientific circles. From the focused efforts of the team he had been part of for the last twenty years, in its various incarnations, the field of ætheric technology had advanced ten-fold. It was strange to think students were now using his work as the basis for their studies, as he had once used Frank Spilling's. But the benefits of government funding were there in the research, both published and classified.

"So," he continued, "Over the last twenty years we have been developing and improving æther-tech, specifically focusing on communications. Have you ever used an Ashphone?"

"Yes sir. Once or twice."

"That was us. One of the first things we worked on. Æther communication has been the biggest leap forward in telecommunication in recent history. The basic model had been rolled out during the war, of course, but most of the time it was worse than useless. They only started growing in popularity after the war, once we had refined them so they actually worked more than fifty percent of the time. Clear, instant communications without wires! That's what they wanted, and that's what we gave them. Hate the damn name of course, but unfortunately it seems to have stuck. Do you know why the government has spent the last fifteen years pushing them into every police and railway station?"

Daniels looked unsure for a moment, sensing a trick question, "To give the public access to the best possible communication?"

Bernard laughed. "No, lad. Never believe anything a politician tells you. You'll do well to remember that. No, this war is the reason. If Europe ever went back to war, as indeed it has, the government wanted a network of instant communications set up and ready across the whole country. And we've been working on more than telephonics, Mr. Daniels. Far more. Things that haven't been released to the public yet. But it is for the field of æther-communications that you are here."

"Yes, Dr. Galbraith."

"And so we come to Project Forebridge," Bernard continued, "My next question: have you used an Ashphone recently, Mr. Daniels?"

"No, Dr. Galbraith. They've been reserved for official communications only."

Bernard nodded, then reached out to the unit that sat on his desk. It was an Ashphone, though smaller than most. He held the receiver to his ear, sighed with dissatisfaction, and then handed it over.

"Here. Have a listen."

The young man leant forward and took the proffered receiver. Tentatively, he placed it to his ear. A look of confusion crossed his face.

"That's not right sir. It sounds," the young man paused, clearly trying to find the most accurate word to describe what he was hearing, "Um… distorted?"

"That's right! Completely. That's the problem. We thought we'd got the technology down pat. We spent over a decade refining this stuff. We haven't had a single significant problem for the last fifteen years. Then, in the last few months, Ashphones have regressed back to the level they were at when we started. Sometimes they will work fine, and sometimes they will be totally unusable. Or anywhere in between. And the Top Brass are furious."

"Furious, Dr. Galbraith?"

"Yes, lad. The army are all equipped with the latest æther-comm units, you see. They rely on them. All their training and planning and preparations for this war were based around having access to clear, concise communications wherever they were in the world. Then as soon as they get out there the damn things became utterly useless. Why do you think things have gone so wrong on the continent so far? This whole mess in Dunkirk is a direct result of our communications strategies completely falling apart. We think we only managed to get so many of our lads out because the Germans have suffered the same issues."

"But how?" Daniels looked shocked. Like everyone else in the country, he had been reading the constant updates on last week's evacuation. Through some miracle of propaganda, the government had managed to turn public perception of it all into a great victory; the pluck and bravery of the English people aiding the escape from the evil might of the Hun. Few people were privy to exactly how badly things had gone, or why. Galbraith was one of those few.

"That's what Project Forebridge is about. To find out what has happened, and to fix it. Ganley House is the headquarters for the project. You're one of the first new bods we've got coming in, but soon this place will be filled with the brightest and best we can get our hands on. Forebridge is high priority right now. We need to know why æther communication is failing, Mr. Daniels. And we are going to fix it."

* * *

Seven months later
25th February, 1941

MEMORANDUM TO ALL STAFF INVOLVED WITH PROJECT: FOREBRIDGE

HENCEFORTH, ALL USE OF THE TERM "ÆTHER SCREAM" SHALL CEASE. THIS IS TO REDUCE IMPACT ON CIVILIAN MORALE SHOULD THE TERM MIGRATE FROM THE PROJECT STAFF INTO THE GENERAL POPULATION.

Bernard looked down at the memo. It had been passed around the Project Team that morning. He wished he'd kept his damn mouth shut. He hated those blasted committee meetings. What had been meant as a light-hearted comment now had the Cabinet thinking that Bernard's team were relying on fanciful day dreams. He was already finding more and more political interference weaving its way into everyday life. He had been lucky so far to avoid having a 'political advisor' forced onto the Project to peer over his shoulder at all times. In the future, he was going to have to be a lot more careful with what he said in his reports.

The trouble was, once you heard it, it was hard to unhear. It had been Daniels who had first made the comparison. When you put your ear to an Ashphone these days, where before you would have heard nothing but the calm absence of sound people had become familiar with, now there was a distant noise that sounded for all the world like a far off screaming. It wasn't obvious, you had to listen carefully; but it was there.

No one had yet deduced what this sound signified, or what was causing it, but soon enough the phrase 'æther-scream' had been adopted to describe it. It was perfectly harmless. Or at least it had been, until Bernard had been foolish enough to mention it outside Ganley House.

Bloody politicians!

Bernard scratched his beard, dropping the memo form onto a desk already covered in paper; a combination of official documents, administration for the Project, and some of it actual work. He remembered the early days back in London, when he would poke fun at old Carter for the chaotic disarray that had been his desktop. Back then, Bernard's habits had been far neater, his papers always filed correctly and his desk ever tidy. These days he barely knew where anything was. With so much going on, and the importance of his task to the military, it was all he could do to keep up with the communications and administration of the Project, let alone try to make a significant contribution to it himself.

With a heavy sigh, he leant back in his chair and picked up

the day's newspaper. A photograph of war-torn Coventry stared up at him from the top page, and he tossed it aside again. He received enough reports on the world situation through angry telephone conversations and telegrams. Bernard couldn't remember the last time he had actually read a real newspaper, even though one was delivered to his desk each morning.

Bernard hated seeing pictures of the war. All they did was remind him how much worse things were because his team had not yet fixed the problem. Ashphones were still next to useless. After years of development and preparation, in which he had played a key role, the country had been forced to completely rework and re-plan its wartime communication strategies. Men were desperately being retrained to use telegraph wires and other old fashioned signalling methods that had barely developed since the last war. The only thing that had saved them was the fact that, as far as anyone knew, the problem was worldwide, afflicting Germany as much as them.

For almost a year and a half, the men and women at Ganley House had been working feverishly to identify and correct whatever error it was that was hidden from them in the æther. But still the problem persisted. The distortion was still variable, but had gradually grown worse as the war progressed, until the chances of an Ashphone connecting were as close to nothing as made no odds. And each day they failed to find an answer brought another General or Minister to vent his anger at Bernard.

He had half expected Whitehall to pull the plug on the whole thing by now, but apparently Churchill himself had decided it was too important a problem to ignore. The side that regained æther communication first, he had declared, would have an advantage that would dramatically tip the scales in their favour. The potential benefits outweighed the ongoing costs, and so Project Forebridge continued.

There was a hard knock at the door, bringing Bernard out of his reverie. He called out an answer, and Daniels and Totteridge came in together. In the eight months he had been here, Terrance Daniels had never quite gotten over his awe of working with Bernard. Greg Totteridge, on the other hand, seemed always at ease with anyone. He had been a radio operator in France, but had taken a piece of mortar shell in his leg early on in the conflict. His combat days over - he would be walking with the stick for the rest of his life - he had been brought into the Project as a military attachment and advisor. An engineer and a soldier, he had nevertheless shown a remarkable intuition for theoretical work and was far more of an asset than Bernard had feared he would be.

"Morning, guv," Totteridge greeted him in his usual familiar way, limping across and taking a seat. Bernard often wondered how the man had managed when he was in the military proper. He had to be one of the least formal people on the team, "How was London?"

"Worrying," Bernard answered. In truth, he hated visiting the capital. The sight of so much damage and death made him feel incredibly guilty that he was getting to spend the war in such comfort. While men and women were braving the Luftwaffe, here he was in this country house, surrounded by rolling countryside, miles away from the bombing raids and evacuations.

"How did the tests on Sandy's ideas go?"

"In theory?" Totteridge answered, "Perfectly. That girl's a genius. No one can find anything wrong with her numbers. She might even be smarter than you, boss."

"We had to build up a whole new unit," Daniels cut in, "A completely new design, almost nothing from the old units. Everything matches up with the numbers, I checked myself. In theory it should offer a far more stable connection and a securer line, but in practice we're still getting exactly the same results as before."

"Damn it all," Bernard had been holding high hopes on Sandy Green's new idea. It had been brilliant; a completely fresh way of looking at the problem, and the last two months had been spent designing tests for it. The girl was one of the smartest people on the Project, with a completely unique view of the fundamentals of æther. When the war was over, Bernard knew that she was going make one hell of a name for herself in the field.

"But the thing is, there's no way it shouldn't have given us the results we wanted," cut in Totteridge, "I know I'm not the maths whizz you two are, but even I can see that those improvements should have been revolutionary. They streamlined the whole process. The new shape of the Bowl means less power is needed, connections should be quicker, everything. It should change the way we look at ætheric technology across the board. There's no reason for it not to work, but it's still screaming."

"Hey now," Bernard held up the memo, "None of that."

"Oh, come on, guv," Totteridge whined, "You know that's stupid. It's just a word."

"I know, and you know, but that's the decision from London. I'm not going to put up with another lecture on public morale just because you like the way the phrase sounds. Now sit down both of you. If Sandy's tests didn't work, then we need to define why."

* * *

Ten months later
26th December, 1941

Bernard's shoes crunched on the grass. The frost had left the ground rock hard, and Carter's wheelchair moved easily across it. The old man himself was bundled up under a thick pile of blankets, a large woollen hat on his head, and two scarves wound around his face and neck.

"Did you read that the Russian's have managed that business in Moscow?" Carter asked, from deep within his cocoon. His voice was wheezy, but retained the air of bright intelligence Bernard remembered.

"Yes, Ron," Bernard answered, with a resigned sigh.

"Of course you did, of course you did. What am I thinking?" Carter mumbled to himself.

Bernard had known about the news on the Russian Front long before Carter had. He had spent a large part of December in his rarely used office in Whitehall, and had picked up the news from Russia as and when it came in. There were some benefits to being close to the top. He was just glad that the German defeats in the eastern front had distracted the Brass from his continued failure to fix his own problem.

The two of them continued to discuss the Russian conflict as Bernard wheeled his friend along the road. He was technically on his way back to Ganley House after spending Christmas Day with his family, but had managed to arrange this stop to visit Ron Carter. The old man was living with his daughter. It was six years since his declining health had forced him into retirement, leaving Bernard with leadership of their team. Bernard wished he could see him more often. Each time he did manage to, Carter seemed a little weaker. But Bernard rarely had free time to visit old friends these days.

Eventually they reached their destination. Carter had managed to browbeat his daughter into letting him go out into the cold with Bernard for a drink at the local pub. Otherwise, he had threatened, she would have been forced to listen to their convoluted science talk all afternoon in her sitting room. As they arrived, Bernard once again questioned Carter's insistence that they sit outside, but the old man was adamant. His daughter never allowed him out, always afraid he would catch a chill. He missed the fresh air, and was quite happy to sit while Bernard bought them their drinks.

"So, how's the Project going?" Carter asked once they were settled, pint in hand, "Any breakthroughs?"

Bernard sighed, staring across the village square. It was peaceful here. So in contrast to the rest of the world. No craters in the street. No gaps where buildings had once stood. No men and women in uniform. Aside from a few public information posters, you could almost believe that the war had not reached this little corner of England.

"Nothing," he answered, "And it still seems to be getting worse. We've looked at everything, from every angle. From the amount of money we've been able to pour into this, and the theoretical advancements we've made, we should have revolutionised the entire technology. Sometimes it gets a little better and I think we're onto something, but then it gets even worse than before."

"Strange how these things work," Carter mused, "You can study and research, and think and think, but nothing will happen for years. Do you remember young Spinks' ideas on adjusting the Farning Lines? He struggled with that one for a year before we took him seriously."

"I remember," answered Bernard. That breakthrough had been one of the team's first big milestones. Archibald Spinks had been a determined man, forever trying to make up for his lingering guilt that his eyesight had kept him from the trenches. In the end, his managing to redefine Farning's earlier work was what had made mass produced Ashphones a possibility. It had been more than a tragedy when he had been killed in a motorcar accident, just weeks afterwards.

"That's what I've been hoping for," Bernard continued, "Something like that would be a godsend, but none of the ideas we come up with seem to stick."

"I sometimes wonder whether we're simply not ready for a thing such as æther communications," said Carter, sadly.

"What do you mean?"

Carter looked at him, his eyes thoughtful, "Well, have you ever wondered at how much more efficient the war machine would be if you had been successful?"

"Of course I have, Ron," Bernard looked at his old friend, confused, "That's the whole point of Forebridge."

"Exactly," Carter waved a glove-clad finger in his direction, "But have you ever considered whether that's what we *should* be doing?"

Bernard looked at his old friend. Carter had never been the philosophical type. He had always been a man of numbers, finding order and ensuring everything was in its place. Bernard' shock must have been evident, as the older man laughed.

"I know, my boy, I know, it's not like me at all, is it? But old age will do this to you, so you better be prepared for it. The body may weaken, but the mind's as good as ever. I can't get about working like you young lads. I don't have the concentration any more. But what I do have is time on my hands. Time to think about the bigger things, eh? Not just the numbers and equations, but the whole picture. So easy to forget about it, don't you think, when you're young?"

Bernard was amazed to hear the old man talk like this. With so many people dying in the world, the thought of not striving to get æther-comms working, to shorten the length of the war, was preposterous.

"You don't think that cracking the æther problem would be worth it to give us the advantage? Freeing troops from wires and unreliable communication? The benefits æther would give to the war effort?"

"Yes, but what *is* æther, Bernard? What *is* it?" asked Carter, his eyes looking up at him intensely, "We've spent the last fifty years working out how to store it, how to utilise it, how to tap it for our own ends. That's all we've ever done. That was all Goldfarn did. That's all Farning did. That's all *we* ever did. I think we often forget just how much of Thomas Goldfarn's success was pure luck. Does anyone in the world actually know what æther *is*?"

Bernard sat there, unable to find an answer. It was true. Nobody was entirely sure what æther consisted of, or how it interacted with the natural world. The processes for capturing it and harnessing it were well established, but there was no way to effectively analyse it. It was an academic problem. Bernard had studied the theories, but like most people it had been the physical applications that had taken his focus. Very few people actually worried about the other side of the coin.

"Sometimes it's worth taking a look from a new angle, my boy, a new angle," Carter continued, "Take a step backwards and look at the whole picture. If a car won't run, you can replace the tyres as many times as you want, but if you're out of petrol, you'll never fix it. Sometimes you can be so focused you forget you are only looking at a part of something. What is it you are playing with? Do you know? I don't. After thirty years of studying the stuff, never once did I give a thought about *what* I was using. Only how to use it."

Bernard didn't answer, but sat there in silence as the older man finished his drink. His mind was racing. He had never thought about looking at the problem from that angle. What if it wasn't a mechanical problem they were facing? That would make so much sense, seeing as how none of the problems had been there three years ago. Had something about the æther itself changed? If so, what? How?

What was it he was missing?

* * *

Thirteen months later
25th January, 1943

Bernard sat in the soft leather armchair and waited. There were two other identical chairs in the room, all three arranged around the small fireplace. Currently, Bernard was the only occupant. He had been waiting now for over half an hour, since he had been summoned and led here by a fussy little man in a dark suit. But he knew, despite the amount of work he had waiting for him in his own office, he would have to remain there until he was told he could leave.

Bernard did not like being left alone with nothing to occupy him. It meant he had nothing to distract him.

Living out in Ganley, sometimes Bernard almost managed to feel as if the war was fading. As the fighting on the Russian Front intensified, the immediate threat of invasion had passed. He had no children or brothers, and what family he did have were too old to be in the Service. While several of his staff had received news of lost loved ones, he didn't have to live with the same fear.

But each time he came into London everything crashed back into the forefront of his mind. As the car that had brought him here glided through the streets, Bernard had looked out over a world so unlike the one in which he was privileged to live. It was a war-zone. Looking out across the dawn-lit streets, people picking their way over rubble and around bomb craters, the holes in the scenery where their homes and workplaces had once stood, Bernard felt guilt stab through his gut. While life in Ganley House was not exactly luxury, he never had to worry about death raining from the sky. He never had to sleep under a table or on a tube station platform, huddled and praying that in the morning he wouldn't find debris and ash where his life used to be. He wasn't under the constant fear of receiving that telegram bearing news of a son or brother gone forever, without even a grave to mourn at.

Before, he had been able to console himself that his work would vindicate this comfort, and that once completed he would be able to say he played a part in bringing about a swift end to this misery. But after almost four years with nothing practical to show for it, these justifications sounded hollow. What use were mathematical workings and theoretical science to people living through all this?

Bernard was pulled from his reverie by the sound of the door opening behind him. He turned and started slightly as none other than the Prime Minister himself entered. He had a presence that filled the room, almost totally eclipsing that of the small man with a pile of papers under his arm who followed him in and shut the door.

"Ah, Mr. Galbraith," Churchill greeted him, as Bernard stood and shook the proffered hand. He had met the Prime Minister numerous times, of course, but never in such an intimate setting. He still felt the same sense of awe. As always it felt strange to hear that familiar voice in person rather than from the wireless.

The Prime Minister sat in one of the chairs, and gestured for Bernard to do the same. The assistant went to a cabinet and brought out two glasses, handing one to each of them without a word and then filling them with brandy. Bernard was slightly thrown by this gesture, quite so early in the day, but the Prime Minister took his drink and carried on as if nothing were at all unusual.

"Now, Mr. Galbraith," he said after a moment, "I've been hearing worrying things regarding Project Forebridge."

"Worrying, Prime Minister?" Bernard asked.

"Yes," continued Churchill, looking him in the eye, "Worrying. We've been waiting for the last four years for you and your team to fix this problem with the Ashphones, and there are those concerned with the amount of progress you are making in this task."

"No, but…"

"Mr. Galbraith," the Prime Minister interrupted, "I understand that this is a large problem. The Cabinet knows that you and your people are doing your very best, and we have full faith that you will find our solution. As much as I want those blasted Ashphones back up and running, I'm not going to insult you or your people by questioning whether you are working to the best of your ability."

Bernard blinked. "Thank you, Prime Minister."

Churchill took another sip from his glass before carrying on, "However, there are some concerns with the direction you have been taking."

"Prime Minister?"

Churchill held out his hand and the small man handed him one of the folders he had brought. As the Prime Minister opened it, Bernard saw that it contained copies of his own reports; weekly appraisals of the Project team's aims, ideas and efforts.

"I have been keeping a personal eye on your work, Mr. Galbraith. If we could only crack the æther problem then we would have in our hands one of the biggest advantages in this war so far. It is no secret, Mr. Galbraith, that without the Ashphone we have been floundering. Our only saviour has been the fact that Germany has been encountering the same problems. The tide of this war is turning, but it has taken far longer than we had hoped. We have held off the threat of invasion, Mr. Galbraith, and the German advance in Russia is being repulsed. We can be confident that there will soon be victory in Africa, and both sides know that the invasion of Europe must come next. For that great undertaking, Mr. Galbraith, we require every resource in our arsenal."

"Yes, Prime Minister," Bernard felt another stab of guilt.

"And some are voicing worries, Mr. Galbraith, that Project Forebridge is being focused in an unnecessary direction," Churchill held up the pile of reports in one hand and shook them, "I need answers, Mr. Galbraith, not theoretical treatises. While I understand the necessity of understanding one's enemy, I require my Generals to do so with a mind to the best way of defeating him, not to have a deeper understanding of the psychology that drives him. Likewise, I do not require our troops to understand the role æther may or may not have played in human evolution, or the greater philosophical ramifications thereof. I simply require them to have working, state of the art communications equipment."

Bernard winced. Over the last year he had been driving his team's efforts in a new direction. After that one final discussion with Ron Carter, God rest his soul, Bernard had been unable to shake his idea that the problem was not mechanical. All that winter and the following spring, the men and women of Project Forebridge had moved away from practical work and devoted themselves to studying the very essence of æther. They knew that theoretically there was no reason why their technology should not work. It had worked in the past, and nothing mechanical had changed. The only logical reasoning was that either their theories were wrong or incomplete, or the æther itself had changed.

It had not been a simple undertaking. Bernard had come under rapidly growing pressure from the War Office to produce physical evidence of their advances. He had managed to hold them off, but with each passing week he sat at his desk and penned his report with a building sense of uselessness. Their work had become almost entirely theoretical, while around them even greater numbers suffered and died in the name of freedom.

"I'm sorry, Prime Minister," he said, "But that is the direction our work is leading us. We have ruled out mechanical failings in the technology. You cannot fix a mechanical problem if you can't find it. We need to have a better idea of the fundamental theory of what we're working with in order to be capable of finding the problem."

The Prime Minister held up a hand, forestalling Bernard's protests, "Mr. Galbraith, I am not a man to tell you how to go about your work. Your team consists of some of the brightest minds in the British Empire. I am just restating that we expect each man to do his duty, and your duty is to do your utmost to fix this problem. There are rumblings in the Cabinet that the money spent on this research would be better used elsewhere. Our resources are not infinite."

"Yes, Prime Minister. I understand," Bernard wished he could explain though. The government could tell him, or encourage him, or threaten him as much as they liked, but the fact was there was no other way he, or any of his team, could see to work on the problem.

Churchill nodded. He held out his empty glass for the small man to take, then pushed himself out of his chair. Bernard quickly stood, again taking the offered hand.

"Obviously, I cannot speak with you of our grand plans, Mr. Galbraith, but let me say that by the end of the year we need your team to have made a breakthrough." He paused, and leant in, his glare emphasising his words, "By the end of the year, Mr. Galbraith."

With that, Churchill turned and exited the room, followed by his attendant, leaving Bernard standing there, his glass untouched.

* * *

* * *

Eighteen months later
7th June, 1944

Bernard looked out of his office window. The morning was low and overcast, the clouds allowing only a dull, depressing light. It had been raining on and off throughout the night, but now it seemed to have cleared.

Looking up at the clock, Bernard hoped that there were better conditions over the channel than there were over Ganley House. Six forty. It would be happening now. None of the others here at Ganley House knew that of course. Along with the rest of the country, they would all learn about it in the news later that day, for better or for worse.

Strictly speaking, Bernard should not have known about the date and time of the invasion either. He wasn't a military man. It wasn't necessary for him or any of his team to know such details. Luckily for him, Greg Totteridge had been transferred to a branch of military intelligence six months ago. Before he had gone, Bernard had taken him aside and explained his plans, and his need to know the exact dates of the invasion. It had been a vague hope. He couldn't expect Totteridge to take any risks for him. If anyone found out he had passed the information on to anyone, even Bernard, he could end up shot. But he had managed it, and Bernard had been able prepare.

No one else in the project knew why they had spent the last two nights awake and taking background readings. All around the main rooms of the house, æthometers were wired up. Ætherbowls of numerous designs were set up all over, from the original Goldfarn design that had to be reset every few minutes, to their own latest versions that could effectively burn indefinitely. His entire team had been working in shifts, taking a vast array of readings. When nothing had happened last night, Bernard wasn't sure whether he had been glad or disappointed, but upon hearing nothing on the wireless about any invasion attempts he had assumed that the bad weather had caused it to be held off. He had had the team continue their readings throughout yesterday and last night, and into the morning.

Picking up the receiver of the Ashphone on his desk, Bernard placed it to his ear. There, as always, were the distant, echoing screams. Was it all in his head, or were they stronger now? They had first used that name in jest; an easy way to identify the sound. But now? Over the last few months, with everything he had come to consider, Bernard had begun to wonder what he was really hearing.

He shook his head. He was tired, but he needed to keep a straight mind. He could not allow any poetic notions to cloud his judgement. Today, he hoped, would answer his questions once and for all. Until then, he had to stay focused. This idea was so ridiculous, he had to keep everything as scientific and clinical as possible if he wanted to avoid becoming a laughing stock.

There was a knock at the door, and Daniels walked in with the latest collation of the numbers.

"Bernard, sir," he began, holding out the paper, "Something is definitely happening."

The young man looked tired, but his eyes held a focus that Bernard hoped reflected the results. He looked over the handwritten notes and saw that, as he had predicted, at almost six thirty exactly the readings had begun to fluctuate again. For the last two days, things had been comparatively quiet. There had even been a couple of points when they had been able to make a connection through their test phones, an occurrence that had become more and more rare over the last four years.

Then, at midnight, the dials had begun to move. Not a

huge amount, but noticeable. These had kept up at a steady level throughout the night, until now.

Bernard quickly went through into the main room. Those currently awake all looked up as he entered, each of them in the process of noting down readings from the various pieces of equipment. He went straight to the main æthometer. Yes, the levels were notably higher and with far more fluctuation than the baseline they had taken two days ago.

He was right.

Suddenly, Bernard found himself crushed by the realisation that he wished he had been wrong. This confirmation of his theories, of his fears, meant a major shift in æther-theory, but also in the prospects of Project Forebridge ever succeeding.

It was also going to take a lot of explaining. He would need to thoroughly test these results, and that would require gaining a higher military clearance. He had no idea how he was going to persuade them to let him know about any military operations in advance. He was already dreading having to explain to London how he had come about this breakthrough. He couldn't allow any blame to fall on Totteridge. He was going to have to pretend that these all night tests had been for some other purpose, and just happened to have fallen on the morning of the invasion.

But there were the numbers, the solid results, staring him in the face. After four years of work, Bernard finally believed he had the answer to why æther communication had failed during both this war, and the last. He just had to hope that others would accept this radical, new explanation.

Bernard looked up, and realised that everyone in the room was staring at him in awe. Belatedly he realised that whatever he told them, they knew that he had predicted something was going to happen. It was the first time anyone had been able to discern even the slightest pattern in the distortions and fluctuations in all the time they had been working on the problem. He could see now that each of them was holding their breath. Their leader had finally made the breakthrough they had sought. Even if they so far knew nothing, they had seen that he had the answer.

That night, at midnight, the guns had started firing. Men had died and the æther had vibrated. Ten minutes ago, the invasion of Europe had begun. At this very moment, men were dying on the beaches of France in droves, and again the æther was vibrating.

Knowing that he had finally solved the greatest problem æther had presented since it was first captured, Bernard felt like a fraud. He now had to find a way to tell people that there would never be safe, reliable æther communication during this, or any war. That the project which he had been leading for so long was a dead end. That he could never say that he had made any true contribution to aid those out there on the front lines.

He had to find a way to tell them all he had failed.

* * *

Ten months later
2nd April 1945

Bernard dropped a few of the remaining files into the box. Placing the lid on top, he took the stamp that lay on the desk, freshened its ink, and struck the thick, red "CONFIDENTIAL" mark on the cardboard.

He sighed. So much work, and for what? Five years they had been here. Five years of research, money and time, with nothing practical whatsoever to show for it. While they may have advanced the science of æther by decades, Project Forebridge itself had been a failure.

After the landings in France, Bernard had explained his theories to the group as a whole and over the following few months they had focused their efforts towards confirming this latest hypothesis. Some were sceptical, but after a while, all of them began to see that it was true; at times of greater violence the æther became disturbed. They had kept taking readings at all times, and throughout the year a clear pattern had emerged that was impossible to deny; that actions in the physical world were directly affecting the meta-physical.

He had, as expected, encountered serious resistance from the War Office in his desire to know about planned offences in advance. In the end, he was granted clearance to know when operations were planned, but nothing else. He would then receive more detailed reports at a later time, allowing his group to match the readings they had been taking against the timings of military action on both sides.

Their work had soon begun to give concrete results, and an excitement had filled Ganley House that Bernard could not remember feeling for years. He, however, had sunk into a depression. As he watched his team run around, documenting their results with vigour and enthusiasm, he could only see how this work was proving over and over again that he had failed. He constantly wondered how many of those who had fallen in this war would still be alive if he had managed to find a real solution, or if he had focused his mind on any other branch of research; on medicine or weaponry. Anything that might have been some practical help.

He felt disconnected from the energy that had overtaken the rest of his team. When they weren't working, they all seemed to spend their time discussing new ideas and theories, and reassessing fringe theories that until now had been largely ignored. He wasn't sure Sandy Green even slept anymore, she seemed so excited about the whole thing.

But of course his discovery, bringing with it the fresh understanding that it did, had brought about the inevitable closure of Project Forebridge. They knew now, thanks to Bernard and his team, that the answer to the æther problem was one that they could not solve with mechanical means. The war itself was drawing to an end, with people measuring Germany's fall in terms of weeks. Having made do with telegraph and electronic communication, the army no longer required working æther-comm methods to ensure victory. People were looking forward to a time where resources would need to be allocated to rebuilding, rather than military research.

This was the official reason, and would go on the reports. But Bernard had been part of those final meetings and was aware of a second reason. Aware, and more than a little worried. Having finally been made to accept how æther had been affected by the actions of the war, the government wanted above all for this to be kept from the public.

Many in London still did not believe Bernard. While officially the government recognised and accepted the results of Project Forebridge, those less scientifically minded accused him of stretching for any semi-plausible excuse for his failures. Even those who understand were already looking to election time, and wished to disassociate themselves with any aspect of the war that would be seen as a failure. But others saw things differently. They saw the truth in what was being said, and it was a truth that they believed should be kept close to Britain's chest. If other countries had reached the same conclusions as Project Forebridge, then they were not publicising it. And if Britain was the only country to have made this discovery, it could mean a great advantage to the nation's science in the post-war period.

And so Bernard was left gathering up all of his notes, rattling around the almost empty halls of Ganley House.

Most of the team had been let go, and had left to pursue their own careers in new fields. As far as they were aware, government funding for the research was simply being stopped. Only a few had remained; those who Bernard had judged would look to continue this field of research whether or not they were working for the government. Daniels would have followed Bernard anywhere, and Bernard would have been prepared to all but beg Sandy Green to stay. As if it wasn't obvious where her passion lay. They, and one or two others, would be the kernel that remained of Project Forebridge; the descendants of that small group Bernard had joined so long ago in 1923. For now, the government wanted to keep this research under wraps, and so they were being moved, under strict secrecy, to a new location.

Bernard sighed. He had begun working on æther technology twenty two years ago. Six years ago he had discovered that half the things he had been certain of had collapsed around him. Three years ago he had stumbled upon the answer to all of it. He had felt once that if finding the answer to the question involved debunking all his previous work, he would have been more than happy to accept that. Yet somehow, having finally found the answer, he only felt a sense of uselessness. People had been counting on them. On him. And all he had was refined mechanics and a bunch of wild theories that showed that the problem had no solution. He may well have uncovered the outermost layers of something far greater, something that might reshape his entire field, but out in the real world men and women continued to die in the greatest war that mankind had ever fought, while he had done absolutely nothing to help them.

Feeling a painful lack of excitement in his task, Bernard took up the box of files and carried them from his room.

* * *

* * *

Five months later
6th August, 1945

At approximately 8:15am, local time, the bomb *Little Boy*, dropped from the US bomber *Enola Gay*, detonated 6800 feet above the city of Hiroshima, Japan, with a blast of sixteen kilotons.

In one second, over seventy thousand men, women and children died in a single fiery moment of violence and fear.

* * *

At the University of Sydney, Australia, a class of students were shocked as the ætherbowl that was the focus of their morning's lecture suddenly flared with white-blue light and burst, showering them with broken glass. Their lecturer, who had been standing by the bowl at the time, was severely injured, as were several students.

* * *

In a top secret military lab, deep in the New Mexico desert, a team of the United States' top scientists were thrown into turmoil as every active piece of æther equipment in their labs exploded at once. All the work they had been undertaking that day had been routine, and nothing out of the ordinary was noticed or recorded until their labs were suddenly transformed into a spinning galaxy of glass and wood.

On later examination, they discovered only those pieces of equipment that had not been switched on and functioning had survived.

* * *

* * *

All across the world, at that one same moment in time, each and every device connected to the Grand Æther-Flow exploded. Every ætherbowl that was under power, whether it was stand alone, part of an Ashphone, lighting, power source, or academic research equipment, shattered in a spray of glass. Whether in schools, laboratories, homes, or public houses, each and every single one reacted to the same unseen trigger.

* * *

By this time, their increasing uselessness meant that Ashphones had been almost completely abandoned. The inability for any government or institution to fix them meant that people had moved over to wired technology. There had been quite the outcry about it at the start, but after five years, people had adjusted and got on with their lives without thinking about unavailable alternatives.

This meant that the moment *Little Boy* detonated over Hiroshima, Bernard Galbraith was the only person in the entire world who had the receiver to an operational Ashphone held to his ear.

Bernard could not have explained why he was up quite so late. Since moving to his team's new quarters, he found that he rarely required more than a couple of hours sleep. He sat up most nights, pondering on the hundreds of questions his five years on Project Forebridge had brought up, trying to fight down the guilt he still held.

On a whim, he had fired up the Ashphone that sat on his desk. It was the same unit he had owned at Ganley House. He couldn't say what made him do it. He just felt the urge to lift the receiver and put it to his ear. He didn't dial a number. He had no one to call. He simply sat there listening to the same sound that had been there for the last six years; the distant echo of the æther-scream. In the silence of his office, the distant buzz sounded cold and frightening, as if it were indeed issuing from a hundred lost and forgotten mouths. He listened, not knowing what he was expecting, and waited.

And so it was, at 8:15am Japanese time, Bernard Galbraith was the only man to hear the searing scream of seventy thousand souls roar across the æther. In an instant, as an entire city died in a maelstrom of fire and agony, the distant wavering sound that had become so familiar rushed towards him through the receiver. Sudden. Deafening. Overwhelming. Bernard heard all of them. Each scream. Every cry of pain. All mixed together in one moment, yet each clear and distinct. The death cry of a city, echoing through the æther in one powerful, destructive, howling shriek.

As the 'phone unit burst in a shower of wood and glass, Bernard felt the pain of every single death course through his body. He felt his own soul blend with that pain, filling and overriding his consciousness before everything pulled away and left him in a overwhelming field of blue light.

* * *

No definitive cause was given for the death of Doctor Bernard Galbraith. His body was found on the floor of his study early in the morning of 6th August, 1945, when his associate, Terrance Daniels, came to inform him of the destruction of most of the operational equipment in their laboratory.

At first it was thought that the explosion of the Ashphone on his desk was the cause, but on examination it was found that his body had received no physical damage from the low key blast. Suicide was also considered, as his colleagues reported he had been suffering a depression. However, as no drugs were found in his system, and no injury was found on his body other than a slight burning on his right ear, the inquest's ruling was inconclusive.

The Collection

1972

Hannah grimaced as the bony hand slid insidiously up her back. As his fingertips caressed the fibres of her jumper she tried to angle her body so that her next steps would move her away from him without seeming overtly rude. He just stepped in closer, putting his arm around her waist and holding her close against him as they walked. His quivering fingers rested on the belt of her skirt, pressing into her flesh through the coarse material. His pervading scent filled her nostrils; the familiar mixture of peppermint and carbolic soap.

"Here you are, young lady," Dr. Goodman drawled in his infuriatingly obsequious yet patronising tone. They had finally reached the door to the Æther Room and as he retrieved the key from his pocket Hannah was at last able to pull away. Carefully he inserted the thick, old fashioned thing into the lock. There was a loud click, followed by a soft grunt as he pushed open the heavy door.

"All there, ready for you as always," he turned back, his eyes roaming her body.

Hannah forced her face into a smile and held out her hand for the key. Instead of simply handing it to her, Dr. Goodman pressed it into her palm and clasped her hand between both of his.

"Thank you, Dr. Goodman," she said, desperately holding her expression as she extracted herself from his clammy grip and backed into the room, "But you know you don't have to escort me here every time. I do know my way around by now, you know."

"Oh my dear, my dear," the old man chuckled, "You modern girls don't understand this sort of thing, but what sort of gentleman would I be if I didn't accompany you? I know it's hard enough keeping up with the boys in your classes. What little I can do to help you along is my pleasure."

Hannah felt her hands clench as she battled the urge to slap him across the face. His patronising tones never became any less maddening, no matter how many times she had to hear them. He smoothed down his thin, oily hair with one hand, before reaching out as if to pat her on the cheek. Hannah hastily stepped backwards, through the door and out of his reach.

"Thank you again," she said hurriedly, "I'll make sure I bring the key straight back once I'm done."

Shutting the door as quickly as she could while still seeming polite, Hannah flicked on the ætherbulbs and bit back a curse. She shuddered as the soft light filled the small room, subconsciously brushing at her back where his hand had rested.

God, she hated that odious, slimy old man! He was the reason most of the girls in the college avoided this library. If only she had that option. She wished, as she had so many times before, that there was something, anything, that she could do about it. But access to the Æther Room came through Dr. Goodman. All making a fuss would do would be to lose her that access. Or worse.

Closing her eyes, Hannah took in a deep, slow breath, held it, and counted to ten before exhaling. Slowly she felt the calming atmosphere of the room allow her to focus. Despite the gauntlet she had to run each time she came here, it was always worth it. She was safe now, shut away from the unwelcome attentions of lecherous old men.

For all that it was little used, the Æther Room held one of the library's proudest collections. Before the war, when the study of æther had been more fashionable, the university had made a point of collecting rare or unique journals and works on the subject. There were papers here by Farning, Carter, Spilling, Galbraith, and even original notebooks by both David and Thomas Goldfarn. There were also several post-war papers by Sandra Green and Matthew Bodine. It was a goldmine for anyone with any serious interest in the history of theoretical ætherics.

But that gold came at a price. As with all the rare collections at the university, you had to have permission from both a professor and the relevant librarian to be allowed access. And the librarian for this collection was Dr. Goodman: a man at least fifty years her senior, with wandering hands and a robust misogyny. His attitudes and attentions towards women were well known in her college. Hannah wished it wasn't totally useless to complain. She knew what had happened to girls before her who'd done so. Her only option was to grit her teeth and endure the long walks through the archives while his quivering hands nonchalantly roamed her body.

Shaking the memory of the old man's hand creeping down her back, Hannah dumped her books on the table in the middle of the room. As usual, she was alone. With no one else currently working on the same speciality, Hannah rarely had to endure any company here. This suited her just fine. She had come to think of this room as her own. A safe place. It was a silly notion, she knew, but Dr. Goodman had never once followed her inside.

She stepped over to the wooden shelves that ran along one wall and placed her hands gently on the books. Touching their soft, worn leather covers gave her a sense of focus. Whether it was the isolation, or maybe her mind actively blocking out the preceding minutes, the distractions of the outside world never found her here. Here she could work for hours without needing a break.

With a contented sigh, she selected the books she required. Taking a seat, she placed them on the table and dug her own notes from her bag. Finding her place, she uncapped her pen and began to write.

Through the view of modern studies it is clear that the single most important aspect of ætheric theory is one that has been either forgotten or ignored for much of the last seventy years; that at all time the æther surrounds us. Thomas Goldfarn states this clearly in his original theories, and his ideas were later confirmed by the studies of both Farning and Eddlestone. However, the attitudes of David Goldfarn, who continued his uncle's work and is widely accredited with establishing the tone of the next fifty years of research, firmly set a focus on application over theory. Through the filter of his work, and social attitudes of the time, an entire branch of study was marginalised. With only a few notable exceptions, development of the science has been firmly geared towards practical application.

While it is true that early technology drew almost exclusively from the Grand Æther-Flow, this was due to the limitations of that technology, rather than the nature of æther itself. Modern advancements, notably the work of Sandra Green, have proven that most equipment can run on the background æther-levels present around us.

Green's work, following on from her time spent with Galbraith in the forties, developed Goldfarn's original theories at a time when research in the field had become unfashionable. After the Æther Event in 1945 no definitive connection was ever made between æther and the radiation caused by nuclear fission, yet despite this lack of proof the agreed orthodoxy is that this connection must exist. During this time, Green's theoretical work focused on the aspects of shared resonance between…

* * *

Hannah woke with a start. The image of a pair of sorrowful eyes floating in a strange darkness wavered in her mind before being displaced as immediate sensations flooded back. She couldn't remember falling asleep. She could feel cold paper pressed against her cheek, and a pair of hands kneading at her shoulders. Looking down, she realised with horror that her face had been resting on one of Goldfarn's original notebooks!

"God, what…?" she began.

"There, there, young lady," came Dr. Goodman's oily voice. Hannah froze, her stomach turning with sudden revulsion at the realisation that he was standing behind her; his hands rubbing her back through her sweater.

"No harm done," he drawled as her eyes widened. The disgust was almost physical. "It's tiring, eh? All this hard work. Got to put the effort in to keep up with the boys?"

Hannah recoiled. He had been in here. Alone with her. While she slept. This was her place. Her sanctuary. The thought of him actually inside with her filled her with such repulsion that she almost retched. How long had he been here? How long had he been watching her? How long had his bony hands been on her back?

She jumped up, bashing her chair against his legs, and

quickly moved to put the table between them. She looked at her watch. It was just past nine. This section of the library closed at nine. When she hadn't returned the key on time she had given him the excuse to come and find her. Stupid. Stupid!

The old man was looking around the room with a look of discomfort on his face. Could he actually be realising the inappropriateness of his being in here? Alone with a young female student? She couldn't imagine him worrying about the situation. He hadn't in the past. It was never *his* reputation that was ruined by the rumours that spread about.

"I'm so sorry, Dr. Goodman," she stammered, "I don't even remember closing my eyes."

She hurriedly gathered up the books and placed them back onto their shelves. She no longer felt focused and relaxed. The tension and revulsion she normally felt in Goodman's presence was magnified by this intrusion. Despite the table between them, he had never felt so unavoidably *close* as he did right now.

"I understand, my dear," Goodman's tone was better suited for a small child than a post-graduate student, "This room has a strange feel to it, I've always thought. I never came here much myself, before you began your studies. It always has an uncomfortable air to it, does it not? Old book collections can have that effect sometimes, you'll find. I can't imagine it's good for a young lady such as yourself to endure it."

"I'm fine, Dr. Goodman, I promise," Hannah said, biting back yet more irritation. Bile was churning in her stomach; a physical sickness that grew harder to fight with each passing second. She hastily slid the key across the desk towards him, keeping the solid table between them. If he touched her again she would probably scream. "I'm so sorry, I promise I won't let it happen again. Excuse me, but I'm running late."

Brushing past him as quickly as possible, Hannah fled from the room.

* * *

"I'm fine, I promise," Hannah argued, trying to keep the desperation out of her voice, "Dr. Goodman, you really don't need to…"

"Nonsense, my dear," he answered, "After your little episode last time, it would be remiss of me not to check in on you from time to time. Just to make sure you're coping with the work, you understand."

Hannah tried to pull the key, and her hand, from between his moist palms but he held on tight. His touch made her stomach churn. The sense of disgust she had felt yesterday hadn't fully faded all evening and she had fallen asleep to twisted visions of him standing in the room, beckoning her inside. She'd had nightmares of his hands sliding over her back as she lay facedown and helpless on the table, his rancid breath unnaturally loud in the enclosed space. Now the revulsion threatened to burst forth again. She had the overwhelming need to step back into the room, but felt terrified that if she did he might follow her inside.

"We wouldn't want you to push yourself too hard, would we?" he said, looking at her with what could almost have passed for concern, "I'll be back in an hour, my dear. How about that?"

Hannah finally pulled her hands away and skipped back through the open door. Dr. Goodman stood there for a moment or two, as if ready to follow her inside again. Hannah tensed. She wasn't sure what would happen if he did. She couldn't fight the irrational fear that it would somehow irrevocably taint the room for her.

Finally, with one last glance through the door, he turned

and wandered away through the stacks. He hummed to himself as he went, the sound echoing softly between the bookshelves like a sinister parody of a lullaby.

As soon as he was gone Hannah slammed the door shut as hard as she dared. Why? Why did Goodman have to be in charge of this, of all sections? It wasn't as if other professors or librarians didn't have similar views about girls studying. And most of the boys in her lectures felt the same way, even if they weren't so open about it. It was just part of life. But Goodman was something else. The others she could deal with and ignore. With Goodman it took every ounce of her will to hold her tongue. To fight the urge to reach out and slap him across his soft, sagging face and tell him exactly how much his inappropriate desire to 'check up on her' disgusted her.

But as infuriating as it was, Hannah knew it would do no good to complain. Girls who had soon found stories spreading around the campus. Rumours questioning their moral standing. It did not matter that there was never any evidence. Once that sort of thing began it was already too late, and it took next to nothing to ruin a girl's reputation and career prospects. In the end it would be the word of a young post-grad student against that of a long-standing and well respected member of staff, and it always ended the same way.

She threw her bag down on the table and pulled out her notes, but didn't go to the older notebooks as she usually did. As much as she needed their calming influence right now, in her current state she did not trust herself with anything so valuable. Causing any damage to the precious collection would be just as good a way of getting her thrown out of the library as a complaint against Goodman, and with more justification. Instead she drew out some of the newer, less fragile works and settled in.

As she sat down and set the pile of textbooks on the table, the ætherbulb above her flickered. Hannah looked up, frowning. That was unusual. All the libraries were fully fitted with ætherbulbs, as the properties of æther-light were far less harmful to paper than electric light. They were also calmer on the eyes, and more reliable. While they did, of course, need changing occasionally, they usually just began to slowly dim. She had never seen one flickering like that before. She watched for a few moments, but the defect did not repeat itself and so she returned to her work:

Green's later work with Sheridan demonstrated, to a far clearer extent than had been seen before, how much æther fills the space around us. It was these studies that effectively disproved Ganding's alternate Strand Theory, showing beyond doubt that æther surrounds us, rather than being pulled down from the Grand Æther-Flow. Strand Theory's assertion that æther was pulled in strands from the Flow to connect with and power correctly aligned devices, was never fully accepted by the scientific community but remained a popular sub-field of study until Green and Sheridan's work in the late fifties.

The significance of Green's work has still to be fully understood. The fact that we can now know for a certainty that all æther technology is connected through the Grand Field, rather than each being separately drawn from a greater source, lends credence to various fringe theories that have grown up in the last few decades; specifically, the theories of how æther reacts and responds with the human body.

Recent advances in neuroscience have shown that the chemicals used in the earliest experiments with æther closely correspond with those found in the brains of mammals. While the technology has developed and been greatly refined since then...

* * *

"How are we, my dear girl?"

Hannah stopped writing and stared down at her notes, refusing to look up until she could master her expression. Her mind burned with exasperation. This was the third time this afternoon Dr. Goodman had appeared at the door, uninvited, to follow up on his unwelcome offer to check on her 'wellbeing'. Each time, Hannah had been forced into several minutes of uncomfortable small talk which had broken both her concentration and her mood.

"Yes, Dr. Goodman," she answered without looking up, not quite keeping the anger and frustration out of her voice, "I'm perfectly fine. I'm just trying to concentrate. Please."

"Hmm, you seem a little strained, my dear," he replied, looking her over with what he clearly thought of as a worried, considerate gaze. He still hadn't entered the room itself. Instead he hovered uncomfortably in the open doorway. She could tell without a doubt he wanted to come closer; to share the confined, intimate space with her, but something seemed to be holding him back. Each time he had turned up that afternoon it had been the same; he would move, then flinch back as if he felt he was being watched and fear of this hidden observer prevented him from acting. Whatever the reason Hannah was glad of it, but having him standing there still gave her the inescapable feeling of being blocked in.

"Are you sure you are not too tired?" he frowned.

Battling to keep her features calm, Hannah finally turned to look at him. All she wanted was for him to leave and go as far away from this room as possible and stay there. Preferably tripping and severely injuring himself on the way.

"Yes, Dr. Goodman," she managed, "I am fine. I'm sorry about yesterday. I'd been working late the night before. It won't happen again."

"Mmmm-hmmm?" The elderly librarian looked less than convinced.

Get out of here, you leery old man! Hannah's face twitched as her mind bellowed the words she wanted so much to say out loud. She said nothing, in fear that she would be unable to prevent herself from snapping. She simply stared at him, waiting for him to read the hint in her eyes and leave her to her studies. He continued to hover in the doorway. With every excruciating moment he remained, the tension in Hannah's body grew until it was almost physically painful.

Above her, the light-bowl flickered.

Looking up, Dr. Goodman shivered. "This room always feels so unwelcoming, don't you think?" he asked, "I worry about you, my dear." Pulling his tweed jacket around him, he at last turned to go. "I'll return to escort you out in an hour." Taking one last look around the room, he finally turned and left.

Fuming, Hannah looked down at the paper before her. The interruption had completely broken her train of thought, just as each of the previous ones had done. She had only another hour before the Library closed, and she planned to leave long before then to avoid giving Goodman the chance to come and fetch her. These interruptions were unbearable. She had deadlines!

Sighing, she roughly pushed the paper away from her and stood. At this rate it was going to take weeks to gather all the notes she needed. In fact, she wouldn't be surprised if she was put off the whole damn subject!

Slamming her current textbook shut, she shoved it back on its shelf. She needed a distraction. Something to bring her mind back to her work. Stepping over to the shelf of original notebooks, she gently placed her hands on the closest one and let her fingers rest on the binding. Slowly, she felt her sense of focus return. She pulled the book off the shelf. It was one of Farning's. Letting it fall open in her hand, she began to read at random. She knew this passage, but as she read she felt her desire to study rise; sharp and focused. Having these handwritten notebooks made her feel as if she had a physical connection to these great men and women, scientists all, that helped her remember why she loved her studies. They reminded her that it was worth the gauntlet she had to run, and helped her to forget.

It was this line of thought that had led her to the focus of her post-graduate studies. Not many people had openly discussed the idea of æther clinging to objects, or how it interacted with the human brain. Despite seventy years of research, it was still a largely untouched field. But as far as Hannah could see, it was the only logical connection. Green and Sheridan's work had proven that æther surrounded everything. It stood to reason that this must have been the case throughout the whole of human evolution. Knowing this, it had to be assumed that æther must have some kind of relationship with the human body. And if so, would it affect people differently? Could some people be more in tune with the æther than others?

Deciding to work on a different chapter for her remaining hour, Hannah searched through the cabinet. Selecting a few of the books, she piled them on the table. She sat down, letting her mind relax and endeavouring to fit in as much work as she could for the time that remained her.

If we accept Green's work as vindication for the various theories collected by Tanning then we can see that æther may well have played a far greater part in our evolution, both biologically and psychologically, than has been previously recognised. The myopic vision of æther as a fuel, suitable only for the design and powering of tools, must now be expanded to something far greater. It is as if we believed that the wind was only used for powering windmills, and suddenly realising that we had been using it to breathe.

The most fascinating application this work has brought about is the concept of æther as an emotional conduit. If we accept that the chemicals in the brain are somehow conductive to the drawing forth and focusing of the æther around us, then could not our own emotions be somehow manipulated to charge the æther? Would it be possible - as Tanning suggested - to consciously affect those around us? Or even affect physical matter? Could we not possibly examine previously maligned ideas, such as telepathy and telekinesis, in a whole new, scientific light?

Another avenue of thought when we consider these ideas is whether people might have varying levels of influence over the æther. It has for years been an old wives tale that some people have more trouble with ætheric technology than others. We have all heard urban legends of people for whom technology powered by the æther will function incorrectly or not at all, or stories of people who have experienced strange effects through using simple machinery. Could these be more than simple conjecture? Could it be considered with scientific seriousness that some people have such a strong natural connection to the æther that they can cause these unexpected reactions?

Taking Tanning's views and filtering them through the implied assumptions of Green's work, could we categorise people into three groups, impactive, sensitive, and neutral. Those considered "Neutral" would be those of to whom æther reacts just as expected, while those categorised as "Impactive" or "Sensitive" would be those rare individuals who have some natural, genetic predisposition to be able to interact with æther, either consciously or subconsciously.

Working on this hypothesis, a series of experiments could...

* * *

The ætherbulb flickered again. Hannah looked up, frowning. Again? She had been a student of æther technology since she was sixteen and knew the workings of æther-bowls inside out. There was no reason she could think of for it to be doing that. If she hadn't been so focused on her current work it would have been interesting to look into further, but she was busy enough without taking on side projects. The problem with a subject as fascinating as ætheric theory was that unless you made an effort to stay focused your mind could get pulled into any one of a thousand directions and offshoots.

Then the door handle turned, rattling loud in the small room. She looked at her watch. *Damn it!* There was still half an hour left before the usual time the library closed. Clearly Goodman had anticipated her plans to leave early.

Desperately she began to shuffle the books together. Maybe if she managed to slip out quickly she could get away before he had the chance to lock the door and catch up to her. The light above her continued to flicker as the handle rattled.

"Young lady?" came the familiar, slimy voice, "Are you alright? The door appears to be locked."

Hannah looked over. The key lay on the desk, and she hadn't locked the door. Why would she? It wasn't as if barricading herself here would have helped her avoid him. He was probably just too overwrought with his ageing libido to pull strongly enough.

"It's unlocked, Dr. Goodman," she called out, gritting her teeth as she slid the notebooks back into their correct places in the cabinet.

The door rattled, shaking on its hinges.

"Young lady, this really is not acceptable. The door is clearly locked. If you would be so kind as to open it."

Sighing, Hannah stomped over to the rattling door, grasped the handle and pushed. It opened easily, revealing Dr. Goodman catching his balance after quickly stepping away. As the old man looked up at her disapprovingly, Hannah was forced to console herself with the thought of how satisfying it would have been to see the door hitting him square in the face.

"Young lady, it is prohibited to lock oneself in these rooms. You know my rules. What would happen should you be overcome and require assistance?"

Hannah stepped aside and gestured at the table, where the key lay quite out of arms reach. "I'm sorry, Dr. Goodman, but the door was not locked," she snapped, "As you can see, the key is over there. With how you were rattling the door to get in here with me, I would not have had time to unlock it and return the key before you could have opened it yourself. You must have not turned the handle fully."

She had spoken far more harshly than she had intended and could see the disapproval in Dr. Goodman's face. The light flickered. Her anger flared. How dare this old pervert judge her!

"My dear, that is not the sort of tone I would expect from a young lady," he frowned, "I am sure that you must be over-working yourself, to speak to me in such a way."

Hannah knew that she shouldn't rise to him, but her temper was building faster than she could control it. Weeks of frustration and anger were threatening to spill out. She fought to hold herself back, but her mind raced with how satisfying it would feel to give in and slap him across his soft face.

The light flickered again. Goodman looked up. His gaze broken, Hannah took advantage of the distraction to turn and gather her things.

"Dr. Goodman," she spoke through gritted teeth, "I think you'll find that I am quite capable of the work I have been set, as would any woman. And quite frankly I find your insinuation that my gender means I have less ability than any other student at this university incredibly insulting. Now, if you will excuse me, I shall be on my way."

She stood in the doorway, with the elderly librarian

blocking her exit. There was a new edge to him. Something had changed in the way he looked at her. She was used to feeling him undress her with his eyes, but now he seemed rather to be sizing her up as an opponent. Hannah had the uncomfortable feeling that she was at last seeing a glimpse of the real Dr. Goodman, the sly old man who had spent a career manipulating his position to harass young girls without fear of retribution rather than the bumbling old man persona he put on to do so.

After a few moments the mask returned and he stood aside. Reaching out he placed his hand on her shoulder as if in a gesture of placation, but it straight away began to slide down her back.

"Young lady, I am merely…"

Hannah turned, knocking his hand away and glaring up at him.

"Dr. Goodman, if you place your hand on my body one more time I will not be responsible for my actions, I promise you!"

It was all Hannah could do not to hit him where he stood. How dare this crumbling anachronism treat her in such a way! For a brief moment she could see shock in his eyes, but it was quickly replaced by a calculating malevolence. She stood firm, refusing to back down or look away. She knew what had happened to other girls who had stood up to Goodman. She knew that she would suffer for her outburst, but right now she didn't care. It would have been too late to defuse the situation even had she wanted to, but now she had finally spoken up she had no desire to do so. She wasn't going to put up with it any more. No more pretending that any of this was acceptable. She had finally reached her limit. She could not, would not, take this insulting, offensive behaviour any more.

Turning, she stormed away before anything else could be

said, leaving the disgusting old man standing in the doorway with the ætherbulb flickering behind him.

*　*　*

As he watched young Chambers storm off, Goodman shook his head. Girls these days. They just didn't understand how the world worked. It was all these foolish women's libbers putting silly ideas in their heads. In his day, girls hadn't made a fuss over such little things. Nowadays they were always so busy trying to play at being men, and then got all hysterical over a little friendly attention. It would be sweet if it were not so tiresome.

He sighed. It was such a shame when one of them got over-emotional like this. And Chambers was a pretty little thing. He would miss their walks. But he had dealt with these situations before. He would have a few words with his staff; make sure a few choice rumours began to spread. He had no worries about himself. If it came down to it, it was the word of an eminent college librarian of forty years standing against that of an unstable young girl who had clearly been overworked in a post graduate program she did not have the emotional fortitude to cope with.

Behind him, the light flickered again. He stepped into the room and looked up at it, frowning. He would have to get someone down to check on that. He didn't like it when something was out of place in his library. Then an idea struck him; it might be worth making people believe it was somehow Chambers' fault. He smiled. Yes, with a little thought he could probably make that work.

The bulb continued to flicker on and off, faster and faster. Goodman's eyes were beginning to ache. He wasn't prone to headaches, but when they did come they were, as a rule, acutely painful and would render him bedridden for the rest of the day. He held up one hand to shield himself from the light. He felt less and less well by the minute. Quite unsettled. This business with the Chambers girl must have struck something within him.

As the pain in his eyes rose, it was matched with a sharp bilious sensation in his stomach. Wincing, Goodman turned to leave. He had barely stepped outside when suddenly the door swung around and slammed shut.

Goodman jumped as the crash echoed around the stacks, and the sudden movement caused the pain in his head to spike. Cursing, he looked around. There was no-one near by. How had the door swung shut on its own like that? There were no windows here, at least none that could open, so it couldn't have been the wind. He shook his head. He must have pulled the door without realising it. Yes, that must have been it.

Away from the flickering light, the pain in his eyes and the nausea that had so suddenly built up in his stomach began to subside. Wiping his face, Goodman looked through the frosted glass in the door. The light was still flickering within. He reached out, meaning to open the door and turn off the switch, but as his hand touched the handle the same pain and nausea washed over him in a wave of discomfort so acute that his legs nearly gave out from underneath him. He cried out in shock. For the first time he could remember, he felt the unsettling feeling of not being welcome in his own library.

Goodman let go of the door and staggered back. The heavy door key fell from his fingers and there was a dull crack as the metal impacted on the hard wooden floor, snapping cleanly in two. Goodman swore loudly, stooping down to pick up the pieces. How on earth was he to keep the girl out if he couldn't lock the damn room?

That bloody light. The rectangle of frosted glass continued to flicker, each flash causing a fresh spike of pain. Grabbing the handle, he fought down the sudden discomfort and pulled at the heavy door. It didn't open. He tried again, with both hands. It simply rattled on its hinges, just as it had before Chambers had unlocked it.

Unable to hold on against the miasma of repulsion building within him, Goodman let go of the handle. He was overcome with the ridiculous notion that something did not want him here. As if the room itself rebelled against his presence. As he looked into the flickering light beyond the glass, he could almost feel a conscious barrier standing alongside the physical one.

Nonsense. He shook himself. The lock must have somehow tripped when the door slammed, that was all. Nothing more. At least it meant the door was barred and he didn't have to worry about Chambers gaining access against his wishes. No one else would either, but that did not bother him too much. He would make up some excuse for closing the room. He could get a locksmith in later to replace the lock. What did it matter to him if a few students were put out for a short while?

Perhaps he could find a way to pin this on Chambers as well? Yes, that could work out nicely.

Pocketing the two pieces of broken key, Goodman turned and walked back down the cool stack, humming quietly to himself. With each step the feeling of nausea faded. After he had gone a few paces, the light around him suddenly dimmed. He turned back and saw that the room's ætherbulb had finally failed, leaving the window in the door once again dark and unremarkable.

* * *

Hannah stood before the tall oak library doors. It was Monday morning; two days since her outburst. She hadn't returned all weekend, afraid to face Goodman's inevitable response and the trouble she knew would be waiting for her. She had spent the time working on her paper as best she could, but now she needed to get back into the Æther Room. She had been hoping against hope that the weekend might have given him time to forget. She knew there wasn't much chance - none of the other girls who had spoken up to the old pervert had had such luck - but she clung to the hope that as she had not yet made any official complaint that he might have decided to let things go. It sickened her that she had to rely on that old man's charity. From now on, she told herself, she would not put up with anything. Next time she would make an official complaint, for all the good it would do. She would use the library on her own terms or not at all. She refused to let herself go back to how things had been.

Squaring her shoulders, she stepped forward. That old fossil wasn't going to stand in her way. She was a strong, modern woman, and she would not allow the world to treat her like this. Marching through the open doors, she made her way straight to the main desk. To her relief, Goodman wasn't there. She was so used to finding him eagerly awaiting her arrival that it was almost a shock to see an attendant there in his place.

"May I have the key to the Æther Room please?" Hannah asked the attendant.

A boney woman in her middle years, the attendant peered at Hannah over thick rimmed glasses. "Would you be Hannah Chambers?"

"Yes."

The woman's look swiftly turned from suspicious to chilly, and Hannah felt a sickly feeling of dread settle in her chest. The look in the attendant's eyes told her everything she needed to know. Goodman had obviously been about his usual business. She should have known it was useless to hope otherwise. She didn't know what story he had begun to spread about her to his staff, and she didn't want to know. All she could do now was pray that it would not spread much farther than the library and ruin her reputation around the rest of the university.

"I'm sorry," the attendant announced, though her expression showed she was clearly nothing of the sort, "But I'm afraid I cannot allow you access to that *particular* collection. Dr. Goodman has had the room shut indefinitely. For maintenance."

"Maintenance?" Hannah couldn't believe her ears. He was locking *everyone* out, just to spite her? That was excessive, even for him. "What about the collection? People need to use those books. This is a university library."

"People will manage. I'm sure I can't imagine what's been going on," she sniffed and glared accusingly at Hannah, "But if Dr. Goodman's suspicions about what *certain people* have been up to in there are correct, I think that it might be in everyone's best interest that it is shut for a while, don't you? As you say, this is a *university*. We do have certain standards that students are expected to maintain. "

Hannah looked around, "Look, is Goodman around for me to talk to?"

"*Dr.* Goodman," the woman emphasised, "Is unavailable."

"But he's the librarian. What, is he hiding from me?"

Venom dripped from the angular woman's tongue. "Dr. Goodman has suffered an unfortunate accident over the weekend. The poor man has broken his ankle, and will be away from us for some time. But he has left us *specific* instructions about certain people who might ask to use that room."

Hannah tried to stare down the old harridan, but she knew it would do no good arguing. The library assistants were notoriously loyal. Turning, she walked into the library, trying to find a dark corner in which she could sit and think.

* * *

Hannah trudged through the stacks. It was over a week since she had been barred from the Æther Room, and the suffering she endured at Goodman's hand was only increasing.

As so few people used the Æther Room regularly she had hoped that news of its closure would cause little bother. But, as luck would have it, just the day afterwards some final year undergraduates had tried to get in. On being rebuffed, they had gone straight to their lecturers who had demanded to know why the collection had been restricted without any prior warning or explanation.

At first, their anger had been justly aimed at Goodman himself. Hannah had even begun to hope that the collective outburst would force him to relent. However, it soon began to spread that the lock had been tampered with and the key itself broken. He was also refusing to have the lock replaced until he returned from his convalescence, which for some reason people also seemed to be blaming on Hannah.

Goodman had been clever. His staff were more than happy to continue spreading his rumours about Hannah, and with his being away on sick leave nothing appeared to be coming directly from him. And then, as she had feared, Goodman's rumours had begun to spread outside the library. While many dismissed them out of hand, especially those who learned Hannah's connection to Dr. Goodman, too many were happy to accept them without any evidence. Hannah considered herself lucky that her own tutor felt disinclined to believe any of the wilder stories he had heard, but while he was understanding he had no inclination to fight on her side to make Goodman change his mind. There was no smoke without fire, he said, and insisted she must have done *something* to anger the old man. The idea that all of this fuss could have been caused by nothing greater than an old man's spite was beyond him.

Hannah had continued her work as best she could, but it was hard going. She wasn't banned from the general library, but without access to the works in the Æther Room it was like a crutch had been taken away. She was reduced to seeking out quiet corners for fear of Goodman's staff seeing her there and causing more trouble. Each day spent skulking around as if she had actually done something wrong left her feeling more and more depressed. She wished she could rant and rail at the situation but she knew it would only harm her cause. Her only hope was to stay out of sight of everyone and hope the rumours died away before they become so prevalent she could never escape them.

But today the library was unusually busy. Everywhere she tried, groups of students were already ensconced. She couldn't stand trying to work with anyone else around. Feeling their glances and hearing the hiss of muted whispers. She wandered between the shelves, only half paying attention, trying to find some quiet spot where she might work alone, until she suddenly found herself facing the doorway to the Æther Room.

She stood there, staring. Her room. So tantalisingly close, yet irrevocably barred to her. She could feel its pull. She found herself stepping forward, watching her reflection in the dark glass of the window grow larger as she approached. She looked tired. She hadn't been sleeping well recently. Sighing, she reached out and placed her palm on the doorframe.

The glass flickered blue.

Hannah gasped, dropping her hand from the door. There was someone inside. Had they fixed the lock? Had someone forced them to lift the restriction?

Hannah eagerly peered through the frosted glass and

looked around. She could not make out any shapes moving within. She pulled on the doorknob and the door rattled on its hinges. Hannah stopped, confused. Was it still locked? How had the light turned on if no one was inside?

She rested her hand on the wooden door just above the handle. The light inside flickered just once. There was an audible click; the sound of a lock mechanism turning. What was going on? Slowly, peering at the lock, Hannah turned the knob and pulled.

The door opened.

Hannah looked inside. The room, her room, bathed in the soft light of the æther-bowl, was empty. She stepped forward and was immediately hit by an overwhelming sense of calm. The weight she had been carrying for the past week, the guilt and shame she had been unable to fight, washed from her shoulders. She stood up straight for what felt like the first time in weeks. Everything felt… right. She was meant to be in here. It felt as if the room had been waiting for her. Waiting to admit her, no matter the petty machinations of an outdated old man.

It was impossible. Or was it? Hannah thought back to her own work. The fringe theories of Tanning and Bodine, and the modern studies made by Green. She herself had been focused on corroborating the idea that æther could be charged, or polarised. That it could gather around objects and people. But her ideas were just theoretic. Could it have actually happened? It was amazing, but was it actually possible?

Walking over to the wooden shelves she carefully ran her hands along the spines of the notebooks and journals. Books actually owned by the great men and women who had driven and led the field of æther-theory. Books handled and written by people dedicated to the study and research. People like her.

She could not quite bring herself to believe it, but as she stood there and caressed them, Hannah felt that they were welcoming her home.

Imprint

1984

"Well, I think it's obvious where the problem is."

Nicki sighed. He was right, of course. Fixed to the light-box in front of them, the patient's torso stood out; a rich blue silhouette against black. As much as she would never admit to romantic fancies, Nicki could never quite help but feel a little awe at the sight. If you let it, you could almost convince yourself that the lines were quietly pulsing in time with some impossible heartbeat. That you really were looking at a person's lifeforce. But it was just an image. In principle only a little different than what a standard æthergraph would give you. And what this image showed was a heart; shrunken and ill, with dark lines threading out into the body as the weakness spread.

"I suppose you're right. Poor Peggy."

She looked over at her companion, but it was obvious he had already lost interest. She didn't like Peter Mallion. He was a short man who believed that physical bulk somehow gave him the authority he felt he lacked from his sub-average height. He wasn't flabby. Quite the opposite. He worked out to the point where he looked out of proportion to himself. But you didn't have to like someone to work with them. Unfortunately.

Mallion stood back and removed his glasses, sliding them back into a thin leather case. He hated wearing them when he didn't absolutely have to. "Well, it couldn't happen to a more deserving person."

A small pit of disgust opened in Nicki's stomach. It was the hospital's role to care for everyone in the community, no matter who they were. Showing such disrespect was not acceptable. They may not have been doctors, but they were still medical professionals. They were still part of the process. She could understand why people sometimes felt irritation towards those in their care, but expressing that irritation in private was, in her opinion, the first step on a slippery slope. If you couldn't be respectful in private, how did you know you were managing it in public? No one was at their best in a hospital. They were scared and unwell. Patients had an excuse for poor behaviour. The hospital staff did not.

But the thing that made it worse, although she could never admit to thinking it even to herself, was that Mallion was right.

* * *

The door thumped open as the heavyset orderly stepped through, pulling the wheelchair in behind him. Nicki had a glimpse of the sickly green walls of the corridor beyond, lit by the soft blue-white of the lights before the door swung shut with a thump.

"Hello Peggy," she stood and walked over, hoping her smile did not look as forced as it felt. "How are we feeling this morning?"

"What do you fucking care?" The wrinkled old woman didn't look up. She was sat huddled in the chair, bundled in a pink hospital robe. Thin, claw-like hands clutched the arms. Her legs barely reached beyond the hem of the robe and her feet were engulfed in thick, heavy woollen slippers. *Like a withered old prune stuck in somebody's dressing gown*, thought Nicki, then immediately chided herself. Thinking those things was the first step in saying them.

"Come now, Peggy. We all care about you. That's what we're here for."

It was an effort to keep her voice light, but it was an effort that needed making. Nicki ignored the orderly as he theatrically grimaced over the old woman's head. She didn't like to encourage that kind of behaviour. Just because a patient was rude didn't mean anyone else had the right to be.

Peggy's eyes were sharp blue points sunken into the folds of her rough skin. She leered up at Nicki from a toothless mouth. "What, you got no man in your life to care for? You stuck here, caring about strangers 'cos no one wants you? What's the matter? You frigid?"

Nicki held her face still as Peggy cackled to herself. There was something about that laugh that set you on edge. Impossible to ignore, it cut into your ears however hard you tried. And Peggy knew it. You could not fight the idea that Peggy had honed and crafted that laugh, working on it until it became a weapon. One more way to make herself unpleasant for her own amusement. Even without words you felt she was somehow insulting you. Every interaction with her was designed as a personal attack.

"Well hopefully you'll feel a little better once we get more of an idea what's up with you, won't you, Peggy." Nicki knew that line sounded patronising, but it wasn't as if Peggy cared either way. As she always did with her more difficult patients, she tried to put herself in Peggy's shoes. How would she feel if she were that old, surrounded by young, healthy people as she slowly felt her body give way beneath her. She knew just as well as the doctors it was just a matter of time. It was more than understandable that someone in her position would lash out.

"It's not like any of you have any bloody idea what's wrong with me," the old woman didn't stop grumbling as Nicki and the orderly lifted her from the chair and manoeuvred her onto the scanner-bed. She didn't fight them, just hung there without moving. She seemed to get some perverse pleasure in this passive hindrance, beginning again with her low cackle. Luckily her thin frame weighed next to nothing so it was no real effort to lift her, and before long her frail body was lying on the scanner.

"There. Comfortable?"

"What the fuck do you think?" spat the old woman.

Nicki didn't reply. Sometimes it was better to just leave them to it and focus on the work. Sometimes a patient needed a friend to reassure them. Sometimes they needed someone to just do their job quickly and efficiently. You didn't have to like your patients, but that was no excuse for sub-par work.

Checking that Peggy was lying as flat on the scanner-bed as her hunched body would allow, Nicki reached over and pulled over the receiving plate where it hung on its articulated arm. She had attached the photo-ætheric sheet before the patient had arrived. She moved it down as far as it could go, until it hung a couple of centimetres above Peggy's body. Then she locked it in place.

"Now if you can try to keep as still as possible, remember?

"What do you care, bitch?"

Nicki purposely avoided looking at the orderly as she moved to the console. She could feel his expression of disgust. It wasn't his place to judge. They had a job to do. That was it. Nothing else mattered other than doing her best for the patient. Settling into the chair by the console she began to punch in the final measurements and focus the lamps. This was going to be a more focused scan than the last one. Now they knew the main problem was in the heart, the doctors wanted a detailed view to determine if there was anything they could do.

"Here we go, Peggy. Just lie still for me."

First she flicked up the switch on the wall by the console and the room's lights dimmed to almost nothing. Then she initiated the scanner. The ætherlamps within the scanner-bed ignited, throwing rich sapphire light around the tiny, gnarled figure upon it. A beacon of fresh, calming brilliance. The timer began to count down the ten minute cycle.

The Chambers Diagnostic Scanner was one of the most modern pieces of machinery in the entire hospital. Cutting edge. The new first line in diagnostic medicine. The scanner itself was about the size of a standard single divan bed, from which specialised ætherbowls shone focused light up through the treated glass top and onto the receiver plate hanging above. It wasn't standard ætherlight, such as you would get from everyday ceiling lights. Like an x-ray, if there was someone lying between the lamps and the photo-ætheric sheet it would superimpose an image of their body onto the plastic. Unlike an x-ray, however, the light generated wasn't harmful in the slightest. It gave off no adverse radiation of any kind or any other unpleasant side effects.

The image generated was also far more useful than an x-ray. The light reacted with the chemicals in the body, highlighting the subtle changes in hormones and body chemistry triggered by an illness or injury. Anything living and healthy would show a rich, thick navy blue. Anything non-healthy, from a tumour to a paper-cut, would be darker. If you had asthma, the vessels in your lungs would be discernible dark lines. Kidney stones would be hard black dots. Anything from cancer to cataracts, the scan would highlight exactly where the problem was. It wasn't perfect. It couldn't tell you the reasons or causes behind the problems it detected. For all the ridiculous fanfare it was getting in the media as a 'miracle', at the end of the day it was simply another diagnostic tool. But no one could argue it wasn't a magnificent step forward in medical science, and was fast becoming the standard first stage in patient treatment.

This universal usage had created a frustratingly unscientific belief amongst lay people that a Chambers Scanner scanned someone's 'life force'. Romantic claptrap. What it did was detect the chemicals released by a body in distress, as part of the natural reaction to illness or trauma. But Nikki supposed that if believing in such unscientific nonsense made a patient feel better then that was okay, as long as the professionals didn't give in to such idiotic fancies.

Nicki sat waiting for the scan to finish. She didn't like to talk during the process, as the scans came out best if the patient lay perfectly still throughout. Even interacting with a nurse or family member in the room could be a distraction, so Nicki had cultivated an air of concentration while she worked. She didn't care if it made her seem standoffish. This was her work, her part of the diagnostic process, and she would do it to the best possible standard she could. She wasn't here to be liked.

Once the timer reached the end of the countdown, the machine automatically cut off. The blue illumination faded and Nicki flicked the main lights back on.

"There we go. All done. Everything alright, Peggy?"

There was no response. Nicki stood, unlocked the receiving plate and moved it aside. She looked down at Peggy's limp, wrinkled form lying perfectly still. Her face hung to the side, mouth open, a line of drool dripping from the corner onto the glass surface. Her eyes were glassy.

"Peggy?"

Nicki grabbed the old woman's wrist and felt for a pulse. She felt nothing.

* * *

Nikki had never seen an image like this. Usually if you put a dead body in a scanner it would give you a black image. Photo-ætheric technology only reacted with living material, and anything dead or inanimate, like metal, would not be detected. But the image she had captured yesterday while Peggy had lain dying on the scanner showed a silhouette pale enough to be almost white. And where in the previous scan the heart had been highlighted in a darker hue, now it hung in the centre of the image as a pure black space, with thick strands sprouting from it and into the body as if sucking the colour and life from it.

She had never realised just how full of life a normal æther-scan looked before. This was something different. Both eerie and beautiful at the same time. A ghost imprinted at the moment of death.

No one else had been particularly bothered at Peggy's passing. An on duty doctor had been called in to officially declare it, and then after a while someone came to take away the body. Other than that, there had been nothing special or unexpected. Everyone knew that Peggy had been incredibly unlikely to ever leave the hospital alive. She had been a sick old woman at the end of her life. The original scans had confirmed how bad her heart had been. In the grand scheme of things it had been a good way to go; slipping away on the scanner with the light shining through her body. No pain. No build up. Clean and easy.

But Nicki hadn't felt right for the rest of the day. Not because the old lady had died. She wasn't so naive that a patient dying would put her off her stride, and it had been simple chance that Peggy had slipped away under Nicki's watch. No, what bothered her, other than how her appointments for the rest of the day were delayed, and in some cases even cancelled, was how nobody had cared. There had been the basic legalities and a quick chat with the head of her department asking if Nicki wanted counselling, but other than that the old woman's death seemed to register as little more than a freed up bed. An unwanted and unpopular patient out of the way. Oh, no one was jumping around and celebrating, but they could have at least shown some remorse. Peggy had been a human being, a life, and deserving of some respect for that alone. So what she had been so unpleasant? You didn't help someone because you liked them. You helped someone because they needed it.

They hadn't even thought it worth sending the scan for development. The technology was still new, and the process of developing the photo-ætheric sheets wasn't cheap. If Nicki hadn't slipped it in with the others at the end of the day it would most likely have been thrown out as rubbish. And now she had come in early in order to pull the image out before anyone else saw it and discovered Nicki had given in to some foolish flight of fancy. She hated how sentimental the whole thing was, but with no one else caring one bit about a patient's death she wanted to complete the scan as a way to give Peggy that one last piece of respect. It didn't matter that she had been an angry, ungrateful old woman who seemed determined to make anyone around her as unhappy as possible. That shouldn't have mattered. And now, because Nicky was the only one who cared, she was the only one who would get to see this beautiful final image of what had once been a life.

For all she knew it had to be medically fascinating, something held her back from showing it to anyone else. She had never heard of anything like this before. There probably hadn't been. What were the chances of someone dying at the precise moment they were in the scanner? But they would turn it into a case study; an interesting anomaly to publish and analyse and discuss, all without any consideration that what they were studying were the final moments of a person's life. It wasn't right. For all her many flaws, Peggy shouldn't be remembered as nothing more than a statistic. While Nicki had never given into such cloying sentimentality in her entire career, she couldn't help herself. That someone so twisted and hateful as Peggy could create such a beautiful, ethereal image was a testament of humanity. She had died unloved and uncared for, in a moment shared with Nicki and no one else. Something so intimately private had to be more than just a scientific curiosity. She couldn't let anyone else dilute that.

Nikki rolled up the sheet and left the lab. As she stepped out into the corridor, the soles of her shoes tapped rhythmically against the hard floor. People joked that she wore hard soled shoes to alert people when she was coming so they had time to tidy themselves up. She didn't mind. She knew it was meant affectionately, for all it was ridiculous. The truth was that as much as softer would be more comfortable, they didn't give the correct impression. People expected a certain sense of professionalism from hospital staff, and trainers were not part of that image. Reaching the scanning room she pushed through the heavy doors and hit the lights. Before she did anything else she went to the corner where her coat and bag were hung on their peg, and slid the rolled up sheet inside.

Once that was done she put it out of her mind and looked around the room. The small desk was as she had left it the evening before, everything in its place. The receiving plate hung locked over the scanner. The frail, elderly body lay peacefully on the scanning-bed.

Nicki's head whipped around. The scanning-bed was empty. Of course it was, but for a second she could have been sure there had been someone there. She shook her head. It must have been a trick of the light. She didn't give it another thought as she sat at the computer and spent the next half hour preparing for the day. Her first task was to run through her appointments and begin working on the calculations for each one. Every scan was different. The exact strength, position and focus of the lamps inside the scanner had to be adjusted depending on the size, height, weight and general health of the patients, as well as of course the part of the body the doctors wanted to see in most detail. Most of the technicians didn't bother working on those until the patient was already on the scanner. That wasn't good enough for Nicki. It left the patient lying there for however long it took to make the calculations. It was far more time efficient to work out as much as possible in advance. She had most of a patient's measurements and weights in the records. That was enough to determine an approximate set up, and then once the patient arrived all she had to do were a few final adjustments. It might only save each patient five or six minutes, but every second meant something to someone going through the diagnostic process.

Her first appointment of the day was scheduled for ten, but rolled in at six minutes to. Nicki smiled to herself. Arriving early and getting seen straight away. No waiting around. No uncertainty. These little touches were what allowed her to make someone's day just a little more bearable.

"Good morning, Mr. Dallot. I'm Nicki."

The man in the wheelchair grunted a reply as he looked around the room. He had a physique clearly built on beer and accustomed to little more exercise than he needed to stagger between bar and bathroom. The skin on his head and neck was red, his nose and cheeks threaded with broken blood vessels. What hair he had was cut short and blended into the fuzz of stubble on his cheeks and chin. Neither had been shaved recently, giving him an oddly furry quality.

"Well, if you can hop on up onto the scanning-bed, we'll get things rolling. Okay?"

Not without some effort, Mr. Dallot pushed himself out of the chair and waddled over to the bed. Even that short distance seemed to leave him winded. Nicki wasn't sure a scan was needed to determine what was wrong. His entire physicality screamed heavy drinker. Nicki stepped over and took his arm, helping him lift himself onto the scanning-bed.

"Get your hands off me, bitch."

Nicki stepped back, dropping his arm. "I'm sorry, what?"

Mr. Dallot looked up at her, "I said, I just lie down on this thing then, do I?"

Nicki stared for a second. She looked over at the orderly who had wheeled him in. The heavyset man was checking his phone as if nothing unusual had happened. Had she imagined it? That harsh, bitter yell? It certainly hadn't sounded like Mr. Dallot, whose every word came as a wheeze of struggling breath.

"Uh, yes," she stammered, pulling herself together, "Just lie back and we'll be done in no time."

"Alright then. Sooner the better really. Hate bloody hospitals." He pushed himself back onto the bed without further comment, wriggling to get comfortable. His body covered the entire scanner, when he placed his arms by his sides they just barely fit. Nicki busied herself positioning the receiving plate, locking it in place and taking notes on the final position.

"I'm only here because of the wife. Last time I complain about gas, I can tell you." His complaints sounded more good natured grumping than having any real malice.

Nicki smiled. He seemed like a nice guy, for all of his poor health choices. "Well, we'll be done in no time. Then we'll know if there's anything to worry about."

Locking everything in place, Nicki sat at the console and entered in the final tweaks to the settings. The machine whirred quietly as the lamps positioned themselves. Then she lowered the lights and fired up the scanner.

With the size of Mr. Dallot's body, hardly anything spilled out from the machine itself, leaving the room unusually dark. As the timer counted down, Nicki found herself thinking on his sudden outburst. It seemed out of character and the orderly didn't seem to have noticed anything, but she couldn't have imagined it could she? But then she'd also thought she'd seen someone on the scanner this morning. Maybe she hadn't slept well.

Her reverie was broken by a sudden hiss of pain from the scanner. She looked over.

"Are you alright, Mr. Dallot?"

"Ah! It's me chest."

Quickly Nicki hit the shut down switch and turned up the lights. Mr. Dallot's face was contorted in pain, with one hand grasping his chest. She leapt up, unlocking the plate and pushing it aside so she and the orderly could lift the heavy man to a sitting position. He was breathing heavily and a sheen of sweat glazed his red face and neck, but the pain seemed to have passed.

"Are you OK?"

"Ah, don't know what happened. Felt like cramp, or something." He rubbed a hand across his forehead and wiped it on his gown. "Bloody hell, that bloody well hurt for a moment."

Nicki took his arm and felt for a pulse. It was fast, but not worryingly so. His breathing had slowed back down to its usual wheeze. Whatever it was that had been the cause of the pain, it seemed to have passed.

"Are you feeling alright? Would you like us to get one of the doctors in to check?"

"No love, I'm fine. Just stress I guess. Not your fault, just hate hospitals. "

"Do you feel okay to carry on?"

"Oh bloody hell, don't let this hold anything up. They'll just keep me here another bloody day. Sorry to be a pain."

"No trouble at all, Mr. Dallot," Nicki helped him lay back down. Once he was comfortable she took the photo-ætheric sheet from the receiving plate and fetched a replacement. You couldn't use the same one again, as you could never guarantee the patient would lie in exactly the same position. You had to start from scratch. Nicky fought back against the irritation of it. She couldn't blame the patient, but something like this on the first appointment of the day would throw everything out of routine. An entire day fighting to pull back the time while patients suffered unnecessary delays.

"Oh, and can you not tell the wife?" Mr. Dallot's eyes pleaded up at her as she moved the plate back into position. "I'll never hear the end of it. You've got that patient confidentiality thing, right?"

"I'm afraid I will have to tell your doctor, Mr. Dallot."

"But not the wife?"

"Not if you don't want me to."

"Please. I'd never hear the bloody end of it."

* * *

The second scan went without a hitch, but starting from scratch meant she had lost the precious setup time between appointments. A couple of minutes here or there might seem trivial but they added up, and ignoring them was the kind of sloppy thinking that led to even greater cumulative delays. Letting things slip at the start of the day could lead to the final appointments having to wait an extra half hour or more. Nicki wasn't prepared to allow herself to let that happen without a fight.

She rushed to wipe down the scanner-bed and put the next sheet in place on the receiving plate, then went out into the waiting area. As she turned and the door swung shut behind her she caught sight of a figure back in the scanning room. She only had a quick glance before the door banged closed of a short figure hunched over the scanner console in a bright pink hospital gown. Nicki turned and pushed the door back open. There was no one there. Of course there wasn't. Nicki had been alone in there once Mr. Dallot and the orderly had left. Nevertheless, she let her gaze linger as she slowly let the door fall shut again. Only once it had closed all the way did she turn away.

There were already a few people waiting when she turned the corner. They wouldn't all be for her, and this early in the day she could remind herself that some at least were those who had chosen to come early and wait. As she looked around, a young girl with short hair dyed blue came through the far door, accompanied by an older man Nicki assumed was her father.

"Cassie Reicherman?"

The young girl looked up and nodded, and Nicki ushered them into the room. She smiled. Right on time. They hadn't even had to wait. That was what patients deserved. To arrive on time and be seen on time. Especially first thing in the day. As she pulled the door open for them she instinctively took a look around the room. It was empty, of course.

Focus. Stop being stupid and look after the patient.

"If you'd like to take a seat, Mr. Reicherman," she gestured to a chair against the wall. He had a face filled with the nervousness of a parent sick with the knowledge that there was nothing they could do to make their child better.

"Cassie, if you can lie yourself down on the scanner we'll get things going, shall we?"

Cassie nodded. From her file Nicki knew that she was fifteen and suffering from unexplained pains in her gut, and so her doctor had sent her for a preliminary scan before any more invasive tests were planned. So far the young girl hadn't spoken a single word. Nothing unusual for a teenager. Nicki knew some of her colleagues would have tried to draw her out into a conversation with the idea of distracting her or putting her at ease. Nicki didn't agree with that one bit. As far as she was concerned, if a patient didn't want to chat that was their decision. Without saying another word she began to set up the receiver with quiet efficiency.

She got the receiver plate locked in position and turned away. As she did, she felt something grab her wrist. Nicki yelped and looked down. There was nothing there. Nothing, despite the fact that she could feel sharp, boney fingers, clamping around her arm, pressing so hard Nicki could feel the joint grind. She stumbled back away from the scanner and the sensation faded.

"Is everything alright?" Mr. Reicherman was half out of his seat, open concern on his face. Cassie remained on the scanner, with her hands by her sides. Nicki looked at her arm. There had definitely been something. Hadn't there? Even now, the memory lingered. Had she imagined it?

"Uh, yes. Yes. Sorry," she managed, rubbing her arm and moving to the console so they couldn't see her face. "Just a bit of static. Nothing to worry about. Now, if you can just lie still for me Cassie, we'll be done in a jiffy."

Without waiting for a response she lowered the main lights and fired up the scanner. As the ætherbowls fired up the room took on the familiar peaceful hue. Cassie was so slight that plenty of light spilled from the table to give definition to the darkness, sending highlights and shadows across every surface. Nicki hoped the light was low enough to hide her features. She didn't want the patient or her father to see how shaken she felt. As the timer marked the seconds she took a few quiet, deep breaths. She had to pull herself together. She was a professional. She had a job to do, and she wasn't going to let some stupid fancy distract her. She checked the dial.

"Half way there, Cassie," she turned to face the scanner, "You're doing great…"

Bathed in the rich blue light of the scanner bed lay a small, wrinkled figure with a devilish grin on its sunken, yellow face. Thin, skeletal arms stretched out of a pink hospital gown and gripped the edge of the scanner. Its eyes were sunk deep into a gurning bed of loose skin. Nicki couldn't move. Pulling itself forward, the figure leant out from the bed, opened its mouth and spat. Nicki felt a glob of cold spittle splatter wetly against her eye, dripping down her nose and over her lips. The shock of revulsion gave her back control of her body. She screamed and fell backwards, toppling from her chair. She heard rather than felt her head hit the hard floor. For a few seconds she felt nothing, then the pain hit. Her vision swam, and the next thing she knew Mr. Reicherman was kneeling over her in the darkness.

"Are you OK? Do I need to get someone?"

"Dad, what's happening?"

Nicki looked around, trying to focus on the last few moments. She'd fallen, but couldn't quite put her finger on why. Cassie was sitting up as far as she could under the scanner plate. The thought floated into Nicki's mind that the scan would be ruined. She'd have to start over. She tried to sit up, then bit back a hiss of pain as the back of her head gave a sharp, stabbing throb. Mr. Reicherman took her arm and gently helped her into a sitting position.

"Everything's alright darling, just stay on the scanner. The lady just fell, is all." He turned back to Nicki, "Look, I'm going to find someone. You just wait here."

Before she could answer he was off and out the door. Nicki sat there, unable to do anything else. As the immediate pain began to ebb, its replacement came as the knowledge that her actions must have caused her patient worry and concern. She had done the worst thing she could possibly do in her job, make a patient's experience worse. And then on top of that how many more appointments would be delayed because of her carelessness?

Then the image came back to her, rising up out of the rippling fog of her thoughts. That face. Peggy's face, bathed in blue light, leering out of the scanner. Her stomach lurched. She put a hand to her face. Nothing. She had felt the old woman's spit hit her. Felt it slide down her face, down her nose and between her lips. Yet, despite the sensations she knew she had felt, her memory told her there had been nothing there. Aside from a sheen of sweat, her face was dry.

"Are you OK?"

She looked up, even though the movement sent a jolt of pain into the back of her eye. Cassie was looking at her from the scanner. The lights were still down, so the girl was backlit with the rich light of the scanner.

Nicki tried to tell herself that the wavering shadow that made it look like someone was lying behind her was nothing more than her vision swimming.

* * *

Nicki silently cursed herself as Marilyn escorted her through the waiting area. She tried not to count the number of people she could see waiting for their scans. Tried to ignore that fact that the queue had grown to the point where some were having to lean against the wall or take a seat on the floor. She had no idea how many of them were waiting because of her. All of them forced to sit out there so much longer than they should have to. Their hospital stay made that little bit worse because of Nicki's moment of weakness. Bile stirred in her stomach at the thought that she had let them all down.

Marilyn lead her through to the scanner room, her hand resting gently but firmly on her arm. Nicki felt herself tense as the other woman opened the door and held it for her to step through, but there were no figures waiting for her, either real or imaginary. Of course there weren't.

After Mr. Reicherman had returned with one of the receptionists, Nicki had been taken to a nearby examination room. Dr. Zwelieg had turned up to check her over. She hadn't mentioned the figure on the scanner; the strange, all too real vision of Peggy and the sensation of spittle sliding down her lip. They had easily believed her story that she had lent too far in her chair and it had slipped out from under her. Even now she wasn't certain anything had actually happened, and she certainly wasn't going to mention it to anyone else. Eventually the doctor decided that she probably wasn't concussed, but told her to rest for a while before going back to work. They had left her with Marilyn, one of the floor's admin staff, to watch over her. It could have been worse. Nikki knew her well enough to know she wouldn't spread the story around the entire hospital. Unfortunately she seemed to be taking her responsibility of care a little too enthusiastically. Nicki at least admired that the other woman seemed to genuinely care, unlike some of the admin staff who wanted to do nothing more than the minimum required for their pay each month. But that didn't help the fact that the focused attention was a little cloying.

"Now, are you sure you're okay?" Marilyn asked, putting her hands on Nicki's shoulders and looking her in the eye in what she clearly considered a comforting yet authoritative way.

"I'm fine." Nicki found it hard to keep the irritation out of her voice. She knew the girl's heart was in the right place. She wanted to get on with the backed up appointments. Just the thought of being forced to go home, leaving all those people to go through a cancellation, delaying their diagnosis by who knew how long, made her physically uncomfortable. She pulled herself away and walked over to the scanner where Cassie's abortive scan still hung. Nicki pulled it down and quickly put it aside. She didn't even want to look at it. Cassie had been told the scan would be rescheduled. That dug at Nicki, but it couldn't be helped. She couldn't have been asked to wait, and calling her back now would just compound the misery. She had to do what she could to fix the remainder of the day.

"Thank you for walking me back, but I just need to get back to work now. I'm very behind." She moved about the scanner, rushing to get everything set up to the next patient.

Marilyn gave her a look filled with fond condescension that Nicki did not appreciate at all. "Okay then, but don't push yourself. If you need a break, take one. You'll only push things back even more."

"I know!" Nicki hadn't wanted to snap, but she didn't need mothering. She needed to work. "I'm sorry. Really, I'm fine. I just need to catch up."

The younger woman smiled. "Alright, but you know where I am if you need anything."

With that, she turned and finally left. As the heavy door swung shut, Nicki turned back to the console to see which appointment was next.

Alone again, bitch?

Nicki spun around, searching the empty room. She couldn't have imagined that voice. That harsh, guttural voice.

It had been right behind her shoulder. She had felt the puff of breath on her neck, smelt the brief lingering scent of halitosis that hit the back of the nose then evaporated so quickly she couldn't even be sure it had been there at all. Her heart raced. She took a moment to look around, but there was nowhere in the room where anyone could be hiding. She went to the door and pulled it open, hoping that someone had called from outside. Before it had moved more than a foot she felt something pushed into her back, knocking her forward so that the door slammed shut. She flinched as the noise reverberated unnaturally around the room. Had someone just pushed her? Or had she tripped?

Nicki backed away from the door until the her legs hit the scanner-bed. As they did she felt a bony hand punch the small of her back, shoving her violently forward. Or did she? The moment the sensation ended she almost couldn't believe it had been there. The sudden movement jolted the bruise on the back of her skull and her vision swam. She turned, but there was no one on the scanner. She was alone.

"What's happening?" she moaned, her gaze sweeping the room for any sign of her antagonist.

What do you care?

The memory of a voice came from behind her again. Almost on her shoulder. Nicki shut her eyes, trying to focus.

"Peggy?" The word was a whisper.

Bitch. In front of her this time. A blast of acrid breath blew across her face, stinging her nose. Nicki stepped back, tripping over her own feet and tumbling to the floor. She pushed herself back until she hit the wall.

"What...?" The word was mumbled from numb lips.

I don't want to be 'ere. Not much fuckin' choice though, is there?

Nicki froze. That was Peggy's voice in her mind. A dead woman's breath tugging on her senses. Someone who had passed away right there on the scanner-bed yesterday, her final moments bathed in the rich blue ætherlight and imprinted on the ethereal scan that was now curled up in Nicki's bag.

The scan that no living person other than Nicki had ever seen.

Without thinking, Nicki pushed herself up and threw herself across the room. She felt something hit her shins, as if someone had stuck their foot out to trip her, and fell face first into the hard floor. She rolled onto her side, her head throbbing and vision swimming. In the brief seconds before it focused she was sure she could see someone standing over her; bathed in blue light, hunched over in a bright pink hospital gown that hung from their body like a cowl, a sunken, evil grin leering down at her. She blinked, the room came into focus, and they were gone.

Was that laugher? The harsh cackle of someone causing pain and misery for nothing more than for their own amusement?

Nicki dragged herself onto her knees, then pushed herself up threw herself at her bag. Tipping it upside down she shook it, emptying the contents over the floor. As the ætherscan landed it unrolled and the ethereal image stared up at Nicki. She could hear laughter lingering on the edge of hearing, faint but impossible to ignore. Despite the fact there was no illumination behind it, the ghostly image was almost too bright to look at. Was the dark hole over the heart larger than before, the black strands thicker, or was it her imagination? Pulling her eyes away, she re-rolled the sheet to hide that mocking image, stood, and threw herself out of the doors and into the corridor. Fighting to keep her face as calm as she could manage she staggered through the waiting area, the laughter following her as she went. She tried not to notice the expectant faces turning towards her. Which ones were waiting for her to call them through? Waiting patiently for someone who cared enough to help them through these difficult times. Someone like Nicki who wanted to help people, no matter who they were or what they were like.

Someone who cared, no matter what.

She managed to fumble open the door to the reception room and staggered inside. Marilyn was sitting at the window speaking with an unhappy looking patient. The younger woman turned as Nicki entered.

"Nicki? Are you OK?"

Ignoring her, Nicki reached over Marilyn's shoulder and grabbed a pair of scissors from the desk. Dropping to the floor she cut the image down the middle, into two jagged halves. Then she held those together and cut again. Then again. Ignoring everything around her, the clean snip of the scissors sounding over and over until the floor around her was littered with tiny pieces of monochromatic photo-ætheric plastic. She kept going, shaking off hands that reached out to try and calm her, cutting again and again, reducing the sheet into smaller and smaller pieces until no piece remained big enough to cut anymore. As she worked the harsh laughter that hung on the edge of her hearing began to fade, until at last it fell silent.

The scissors dropped from fingers stained red where the blades had cut too close to the skin. There were tears on her cheeks. When had she started crying? She hadn't cried since she was a child. Looking up, she saw Marilyn crouched next to her, honest concern on her face as she carefully pulled the scissors out of Nicki's reach. She was saying something, but Nicki couldn't make out the words. She felt numb. She could see the faces of patients staring in through the glass window of the reception area. She turned away. She couldn't face them. What was she to them now? How could any of them ever want to be treated by someone like her?

She looked down, and swept her hand across the shredded

sheet, scattering the pieces across the floor. All she had wanted was for her patients to know that she cared. That no matter how unpleasant they were or hopeless their case, someone cared enough about them to treat them as a human being, rather than a statistic.

Was that laughter, just beyond the edge of hearing?

Locked Out

1985

"For fucks sake! Can that man-child not handle anything on his own?"

Mel placed the handset on the table in front of her, ignoring the nearby diners looking over at her outburst. Her fingers thudded on the rubber keyboard as she typed out her reply.

- [Mel Anders] *I don't care, Clive. You either work with him or not at all. Frankly, with the client signed and locked I couldn't care if they never see you again. Stop whining.*

She watched the status bar change from SENDING to DONE, then pushed the handset to one side. Picking up her glass she took a long sip and felt the glorious sensation of the bubbles caressing her tongue. She looked across the table and rolled her eyes at the slim, neatly dressed man sitting opposite her.

"Are you being mean again?" he chided, smiling.

Leaning back in her chair she slid one foot out of her

stiletto and ran it slowly up the inside of his leg. She knew Joshua didn't mind the way she treated her team. He was one of the few men she had ever met who honestly preferred powerful women. Oh, there were plenty out there who claimed they did. She'd been through her share of those, but that inevitably wound up meaning they wanted kinky stuff in bed but a submissive piece of arm candy in public. She'd learnt not to expect much more, but after seven months Joshua still honestly seemed happy with her being in a better job, earning more, and taking the lead in their relationship. And he wasn't turned off by her treating people in the same way any man in her position would without anyone giving it a second thought.

The handset vibrated as a new message came in. It took him this long? Was Luscombe typing with one finger?

- [Clive Luscombe] This isn't fair, Mel. I put in at least half the work pulling in this account. I don't see why Devinson should be put over me.

- [Mel Anders] Go and bitch to HR if you don't like it. Maybe mummy will hold your hand. One more word to me and Devinson gets the account solo.

"Idiot," she growled.

She shut the handset with a satisfying thud. When she looked up she could see people on neighbouring tables turn back to their own meals, too embarrassed to look her in the eye. Mel smiled. She enjoyed seeing people feel uncomfortable around her. If it had been a man acting so obnoxiously in the middle of a restaurant none of them would have batted an eyelid. Well, maybe they would have, but they wouldn't have thought it unusual.

"Is someone enjoying their new toy?" teased Joshua.

"Whatever do you mean?" she purred. She rested one

hand on the closed handset.

"You could have showed it off to me at home?"

"I didn't get it to show off. I got it for work."

That was only partly true, but as much as the ashphone was essentially a tool, what good was a tool if it wasn't worth flaunting? The handset was the latest advance in a technology thought all but obsolete. It had been decades since anyone had taken ætherphonic communications seriously. Its reliability had never improved since it fell out of fashion in the forties and fifties. But why bother speaking when you could send information? Now it was possible to use the same connections to send data to people all over the world. It didn't have any of the irregularities that people suffered while transferring sound. You typed in a message and sent it straight to another device, wherever it might be in the world. It was clean. It was simple. It was the tool that was putting Mel on the way to the top.

It also helped that the handsets were now small and efficient enough to be completely portable. Her handset was a little smaller than a standard house-brick, split into two halves that opened on a hinge. A bit big for a pocket, but perfect for anyone with a handbag. The bottom half had a small, rubber keyboard. The other a glass screen, behind which fitted the ætherpod which doubled as both the backlight and the power source. Each pod could last up to two weeks use before it needed changing. The pod was also what connected the handset to the 'æthernet': the cloud of information that was there for the taking for anyone smart enough to realise the potential.

And Mel had been one of the few who had. From the day she'd first read about them she had badgered the company until the board had approved the money for her to buy enough for her team. It hadn't been easy. Not everyone had recognised how much of a game changer this technology would be. The board had seen them as little more than a novelty, and not a cheap one at that. But she had fought her corner, as always, and since then her team had been running rings around their competition. Now, with the Mason-Riley account all but signed, the firm had begun almost literally throwing money at the technology.

Joshua reached over and picked up the handset. He turned it over in his hands. "It's amazing how small they get them."

"I'm not interested in small," Mel purred. She watched his eyes widen as her foot reached the top of his thigh, "So why don't you put that thing down and tell me what you've got planned for this weekend?"

* * *

- [Chris Devinson] Contract's arrived. Everything checked. Mason-Riley is all yours.

Mel looked up at the group of men waiting on the other side of her desk. All of them wearing expensive suits that screamed status and aspiration, trying to give off the appearance of affluent masculinity, desperate to stand out in a city full of wannabe big fish. All of them willing to work together only until the moment where screwing the others would gain them the tiniest advantage.

"They're ours."

Their cheer filled the office like a post-game locker room. Hands slapped in celebration. After weeks of work it was finally a done deal. Mel had expected to feel exhausted at this point. She had hardly stopped in the last week, but her mind was buzzing.

There was a loud pop as a bottle was opened. The discarded cork rolled into a corner as froth fizzed carelessly down the neck and onto the floor. Mel didn't care. With the money she'd just brought in, the partners wouldn't complain about her replacing a carpet. Hell, if she asked them today they'd buy her a whole new apartment and furnish it too. As her intern, Patrick, began filling the glasses she tapped out a quick reply to Devinson, then a slightly more formal one to Mr. Canderbill's assistant. She wanted that meeting with him sorted before any of the others had a chance to beat her to it. They all knew who led this team, but she had no doubt any of them would eagerly leap in and oversell their contribution if they had the chance. It didn't bother her. She'd do the same to any of them. This wasn't a family. It was a business. She had no interest in anyone not ready to play the game. She just had to make sure she would always be the better player.

A glass was thrust into her hand and she drained it with one long, luxurious pull. The bubbles tickled her lips as her lipstick transferred to the glass, combining with the elation of victory to make her head spin. Holding up the empty glass elicited a cheer from the guys. She knew some of them bitched about having to work under a woman, but there were never any complaints when things were as good as this. While the champagne lasted, they were happy to drink.

"I don't know how you did it, Mel." Daniel was standing right by her desk, positioning himself to be the first to congratulate her. The oldest one in the room, his attempts to ride Mel's coat-tails were almost painfully obvious but at least that meant he never tried to sabotage her. They both knew that he'd reached as high up the ladder as he ever would, and he was smart enough to recognise when to hitch himself to the winning team. "After Luscombe screwed up I was sure they'd walk."

"If I had a body like Mel I could have got them to sign anything as well," called out Alistair, getting a hefty laugh from the room. Mel smiled but hid her face by signalling Patrick to refill her glass. Alistair was a smarmy bastard who never had a good word about anyone behind their back. Especially a woman. His problem was that he utterly failed to hide it. She knew full well he'd been behind Luscombe's bungled attempts at sabotage. If Luscombe had only been even slightly competent he should have been able to easily turn things back on Alistair, rather than losing everything. Mel wondered how much it grated on him that the way she had handled the situation had only made her look even better to the Partners. She raised her glass in a mock salute, seeing the hatred glimmer behind his fixed grin.

Yes, she knew how to use her body to her advantage. If you wanted to get anywhere in life you used every weapon you had. So many girls trying to get ahead thought that was all they needed, but a pair of legs and a tight blouse didn't land contracts on their own. The type of men you dealt with in this world were happy to have something pretty around the office but if you started to out-achieve them, that's when things would turn ugly. If you wanted to be a success you had to be the best and not allow anyone to take anything from you. Sexy *and* intelligent was a combination most men didn't expect, and by the time they clued in to the situation Mel was already several steps ahead of them.

She looked up at Patrick as he leant in and refilled her glass, her fingertips rapping on the case of her handset. She saw his eyes flicker towards her as she gazed at him. She smiled. Well, why not?

"Right, I think we can afford an early day," she announced, "Archer's Bar?"

This got another cheer and they moved eagerly towards the door.

"Patrick," she called out, draining her glass and waving it in his direction. There were one or two chuckles at his being called back. As an intern he put up with a fair amount of ribbing. It was part of the job. It was how you dealt with it that got you noticed. Among other things. She looked him over. He was slim, with broad shoulders and thick black hair. His suits always looked cheap compared to the others, but then he was only an intern. Anyway, she wasn't interested in his clothing.

She had a brief moment of doubt, but as she reached over and closed her ashphone a burst of adrenaline surged through her. Her head buzzed with sudden excitement as her inhibitions faded. She deserved a real celebration.

His eyes followed her as she stood and walked around the desk to shut the door. Leaning back against it she stretched, arching her back. "I'm afraid I'm going to be late leaving for the bar. I need to go over a few important things with you. You think you'll be able to keep up?"

Surprise showed briefly on his face, then he smirked and stepped forward, placing his hands on her waist and pressing her up against the door.

"I think so," he grinned. The raw impudence in his voice was enough to make Mel laugh. She shoved him back and down onto the couch behind the door. She could hear the sound of the office emptying as the others trooped out. They wouldn't notice them turning up late. And she didn't care. Straddling the younger man's lap, she lowered her face and kissed him hard.

* * *

Mel stretched, groaning in pleasure as the silk sheets slid from her body into a pool on the floor. From the bathroom she heard the crash of water against tile as Joshua switched on the shower. She briefly considered joining him, but wasn't sure she had the strength. Instead she dragged herself from the bed, pulled on her robe and made her way to the kitchen. The empty bottle stood on the side, a reminder of why her head felt so foggy this morning. She poured herself a glass of water and switched on the coffee machine. While it warmed up she moved into the living room. Tugging open the curtain caused her to flinch as the late morning light spilt into the stuffy flat. She cracked open the window, letting in a breath of air that puckered her bare skin.

Mel dropped onto the sofa. Her ashphone and handbag sat on the coffee table in front of her, next to the two discarded champagne flutes that were surrounded by various items of clothing. She lifted a leg and kicked Joshua's shirt from the table. It caught one of the glasses, knocking it over and sending its contents across the hard wood surface.

Mel cursed, sitting up to pull things out of the way of the spreading pool. She swiped her handbag onto the floor then grabbed her ashphone. Dropping it in her lap, she managed to stop the glass before it rolled onto the floor. Then, using Joshua's shirt, she quickly wiped up the liquid before it stained the wood.

She looked over the scene. No disaster. She picked up her handbag and checked it over. No marks. The champagne hadn't reached the expensive material. Joshua's shirt wasn't so lucky, but if it didn't wash she could buy him a new one. She picked up the 'phone from her lap and checked it over. Not a drop on it, but she flicked it open and booted it up anyway, just to check. The screen shone blue. She had no idea how water resistant the thing was, but she had no desire to become the joke who had drowned her ashphone in champagne.

The sound of Joshua showering continued in the background. He'd be a while yet. As it was already open and connected, Mel settled back and began checking through her messages.

* * *

* * *

Mel leant forward in her chair and began to type one-handed into the handset as the whiney-voiced man on the other end of the phone-line continued to speak.

- *[Mel Anders] Chris. Thursday's meeting moved back to 11 tomorrow. Can we do that?*
  - *[Chris Devinson] Yes. Will be ready.*

How long would that exchange have taken in a telephone call? One minute? Two? That that was assuming Devinson was near a phone. Then she would have had to call the client back to confirm, wasting even more time. Instead she'd been able to type the message while still on the phone to the chump at Mason-Riley. She could hear the poorly disguised surprise in this voice that she had an answer so quickly. It was almost sad. Had he really through as weak a power-play as moving the meeting time at the last minute would phase her? Wrapping up the call, Mel opened a new message on the handset.

- *[Mel Anders] Patrick, I'll be staying late tonight to wrap up plans for tomorrow's meeting. I'll need to you hang around until I'm done.*

Double checking that she wasn't including anyone else by mistake, she hit send. Not that the message would seem incongruous since she had made the young intern her PA. But you didn't get far in life by not being careful of who knew what. She'd done her own share of blackmailing to get to her position, and she'd do it again if she had the chance. If you were weak or careless enough to let people learn anything they could use against you, you deserved to fail.

She knew he would receive the message straight away.

She'd made it clear her team had to have their a-mail open at all times. Other teams had been slower or reluctant to implement the system, but that's why they were all racing hopelessly for second place while she rocketed up the ladder. Her team had their ashphones on them twentyfour seven.

She pulled over her date book. There was nothing in there for tonight, but she supposed she better tell Joshua she was working late so he didn't try messaging her while she was… busy. When your boyfriend knew you had your handset on all day as a matter of policy, it was hard to find excuses for not answering.

- [Mel Anders] Hi Joshua. Meeting moved up so working late. Sorry. Maybe see you Friday? M x

She knew he wouldn't respond for ages. He had his own ashphone. It had been a gift from her. An attempt to soften up his attitude to her always being on hers. He never turned it on unless he wanted to send a message, so sending him anything that needed an immediate response was pointless. But if he tried to get hold of her tonight then he knew to check a-mail and he'd see and know not to bother her.

Mel couldn't understand how anyone could not see the potential in ashphones. Messages zipping around the æther-cloud. The ability to contact anyone she needed anywhere in the world. There was nowhere she couldn't talk to her team. No place she couldn't connect personally with her clients. Data. That was the way of the future.

If Mel had been the superstitious type she could almost have thought of it as her lucky charm. Nothing had gone wrong since she'd begun using it. Freed from worries about ever being out of the loop she had discovered an almost limitless drive that more than matched her ambition. She was working at a level she had never experienced before. Nothing stopped her. Nothing phased her. She felt so confident. So energised.

A reply sprung up on her screen.

- *[Patrick Blass] Yes ma'am. As long as you need.*

She smiled. That should be a rewarding end to the day.

* * *

As they were escorted to their table, Mel curtly ordered their drinks before she had even sat down. Once they were both in place the young girl glided away without a word. They knew Mel here. The restaurant prided itself on its good service and the staff knew that with people like Mel tips came easily if they did their job quickly and without any fuss. They didn't bother their patrons with chit chat or wasted time. It helped that they knew a harsh word to the manager would get them fired in a moment.

Mel took out her Ashphone as soon as she was seated and placed it on the table. She rapped her fingernails on the thick white cotton of the tablecloth as she stared at the tiny blue screen, waiting for the connection. Leaving the office for lunch always made her irritable these days. She had so much to do, so much that could go wrong. However unlikely the possibility, the fact was that if something did go wrong and they couldn't contact her any one of her team could use the opportunity to try and take a piece of her authority. For all her success, no one's position in this world was secure if they allowed themselves to get weak. The second the handset connected she hit the buttons to open her mail. Relief filled her as the menu populated. Eight messages already since leaving the office. Three were from Tallahan, her counterpart at Mason-Riley. Another was from Devinson. One other was from Mr. Canderbill's assistant. She pulled up that one first, and began to read.

"Ahem."

She looked up. Joshua was looking over at her.

"I thought this was your lunch break."

He actually had the audacity to look annoyed? He had been the one insisting she come out to lunch. She kept reading. The assistant's message was just a confirmation that Canderbill would be at tomorrow's meeting. She moved on to Devinson's, which was an update on the progress of the report for that meeting. It should have been done already. Mel was not happy. Something had gone wrong and the entire thing had now slid at least a day behind schedule. The rest of her day was going to be spent going over the whole thing to work out whose fault it had been. Whoever it was, they were out. She didn't allow weak links on her team.

"Look," she answered without looking over at him, scrolling quickly through the remaining a-mail, "If I wait an hour then I've got fifty messages to get through when I get back. I get through them, and I have another fifty. I'm just keeping on top of things. Is that okay with you?"

"I know you've got a lot on. Surely you can leave that thing off for one lunch hour?"

"God, alright." She pushed the open phone to one side. She didn't close it. "Better?"

"Sorry I spoke."

Mel bit back her response as at that moment the waitress returned with their drinks. The two of them sat in silence while she poured, her practiced hand bringing the frothy head right to the rim without spilling a drop. Mel had learned to notice these things. It was important to pay attention to details like that. During that time two more messages floated up the screen. Neither looked important, so she let them go.

"Look," Joshua said once the young girl had left, "I don't

think I ever see you without that thing anymore. I know your career's going well, but you were one of the best before you ever had an ashphone. Stopping for an hour to have lunch with me never bothered you so much then. I just don't see why turning it off for an hour or two is somehow going to change that.

Mel looked at him, her hand resting on the warm plastic of the handset. She knew he was right. The fact was she hated taking downtime. That unscratchable itch of knowing that there had to be a more effective way for her to use her time. For the last few months she had been a machine. Nothing could stop her. She could work all day, spend the night with Joshua or Patrick and be up at five ready to go again. A-mail had revolutionised her life. Her mind was constantly buzzing; plans for the coming weeks, ideas of what the client might want in the near future, innovations to improve processes, insights into who in her team was trying to undercut her. And so far each and every hunch had been right. She could tell what the client wanted before they told her. She could tell when someone was trying to trip her or move behind her back.

Just the thought of letting go of that, even for just a couple of hours, made her physically uncomfortable.

For Joshua's sake more than anything else she forced herself to make small talk as their food arrived. Each time a new message appeared on the screen her eyes strayed back, eliciting a sigh of vexation from her dinner partner. God, did he have to be quite so petty? She wouldn't have agreed to come out for lunch if she'd known he was going to sulk like a little boy.

Then a new message popped up. It was from Tallahan. That was probably worth checking. Before she could reach over to check another followed, this time from Van Burrel. Why was the CEO of Mason-Riley messaging her directly?

And straight after Tallahan. She reached over and hit the open button for Van Burrel's message. The moment she did the screen went blank.

She stared in horror as the text faded from the screen which then shrank to a blue pin prick in the centre before dying completely.

"What? No!"

Mel reached out and grabbed the handset, knocking over her glass and spilling champagne over the pink cotton table cloth and into Joshua's lap.

"Shit!" Joshua pushed his chair back, trying to avoid the spill.

Mel wasn't listening. She tapped futilely on the keyboard. The æthercell had died, leaving her handset dead and useless. How had that happened? They were supposed to last up to two weeks, on normal use. She changed hers every week, just to be safe. She'd done so first thing on Monday, as she always did. No, wait. Her face paled as the memory came back to her. She'd come in early and found Patrick was the only one in. They'd… got distracted. She'd forgotten to change it.

A pit opened up in her stomach, sucking the life from her body. Her head felt heavy. She tapped wildly at the keys. Nothing. What had been in those messages? What if she needed to answer straight away? What if someone else had been included and was able to answer before her? Blood rushed in her ears, drowning out all other noise around her. She tried to think, but her thoughts were jumbled and sluggish in her head.

"No, no, no!"

"What the hell, Mel?" Joshua was wiping at the stain on his trousers with a napkin.

"Shut up, Joshua. Just shut up." Mel stood, shoving the useless brick into her handbag. Her clumsy fingers fumbling with the clasp, almost tipping everything out across the floor.

"What? You're leaving?"

"Get off my case, all right?" She was furious, and scared. She had no connection. Anything could be happening. Her whole team would be using the information against her. She felt naked. Cut off. Panic rose in her throat, threatening to overwhelm her. The world seemed to be pulling away, retreating from her senses. She had to get the ætherpod replaced. The office. She had to get back to the office.

She stumbled away from the table, colliding with one of the waiters and sending the tray in his hands tumbling to the ground. She had to fight to stay balanced. Her body felt thick and heavy, as if she hadn't moved for a long time and was suddenly attempting to sprint. She managed to get herself out of the restaurant and looked around. Why had they gone so far from the office? How long before she could get back? She couldn't catch her breath. Why couldn't she think straight? She couldn't remember the last time she had felt this tired.

A black cab pulled up in front of the restaurant. Mel pushed past the couple getting out, barking the address of her office to the startled driver. A seasoned London cabbie, he pulled away without comment. Mel sat in the back, her breathing hard and fast as she clutched the useless handset through the thick material of her bag.

The lunchtime traffic was thick on the narrow roads. Every light in the city appeared to be red. People filled the streets. Mel couldn't sit still. She felt sick. A small rational part of her mind tried to tell her that it was fine, that nothing was going to happen in one lunch time, but was overwhelmed by the desperate need to get connected. Her mind rebelled at the very idea of not being within a button's touch of the æthercloud. How long had it been since she'd been so cut off from the world? Weeks? Months?

After what felt like hours the cab finally pulled up outside the office. Mel jumped out, throwing a handful of notes at the driver. She had no idea how much. It didn't matter. Her heels clattered on the hard tile floor as she ran through the large doors and to the lifts. As the doors closed she leant against the wall, panting as it began its glacial ascent. She had to read that message. Had to stay on top. Had to reconnect.

The lift eventually reached the end of its agonising rise. Mel shouldered through the two men who had been waiting for it and ran to her office. A couple of people called out to her but she didn't pay them any attention. She couldn't let anyone see her like this. Reaching her office she threw her bag on the desk and pulled open the bottom drawer. There they were, like a lost treasure: an open pack of æthercells. Ripping one out of the packaging she fumbled the handset out of the bag and began the swap. It wasn't usually a hard job, but her hands were shaking so much she could barely get a grip on the case. She finally prised the back open, snapping off one of her fingernails as she ripped out the dead cell and tossed it aside. She fumbled the fresh one in its place and her clumsy fingers hit the switch.

The screen flooded with blessed blue light. She held her breath and felt her body relax. As the phone connected to the ashcloud and the menu came up on the screen, air filled Mel's lungs for what felt like the first time in hours. She inhaled deeply, feeling her mind begin to clear. The blue light bathed her face, washing the tension from her body. Her heart slowed. Colour returned.

Once she was able to think she opened her messages and quickly found the ones from Tallahan and Van Burrel. Tallahan's was just a preliminary note about a planned meeting next month. Van Burrel's was a mass message to the high ups on the project, thanking them for their hard work.

Mel leant back in her chair. Everything was all right. She began to laugh. A shrill, uncontrollable laugh as the last of the nervous energy left her. It had been nothing. She'd been panicking over nothing.

She leant back in her chair, her mind once again her own, but her hand did not leave the hard plastic of the handset.

* * *

The fist swung out of nowhere, taking Patrick hard in the jaw. The younger man dropped instantly, crumpling to the pavement. A hand grabbed her throat and she was shoved backwards against the corner of the wall. Something hard dug into her back, sending a wave of agony through her body. She yelled, more in shock than in any conscious effort to summon help.

"Shut it, bitch."

She had a vague vision of the man before her. Scruffy dark hair. Thin beard. Leather jacket. A knife being held to her face. As her mind focused on the blade it swiped down and to the side. Mel screamed, but instead of pain she felt a weight drop from her shoulder. He had cut through the strap of her handbag, pulling it away from her. Instinctively she grasped for her belongings, but all she managed was to wildly swipe the bag from her assailants hands, sending its contents tipping from the open top. She saw her 'phone slide free and fall to the ground. It impacted on the pavement with a sickening crack. Both halves flew apart as the plastic casing shattered, giving off a white-blue flash as the æthercell inside burst.

A searing pain stabbed behind Mel's eyes. Time seemed to freeze, and for a moment the scene stood still in a sickening tableau before slamming her back into the world. Before she could react the hand left her throat and a fist slammed into her gut. Her vision swam, agony reverberating around her mind as her body went limp and she dropped helpless the the ground. Footsteps echoed down the alley.

It was over in a few seconds. He must have been waiting in the alleyway. They had just left the bar, where her team had been having their usual Friday evening drinks. As far as the others were concerned she was having Patrick escort her to a taxi, while in reality they were heading back to her apartment together. Now she was fighting to breathe on the cold, gritty pavement. Patrick was lying on his side, unmoving. More footsteps. Mel flinched as a group of late night revellers came jogging over. Hands took her shoulders, gently pulling her up into a sitting position and leaning her back against a wall. An older man was clicking his fingers in front of her eyes while the others checked Patrick. One ran off, saying he was going to call the police.

Her phone! The full realisation of what had happened cut through the shock as sharply as the blade had cut through her bag's strap. She tried to slow her breathing, but couldn't get herself under control. Her eyes were watering from the flash of the shattering æthercell. She began to shake. A young girl knelt down and hugged her, whispering that she was alright now, and that the police were on their way. The words meant nothing. It wasn't alright. Only a deep sucking wound remained where part of her had been torn away. The rational part of her mind was telling her that it could be replaced. Anything could be replaced if you had the money. Anything the company or insurance wouldn't cover she could easily afford herself. But rationality had no place in her thoughts. The adrenaline from the attack was no longer a sudden burst but a constant, steady flow. Her senses were heightened, yet her thoughts came slow and sluggish. Her fingers itched, reaching out for something that wasn't there, desperate to feel the hard edges of the heavy handset.

* * *

* * *

Not once in her entire life had Mel allowed herself to be a victim. No matter what happened, no matter what anyone had done to her, she had refused to allow anything or anybody to dictate who she was or what she could accomplish. Every set-back, every attack, every person who thought they could trample over her because she was young, or pretty, or a woman, had been turned around to her advantage. Every single set-back used to show the world exactly why Mel Anders was destined for the top. More than a few people had made the fatal decision to underestimate her, or believing that once kicked she wouldn't kick back, and harder. Everything life had thrown at her she had faced and come through stronger.

But this time something was different. When she had got back from the hospital early Saturday morning she had climbed straight into bed but barely slept a wink. Every movement in the corner of her eye made her flinch. Her pulse had been racing ever since the attack, and had shown no signs of calming. Strangely, considering her lack of sleep, she felt oddly wired. Not the useful buzz that came from working late on a deadline, but the constant alertness of an animal stalked in the night.

She would have preferred to keep the whole thing private, but with both her and Patrick being attacked the police had followed up by contacting everyone they had been in the bar with beforehand, and it had only been a matter of time before the news had been spread throughout the company. When one of the Partners called she had been forced to sit through his fake concern. They both knew the call was nothing to do with her wellbeing but rather to assess any possible implications for the company. She immediately turned down his offer of as much time off as she needed. As bad as she felt, she couldn't contemplate not going in on Monday. By now, she knew, everyone in the office would have heard about what had happened and each and every one of them would already be thinking about how best to use this to their own advantage. Taking sides. Jostling to undercut her. Manoeuvring to make sure they were in position to carve away their own little piece of her empire. It was exactly what she would have done in their place.

She had felt no better on Sunday, but on Monday morning she forced herself out of the flat. She jumped at every noise and movement around her, flinched at every person who entered her eyeline. Each blaring horn created a fresh burst of fear. She managed to find a free taxi and spent the journey into the city huddled in the back, teeth clenched, forcing her body to stop shaking. Once she reached the office it took all of her self-control to march through the lobby to the lift, returning greetings that were little more than barred teeth. Waiting, poised, ready to pounce.

A new handset sat on her office desk, waiting for her. She stared for a moment. Being cut off from the world these last two days had been almost as bad as the attack itself. Tears stung her eyes as she dropped her handbag and slid into her chair. It was the latest model; lighter, with a wider screen and a much more defined keyboard. It even had a calendar function so you could keep track of meetings on the go. She didn't know if it was a gift from the company, or if one of the more loyal members of the team had put it there for her. Right now she didn't care. All that mattered was getting back to work. To gaze into the fresh blue light of the screen and calm the incessant buzzing that would not fade from her mind.

Ripping opening the packaging, Mel grabbed a fresh æthercell from the drawer in her desk and clicked it into the casing. Placing the open unit in front of her, she leant forward and hit the power button.

The screen booted in the familiar flash of blue, but instead of the sense of calming focus she expected, Mel felt an agonising stab of white-blue pain behind her eyes. She could feel the rough hand clamped around her throat. Smell the stale cigarette smoke on his breath. The edge of the knife blade against the skin of her throat. All the memories and sensations from Friday night, all the terror and helplessness condensed at the instant her phone had hit the ground, condensed into a single, frozen moment.

Mel fell back into her chair, eyes wide, breath hard and fast. Her heart raced, and her gaze darted around the room. What the hell was happening? She gripped the desk in front of her, closing her eyes and fighting to force her body to calm itself. Struggling against a flood of adrenaline as the screen in front of her shone blue. In the past, staring into the screen had made her feel alert and secure. Now it mocked and terrified her. Desperately, Mel reached out and slammed her finger onto the power button and held it until the unit switched off. As the cell cut off and the screen faded to black, the fear and sense of immediate danger slackened, leaving her panting in her chair.

What the fuck? What the hell had that been? She lifted her hand to find it shaking uncontrollably. Gripping her chair she made herself take several long, slow breaths, fighting down the bile that threatened to rise from her stomach. Her heart was pounding, but eventually it began to slow and she felt her body begin to relax. Bit by bit, it came under her control again until she was able to think and the immediate sensations of the office returned; the murmur of voices through the door, the occasional sound of laughter or footsteps thudding between desks.

Had it been her imagination? A flashback? It had felt so real. So much more than a memory. Her body had been sat in her office, but every thought and sensation had been back there in the dark alleyway.

Tentatively she reached out again. The shaking had faded, but her finger quivered as it hovered over the power button. Chiding herself for being a coward, Mel leant forward and pushed down hard, daring her body to respond.

A stab of white-blue agony. The callused hand around her throat. The knife blade sharp against her skin. Patrick unconscious on the ground. Her handset hitting the ground, the æthercell shattering. Alone. Afraid. Helpless.

Mel fought against it, but her body was frozen in a rictus of horror. The moment dragged on as she sat there, her finger pressed down on the button. Never fading. Never moving on. Each second the same skin pricking, heart racing moment of pain and fear. That one moment drawn out as if somehow etched into her mind. The screen in front of her was not even loading. It remained stuck on the bright blue of the initial start-up; a field of azure from which she could not look away. It drew her in, no longer a tiny plastic window but a gateway to something greater that threatened to engulf her.

Finally she managed to pull her hand back, and then hit the power button to free herself. The blue light dimmed, leaving the screen a dark, black hole waiting for that one moment of weakness when it could draw her in once more. Mel slammed the thing shut and tossed it across the room. It hit the sofa, bouncing off and clattering onto the floor. Her breath came in quick, open mouthed bursts. Her fingers dug into the wooden surface of the desk. Her blouse clung to her body, sweat trickling down her neck.

What was she going to do? If she couldn't even turn on her handset, how was she supposed to work? She could feel her life crumbling around her. Her entire position had been built on using the a-net. She couldn't just stop using it. Even if she could come up with an excuse that didn't make her sound crazy, that wasn't how things worked anymore. No one in the company went without one now. Because of her. She'd been the one to introduce them. To insist the company invest in them. To force her team into using them until it had become second nature.

Only the strong deserved to survive, in life and in business, and Mel had spent the last six months making sure that her position rested on being the strongest. She had found the tool to make that happen, and had used it to its full potential.

It hadn't been supposed to turn on her like this.

Our Eternity

1995

There we are. I can see the five of us emerge from behind the hedges that stand tall around the garden, dividing it from the world. The brisk air of early morning twilight doesn't bother us. We fizz with the artificial high still burning within us. Our minds run with the kinetic buzz of the dance floor. We are young. Each night is an eternity. The world is ours.

Empty streets stretch away into a city whose twenty-four hour bustle lays subdued. No life reaches this quiet side street except that which we bring with us. There is no one to notice as we climb into the secluded square. What is a locked gate to those such as us? The world is ours; freshly inherited, lying open to exploration. Five friends seeking a hidden place to ride out the end of the night. Even though the sky begins to lighten, the day is still far off. The clubs won't have shut yet, but we have left those artificial hedonisms behind us. Not for us the depressing intrusion of raised light and open doors, as tired staff brush out those last, sad dregs. The desperate, the drunk, and the pathetic, all hoping to somehow salvage their lonely night. Not for us. We choose the ending of our revelry.

We who sit as rulers of the night choose our own thrones to see in the dawn.

I'm climbing over first. Too short to reach the top unaided, the others lift me. Nick's hand is on my ass, pushing me up. I'm laughing, trying to bat him away while not daring to let go of the rails for fear of tipping over. I'm wearing that stupid tie-dyed crop top, and my loose denim phats which catch and rip on the railing. I haven't noticed, too busy squealing as the boys grab a leg each and hoist me over the top. I swing around, dangling awkwardly for a few moments before my fingers slip and I drop the final foot to the ground. I turn and step back as Shannon and Alice follow. Each get the same treatment, Nick and Lance cheekily taking advantage of their vulnerability to cop a feel. As much as we yell and play up, none of us mind. On a night like this, when we ride the heights of the chemical buzz, all of us have been more handsy than a slap on the ass.

Alice lands first. She stumbles and I grab her arm, holding her until she catches her balance. Her ridiculous platform boots under those neon green and black fluffies are hard enough to stand in as it is. She's starting to crash now, swaying and holding onto my arm. She's in her full cybergoth outfit, of course. It's the whole hog or nothing, with Alice. She likes the attention. Without her getup Alice is small, mousey and uninteresting. But when we go out, she can recreate herself.

Shannon drops down far more elegantly. At least half a foot taller than me. Graceful. Athletic. Sweat makes her legs glisten in the early twilight. She's wearing a pair of green shorts, green tank top and that black, loosely knitted crop top. It's the perfect outfit for the club, when we're moving and sweating and heaving in the shared heat of the dance floor, but once the buzz fades she'll soon feel the cold. Still, she looks gorgeous. She's always gorgeous, whatever she wears.

Even having watched this scene so many times now, I can't help but feel a small stab of jealousy. How easy it would have been to hate her if she wasn't the best friend I'd ever had.

Shannon takes our hands and leads us off into the enclosed garden as the boys make their own way over the gate. By the time they join us we've settled in a quiet corner. The hedges and the iron railings shield us from the streets. With the gate out of view and the sky stretching out above us, this could be the whole world. I am sitting up against a tree, my legs curled up in front of me. Alice is beside me, her head on my shoulder. Her mouth works on the dummy she's been chewing all night, its bulb flashing lonely in the twilight. Shannon is lying on the grass beside us, her arms stretching out languorously above her head. I'm not able to keep still. The hard bark of the tree rubs at the skin below my top, sending sensations dancing along my body with each movement. I'm laughing at Alice, making fun of her as she nods on my shoulder. Grabbing her face I pull her dummy away and kiss her on the mouth with a loud, playful smooching noise. The boys cheers us as they walk over. Alice pulls away from me, laughing and punching me on the arm.

Nick lifts Shannon's head and sits underneath her so it rests on his lap. They've been together for a couple of months now, if by 'together' you mean they each have a guaranteed pull whenever we all go out. There's nothing exclusive between them. Neither of them care if the other hooks up with someone else, or that they both spent the night dancing and grinding and making out with a dozen other people. None of us really care about that sort of thing. Life's too short. But their unspoken arrangement is the closest to a real relationship any of us have.

Lance sits cross legged across from me and Alice. None of us notice how he positions himself to look away from the other two. Maybe even he doesn't. I can see it. After watching this scene so many times, how could I not? How he sits so their comfortable intimacy is outside his vision. The slight tightness around his eyes the moment before he looks away. I remember he had confided in me earlier, while we were cuddling in the chill-out room, how he really liked her. Trust him to be the first to let feelings spoil what we all had. I sometimes wonder how that turned out, in the end.

I reach under my top and pull a joint from the cup of my bra. Keeping them there might be a little uncomfortable, but no bouncer is going to pat down the boobs of someone who looks like they could be their little sister. It's one of the reasons I put my hair in pigtails when we go out. Yes, it means that I have to have my drivers licence on me wherever we go, but when bouncers are scanning the queues they're not looking for cute little blondes who smile and wave like it's their first time out. They're definitely not going to risk patting her down in front of an entire line.

Nick tosses me his lighter. I light up, take a drag, then pass it to Alice. I hold my breath for a few moments before slowly exhaling through my nose. The smoke drifts free, floating and curling into the night air. The weed allows me to settle at last. I lean back against the tree trunk, looking up at the sky. I remember how it was so clear; not yet dawn but bright enough that the stars were hidden. The rich glory of the night giving way to the promise of the day. Silver twilight and golden sunrise verged at opposing edges of the sky while above us the pale blue of day emerges. The fragrant smoke builds, lingers, hangs in the still air. We sit in silence, feeling the warm embrace of our shared experiences. The energy and passion of the dance floor begins to seep away, giving way to the luxurious comfort of good times and good friends. We are experts at managing the end of the night. On slowing the harsh encroach of day. These times that are neither work nor play, but something different. We lie together between the death of night and birth of day. The world consists of the five of us and nothing more. What else could possibly exist beyond this garden? How could it? It is our Eden. We hang in a state of wilful bliss, before knowledge and all its temptations expel us out into the world beyond.

The joint circumvents the group twice before any of us speak. The echoes of the night's music hover in my ears. Lance swats at Alice's boot, telling her to stop being lame. I hadn't even noticed her head lolling on my shoulder again. She jerks up, her eyes opening. She tries to kick his hand, but he pulls himself out of reach. Nick's hand rests on Shannon's stomach, his fingers sliding uncontested under the black wool lace of her top. Lance's gaze stays firmly on me and Alice. Roused, Alice sits up. She's reaching into her boots. I can't hear the words anymore, but I remember them. She'd met some dealers on the dance floor. Looking the way she did, with her neon hair extensions and outlandish outfits, she always attracted the ones looking to sell. We laugh at her about it during the day, but if we've not been able to score beforehand we always know she'll meet someone before the night is out.

She pulls out a clear plastic baggie containing a thin, perforated sheet of paper. She's telling us that it's something new. Ash. I'd heard of it. Not much of a rave drug. A chiller. It allegedly gave a quick high with mild hallucinations. The perfect experience to end the night. None of us had tried it. We had an agreement not to take anything if we couldn't get enough for the whole group, and Ash was expensive. I hadn't even met anyone selling it before. Alice is telling us how the guy had been boasting about his connections to impress her. He'd been hot, so she'd made out with him for a while to entice him into giving her a discount. Shannon squeals, sitting up and slapping Alice on the arm. She jokingly calls her a whore, then shuffles over to sit next to her. She's keen to try it out. So am I. Ash is new, but from all accounts it's safe. Made from chemicals found naturally in the brain so the body knows how to handle it and wash it out, hence the quick high. Under the pretence of getting next in line Lance moves over and sits next to her, placing himself between her and Nick. Nick doesn't seem bothered and comes over to me, laying on his back with his head on my lap. He comments on the rip in my trousers. I pull up my legs and exclaim in annoyance. I hadn't noticed when they had caught on the gate. He's laughing, and comments on my legs looking nice. I swat at him, then begin to absent-mindedly stroke his hair. He has nice hair. I kind of like him. We'd hooked up once or twice, on nights Shannon hadn't been with us. He was fun, but I wasn't really into him that much and I knew he'd always pick Shannon over me if he had the choice. Most guys would, and I wouldn't blame them.

Alice is opening the baggie, taking out the sheet of paper and tearing it carefully along the perforations. There are six pieces, so she hands us each one before returning the last to the bag and the bag to her boot. I hold my piece between my finger and thumb. About an inch square, it has a consistency like toilet paper but with a weight to it. I know it's soaked in the chemicals that make up the drug. I raise it to my nose. Free from the bag it gives off a slightly stale aroma. I remember how it cut through the haze that hung around it, almost at if it didn't smell of anything itself but rather muted the scent of marijuana smoke. The others have taken theirs already. I'm the only one still holding. Shannon reaches over and grabs the tab out of my hand. I object, but she holds it back, grinning, and orders me to stick out my tongue. I protest, rolling my eyes at her being so childish, but do so. Sticking the paper on the end of her finger she places it in my mouth. I close my lips around her finger as she slowly slides it out, leaving the small piece of Ash soaked paper behind.

For a moment we hold each other's gaze, before both bursting out laughing. It's impossible to keep a straight face with the way the boys try to pretend they're not staring. They live in constant hope that one day they'll see something more than our teasing. I slap at Nick's crotch, telling him to calm down. He rolls aside, grabbing my hand and jokingly trying to hold it there. I shriek in amusement, flailing at him with my free hand. Shannon takes hold of Lance's arm and leans her head on his shoulder. Alice relights the joint. Nick finally lets go of my arm to take it, and I lean back against the tree.

The paper tab slowly dissolves in my mouth. It feels like kitchen towel that was stuck to a piece of food. I roll my tongue around, feeling it disintegrate. An odd senselessness fills my mouth. Like inhaling fumes. It isn't a numbness. It doesn't deaden my nerves, rather it removes the sensations they were feeling. It's nice. Calming. Nick passes me the joint and I take a drag. I don't feel the smoke in my mouth or nose, but the smell comes through, rich and satisfying, but doesn't linger once I exhale. The joint is nearly dead, and when I pass it to Alice she has the last puff and grinds the roach against the tree. We're all reclining back, waiting together to experience this new high. Alice and me, hand in hand up against the tree. Nick with his head warm on my lap. Shannon and Lance side by side on the grass. The five of us sharing this moment of experimentation, potential and intimacy.

First, my head begins to buzz. A soft, reassuring feeling of relaxed alertness; the same feelings as those nights when you lie curled in bed on the very edge of sleep, yet still awake enough to luxuriate in the complete relaxation. Then colours begin to change. A wash of blue swims before my eyes, saturating the world in eggshell highlights. Everything seems more real. More in focus. I'm looking around, grinning at this new perspective on the world. Nick is waving his hand in front of his face, giggling. I feel disconnected with the world, as if my body and my mind are no longer entwined. I can both feel Nick's head on my lap, and not. I can feel Amy's hand clasped in my own, and not. My brain knows the contact is there, but my nerves have been softened. Physical sensations have become academic. Yet I feel safe. Wrapped in a blanket of my own awareness. When I turn my head everything blurs with sudden motion, yet if I keep still everything appears sharper and clearer. I can see things in minute detail. Feel the textures of my clothing against my skin. The world is both more immediate and more distant. I swallow. There's a weightlessness to the world. I'm rising from my body. Floating above the ground. I can still feel Amy's hand in mine, the weight of Nick's head on my thighs, the rough bark scratching at my back where my top has ridden up, but the sensations are no longer immediate. My mind reels. I can feel myself laughing, but the sound comes to me as an echo of my own voice. Blue light suffuses the world. Not the blue of the sky. It is softer, yet more intense. Uniform. It comes from deep within each object and person. My gaze turns. I can feel that my body stays in one place but my perception floats and moves. It's jarring, as if I'm teetering on the edge of a steep drop. I am not controlling it. As my view alters the world blurs and shifts. I will myself to stop. The scene focuses with renewed clarity on the five young bodies draped over each other in the still morning. I can see myself smiling, but I cannot feel the pull of muscle or stretch of skin. We lie reposed in our secret kingdom. Smoke rises up in the air around me, thick and dull against the rich blue. I cannot smell anything. I have no sense of time. Seconds could have passed, or hours.

My body, small and fragile looking, shudders. A small movement, as if from a sudden chill. I feel a lurch.

Each time I have watched this scene I feel that jarring lurch anew. That sudden uncomfortable shift of being. All in an instant I go from warm embrace to cold disconnection. I can see the five of us below, including my own still body, but I no longer feel that echo of sensation. I can see Alice's hand in mine and her head on my shoulder, but I feel neither. I can see Nick turn onto his side and say something to me, but I cannot feel his head shifting on my legs or hear his words. I feel like I should be panicking, but the emotions have been dulled. I cannot grasp what is happening. I simply watch. I still don't know how much time has passed since I placed that thick shred of paper between my lips.

Then, as I hang there watching, I see myself sit up. I stretch, my arms reaching up above my head. The motion pulls my cropped top upward, revealing my belly. Nick's head turns, looking up my top and saying something I cannot hear. I swat at him. I'm saying something to the others but I cannot hear my own words. Alice reaches around me and hugs me hard, cuddling in the languorous luxury of a waking dream. I know I should be feeling the pressure of her arms around my body, but I feel nothing. The others begin to move and speak. I watch those familiar movements and habits that come unknowing to us, so recognisable that they go unseen. How can the trip be over? I'm still here. Still disconnected from my body, which seems to notice no difference. I try to move, willing myself to float downward but I no longer have any influence over my perception.

Do we look darker than before? The world remains infused with the same rich, blue light, but we seem to stand out as if something has drained from us. I cannot be sure. I have never seen any obvious change. I have not once seen a point where we go from one state to another. Only now does it ever strike me. I never think earlier to watch for it.

Lance is looking at his watch. He stands. Reaching down he takes Shannon's hand and helps her up. He does not offer to help the rest of us, instead slipping his arm around her bare waist. I'm standing, pushing Nick off my legs. Alice, childlike, holds her hands up to me and I pull her up. We begin to move away. I will myself to follow but all I can do is watch. We head back to the gate and begin to climb over. Once again Nick takes the chance to grab my ass as he lifts me over. Alice's too. Lance is more courteous with Shannon, carefully holding her waist and lifting her up to hoist herself over, but once she is over she links arms with the two of us and marches down the street without looking back. Now the hedge is between us. I've gone. I'm left watching as the boys jump over and follow until they too disappear from view and I'm left here alone.

We've gone. I've gone. Yet I'm still here. The echo of panic flutters through me, but there is no emotion. More a memory of how I believe I should feel. I can't understand what has happened. It is too unreal for me to comprehend. Is this simply an intense hallucination? I try to close my eyes and tell myself it's just a trip. A bad trip that will soon be over and I will be able to laugh and hug my friends to bring myself back into the real world. But I can't. I don't even blink. The physical everyday actions that we don't even notice become blatant in their absence.

I don't know how much time passes before we appear again and I'm able to watch the entire scene play out below me. First we appear from around the hedge. There I am. The boys are lifting me over the gate. Shannon is leading us to the tree. I'm taking out the joint and passing it around. Every action identical to my memory except this time I observe from above. I tell myself this must be it. That this unnerving experience will end once the scene plays itself out. This must be the effect of the drug, tricking the mind into playing out memories in some unnerving loop. I wonder if the others are experiencing the same thing; floating above themselves in this unsettling limbo. I watch, eagerly waiting the conclusion. The need for the feelings and sensations of the world becomes almost painful. But then that point comes again. I see my body shudder, and then nothing. No return. I desperately try to urge myself down, to open my eyes and see everything from my own perspective once more, but again I am forced to watch the full scene play out until we march out of sight behind the hedge.

Then, after another period I could not measure, we came again. And then after that again.

I don't know how many times I have watched the night play out. I know every movement, every echo, every gesture by heart. I have no idea how much time passes between each visitation, but once I see myself manhandled over the gate, the sharp railing catching and ripping my clothing unnoticed, I can predict and follow each step, each silent word, each glance and movement.

What am I? Am I dead? I don't know. I simply watch. I try to tell myself this is all just a trip. That the Ash has twisted my perception and sense of time. That soon I will wake up and this entire experience will fade like a bad dream, leaving me with nothing but the unease of a nightmare I can't quite recall. I tell myself that this is not the eternity that it seems to be.

I no longer know if I believe myself.

There we are. Once again I see the five of us emerge from behind the hedges that stand tall around the garden, dividing it from the world. The brisk air of the early morning twilight doesn't bother us. We fizz with the artificial high still burning within us. Our minds run with the kinetic buzz of the dance floor. We are young.

Each night is an eternity.

Connections

1911

If you are reading this, then you hold in your hand the last extant copy of my life's work; the fruits of over a decade of research and study. My name and reputation may be beyond saving but it is my futile hope that perhaps, if these papers are ever discovered, my work might one day be remembered with the merit it deserves. I know it does not truly matter who retains the credit for our work, but I would like to think that there might be some small redress of the histories being re-written by David Goldfarn. It would be glorious if I could believe that one day mankind might evolve past the point where a man's worth and contributions to the world can be erased for a quirk of his birth. Yet today my work is redacted, or attributed to those who have turned their backs against me, and tomorrow my name will be forgotten. In the eyes of history I am nothing. A wisp of memory soon dissipated by the winds of prejudice and the will of callow men.

To you who may read these words, I sincerely hope you are not a man of science. I have learned, to my cost, that even now, at the dawn of the twentieth century, the ideals mankind claims as sacred are nothing but hollow words swiftly drowned by our petty prejudice and jealousy. In seeking to understand the universe I have proven only that mankind is yet barely more than the sum of our basest natures. So I pray that you are one with no stake in the established histories. One who has no interest in extolling Goldfarn's name and reputation. One naive enough to hold that the truth stands over all, and who might make my story known for its own sake.

The only task that remains to me is to bind this, my collection of notes and research, and add my own personal account. This will likely be the only version of history told from my perspective. David has been thorough and none wish to stand against him. Daniel has given up. My only pitiful hope for redemption lies in the possibilities of a distant and unlikely future.

* * *

It has been over a decade since I began working in the field of theoretic ætheric study. I had known of Thomas Goldfarn's work for some time, of course. While his ideas may have been on the fringe of respectable science, such radical ideologies always attract the attention of those young enough to question the certainties of their teachers. I believe most students of science for the last thirty years must have held at least some interest in his theories for a time. For most it became just a passing fancy, and they soon moved on to more established areas of study as their education and careers progressed. We were simply those lucky few for whom that period of interest corresponded with his final, groundbreaking experiment.

When news of that grand work became known the reaction was more muted than it deserved. While established men wasted their efforts recreating and reviewing Goldfarn's work, with, I believe, more intention to disprove than otherwise, we flocked to his banner as eager disciples. Frank Spilling, Terence Farning, Daniel, and myself.

When I met the professor he seemed distant and distracted. Of course his dislocation from scientific life once he had made his discovery is now well known, but to our young minds we could not understand his lack of energy and drive for such a thrilling new branch of science. With Professor Goldfarn seemingly uninterested we instead gathered around his nephew, David. Only a few years our senior, he held the same eagerness and excitement as ourselves and welcomed us into his inner circle. Despite his enthusiasm I recall him even then being a little stand-offish, though never to such an extent as to invite accusations of impoliteness. As welcoming as he was, we were never allowed to forget that it was he who stood as the inheritor of his uncle's work, and led our endeavours in this new science. But why would this attitude have bothered us? None of us thought to usurp his place. The Goldfarn name was indelibly linked to the very concept of ætheric study. We simply wished to join him, to learn and study at his side as the pioneers of this grand experiment.

The only one of us who took any umbrage at David's attitude back then was Daniel. Always one who found it hard to remain politic in social situations, he found it hardest to grant David the soft touch his moods sometimes required. Daniel saw no need to hide his opinion that luck had played a large part in Professor Goldfarn's final experiment. This was the subject on which David could be the most sensitive, and even casting the slightest aspersion upon his uncle or his work could be enough to fire his anger. This is not to say that we did not share Daniel's opinion, to varying degrees, but we were at least careful not to mention it in David's hearing.

But even if those two were never destined to be the

greatest of friends both were adults, and men of science at that, and so more than capable of working together. Those were golden days. Our souls gorged on the mana of discovery and potential, charging forward in the passion of youth with little heed of what might lie ahead. How many men throughout history have been able to say they were at the forefront of such great discoveries? Professor Goldfarn had set the foundation stone and together we five would build a temple to our new science.

We did not always agree, of course. Our early work remained based largely on theory and supposition, and we were unified in the first task of refining the original experiment and stabilising the containment principles. This yielded still greater knowledge and ideas and once complete our discussions soon moved towards the direction our study should now take. David, Frank and Terrence were adherents to the path of practical application. They argued that the most effective way to create interest and generate capital would be to demonstrate to the world the many possibilities this new science offered. Frank and Terrence raved on about the possibilities they saw in communication, and David, in his solid yet unimaginative way, talked of the benefits and possibilities of ætheric illumination. But Daniel and I were convinced that the next steps should remain theoretical. Man should not seek to run before he has crawled, and stood, and then walked. Æther remained an unknown quantity in almost every respect. While the two of us agreed that these proposed technologies were possible, indeed eminently desirable, if we first grew and developed our fundamental knowledge, then the creation and utilisation of such technologies would be easier and more complete.

Having determined on our own areas of research, the group began to work more often apart than together. This did not mean we no longer collaborated. If anything, having the others driving in different directions only spurred us on. You could never know who would come up with an idea that would inspire another, or who could break open a problem by looking at it with fresh eyes. We met, all five of us, at least once a month. Over dinner we would outline our latest ideas, successes and failures; deep, enthralling conversations that would last long into the night. Often Frank or Terrence would bring some of their more promising students. Most appeared overawed by the company - I pride myself that at this time we had garnered a small amount of celebrity in scientific circles, especially amongst those young enough to lack the hidebound ideals of their teachers - and contributed very little. Others showed in themselves the promise of a bright future; such as Ronald Carter and young George Sandringham.

If there was any time in my life where I knew true joy, it was these years.

So while the other three began their work developing the practical applications that now become more and more familiar in our everyday world, Daniel and I strove to further our understanding of the mysterious substance that gave them their power. Our main point of study came from the understanding that the nature of æther was different than how we had at first believed. Today any student can tell you how ætherbowls draw their power from the grand Æther-Flow in the upper atmosphere. But despite prevailing opinion, this is not the whole of it. We had noted in some of Professor Goldfarn's more philosophical research essays the concept of there being a background level in the world around us at all times. Not as concentrated as that above, no doubt, but still an unseen factor of our world. Should this idea be true then it would vastly alter the way æther could be gathered and stored. Perhaps we would not need to store it at all, should there be a way to reduce the amount needed to the point where the local, background level should be enough. To perhaps do away with ætherbowls and containment entirely.

This then was the goal to which we set ourselves. The others found our ideas intriguing, but endeavoured to continue their own work along the lines of current thought. So while they did so, Daniel and I closeted ourselves together. We spent countless hours in our workshop, mixing and testing the compositions of both æther and more environmental chemicals, trying to find the connections and distinctions that might verify our work.

As the next few years passed, our ideas continued to develop. By this time even the most ardent deniers accepted Professor Goldfarn's work, although he had not survived to see this acceptance. Though others around the world now began their own studies into the ætheric, we had well established ourselves as the foremost men of the science. Frank and Terrence were welcoming a flood of students wishing to study under them, and had begun building the first prototypes of their ætheric communicators.

David travelled more and more, giving guest lectures and interviews with periodicals and magazines. He had become the natural spokesman for our cause, and a minor celebrity even outside our own circles. This work did not allow him to conduct much research of his own but he still contributed to our monthly gatherings and played an active hand in our work. None of us would have considered working without his influence. For all that it could be said that we were contributing more to the development of the science than he, the idea that we would exclude David from our conferences was inconceivable.

Daniel and I continued delving deeper into our theoretical works. We may not have been creating flashy mechanicals to display to the adoring world, but we remained more than satisfied with our progress. That our area of expertise remained niche compared to the attention the others received did, I will admit, cause a small amount of chagrin, but it did garner some attention. As hard as it is today to believe, at that time our names were both well known and well spoken of.

Our big breakthrough came during a particularly dank and dreary October, when I, for the first time I think since this enterprise had begun, attended one of our group's regular gatherings alone. A day or so prior, while walking home in a ferocious downpour, Daniel slipped on some fallen leaves and badly turned his ankle. With travel proscribed under the doctor's instruction for at least a week there was no chance of him attending. I would have stayed to tend him but he insisted that I go. We had several new ideas we had been excited to share and he argued he would rather one of us go alone than neither. He was a grown man, he reminded me, and in the capable hands of our housekeeper more than able to manage without me.

It felt odd, travelling alone. Daniel and I had been companions since university, and since then neither of us had worked on anything without the other. Being without his companionship left me feeling strangely uncomfortable. I tried to read my paper but found myself unable to concentrate so gave up and gazed out the window at the wet, autumn countryside rushing by. While later I would know better, at the time I put my malaise down to the break in habit; a fancy that would pass once I had a warm dinner inside me and the good company and educated conversation of my friends.

But after my arrival at David's home my mental acuity continued to fade. As we sat at dinner I found myself struggling to follow the conversation. My attention wavered uncontrollably, my mind wandering from one tangent to the next. Every thought seemed heavy and immovable. My condition and discomfort rapidly become obvious to my friends. Their concern left me feeling as pitiable as a child, utterly unable to put my worries into words. I apologised, claiming I must have been struck by a cold or some such, and took to bed early, something none of us had ever done at one of these meetings before.

As I write these words I realise the description my symptoms seems little more than those one might suffer from a heavy cold or other ailment, and my reaction to them little short of hysterical. I struggle to put into words exactly how this affliction felt. Perhaps I may better explain by describing how it so closely mirrored one of my greatest fears; that I might lose that which I held to be my identity. For all my adult life, my mind has been the one feature that defines me. I do not come from a large or wealthy family. I have never been charismatic, nor did I ever excel at sport. It it only through my talent for science that I make any headway in the world. It was through university that I first met Daniel, and my friends with whom I had now reached the forefront of this great new field of study. My greatest fear, one that I had never admitted to anyone, even Daniel, was of losing this one defining ability. To have my mind drift away. To lose myself and become little more than a burden to my family, with nothing but lingering memories of that which I once was. There are such afflictions that can cause just such a fate, and that night I spent in terror that I these fears had come true.

I left on the early train the next morning, and spent the entire journey attempting to wrestle my mind back to myself. It was not until I reached home that the fog finally lifted from my thoughts. My distress being evident, Daniel insisted I explain what had put me in such an uncharacteristic state. With my hand clasped firmly in his I recounted my experiences since leaving him the previous day. At first I found it difficult to express myself with any clarity, as my mind remained stagnant and moribund. But as I spoke I felt my thoughts returning to me like long lost friends and by the time I finished my tale I was myself once again.

My most fervent wish at that point was to put the entire event behind me and never think on it again. But while Daniel did not push me to do so, his own mind had been prodded into motion. For the next few days he remained quiet and thoughtful, uncharacteristically keeping to himself. I could easily recognise the signs that he had an idea developing he did not wish to share until he had thought it through, and so I left him alone to think.

When he announced that, now his ankle had healed, he intended to visit an old school friend for a few days and wished me to remain behind, I freely admitted my concerns that I would suffer a relapse of my previous ailment. To allay these fears - or so he let me think - Daniel made me promise that I would do no work while he was away. He convinced me that after my experience I needed a holiday to allow my mind to recover from whatever fever had struck me. Neither of us worked more than rarely without the other, so he said, and so his absence was intended to remove the temptation to slip back into habit and begin working before I had time to recover.

His visit kept him away for three days and in that time I kept my promise, however much my nature rebelled. I am not one who easily takes to inactivity or any time spent unproductive. The house seemed empty on my own so I busied myself by taking long walks out into the country, and despite my misgivings I believe it did me some good. I felt rejuvenated and eagerly anticipated Daniel's return so that we might begin our work again.

On his return, however, I found him in a state of great agitation. As he came through the door he babbled excitedly, clearly finding it difficult to express his thoughts. With a sinking horror I recognised the reflection of my own symptoms. A stab of panic ran through me at the thought of my dear Daniel suffering the same malady as I, but remembering how he had talked me through my own recovery I did my best to calm him and his mind gradually regained itself.

Upon recovering, Daniel told me that the experience, while unpleasant, had been no surprise but the intention of his entire trip. It had been an experiment to see if he could replicate my experience himself. For the first twenty four hours away from me he had purposefully refused to think about our work, or anything close to our field. He had stayed with an old school friend, and they spent their evening recalling shared memories of their childhood and swapping news of those they had once known. Then, the next morning, he had asked his companion to listen as he explained our work. Before he had managed his first sentence he had felt what he could only describe as his mind slumping into inactivity. His thoughts became slow, and he was left with nothing but the ability to recognise how much he had lost.

I shuddered at his description. His words recalled so clearly an experience I had truly wished to forget. But where I had been terrified, Daniel had felt the excitement of a theory proven. He told me how, when I had returned home that day, the description of my symptoms had caused his mind to make an intuitive leap. The thrust of our research over the previous few months had been around the idea that if - as we believed - æther surrounds us at all times, then it can only be assumed that it must have played a part in human evolution and therefore be intrinsically bound to our biology. Simple logic dictated that if this were the case then there must be ways that it could affect the human body, and vice versa.

Daniel's idea was this: as the two of us had been living and working together almost exclusively for so long in such intimacy, was it possible that in some way, through the æther around us, we had charged our minds so that they could only work together? Other thoughts seemed to remain clear, as did our motor functions. Only when we tried to think about our work in ætherics did our minds fail us. Could it in fact be that as neither of us had ever worked on ætheric theory without the other, amplified by the long hours we had spent in close confinement with experimental chemical solutions designed for ætheric conductions, mean that our minds *could no longer understand the subject without each other*? It was obvious this could not be a natural process. Multitudes of people throughout history must have spent longer in each other's company than we had, but there were no reports or stories of such effects. Therefore we had to conclude that some outside amplifier must have been in play. It was a simple matter to deduce that this must have been our work, and the close contact and experimentation with ætheric chemicals it entailed.

My mind raced. This was such a bold leap forward in our research. Such a radical hypothesis. Yet the longer I thought on it the more sense it made. It could only be the next natural advance in our theories. What possibilities it opened up! Could the connection between æther and the mind be so deep? How much were our emotions tied to it? Can not one person's mood raise or lower that of an entire room? Will not anger spread and multiply through a gathered crowd? Do we not develop the ability to sense the emotions of those closest and dearest to us without them having to say a word? Could this be more than just familiarity and social awareness, but rather an actual biological ability? The ancient Greek scholars spoke of æther as the fifth of the elements; the divine spark that granted intelligence and emotion to otherwise mundane matter. Could they have been closer to the mark than any of us had granted?

As excited as these ideas made us, we knew we had to

keep them to ourselves until we had the time to go through them scientifically and methodically. We were under no illusion to how radical these ideas were. So far-fetched and bizarre. Even our close friends, no strangers to rebelling against the hidebound opinion of established science, would balk at such wild supposition. The greatest lesson taught to us by Professor Goldfarn had been to always test any ideas with the most vigorous scientific methods. Every idea he had ever published had been tested and verified as far as possible. The only way to gain legitimacy of thought was to follow every step along the scientific path, so that while they may question your ideas they may never question your methods.

The following months were possibly the most industrious I have ever spent as we set about devising ways in which we might test our theory. We had such drive! Such ambition. We decided to test the limits of our connection, and discovered that the debilitating effect began at just greater than half a mile, but otherwise distance had no obvious impact on the severity. Being one mile part or fifty affected us the same. We did, however, discover that whichever of us stayed at home found the effect far less intense. This only served to excite us further, opening up as it did the possibility of places having the same hypothetical charge as people. We theorised that if we spent long enough apart then eventually the affliction would fade, but neither of us had the inclination to push ourselves so far. The most we managed was fourteen days; the longest either of us had spent apart since university. The discomfort, plus the detriment the separation caused our work, outweighed any benefit of continuing that line of experimentation.

As much as it excited us to be the first people to share such an intimate bond, neither of us considered it an ideal state of affairs. For better or for worse we were effectively shackled closer than any husband to his wife. We literally could no longer exist one without the other. But what if we could recreate the phenomenon on a temporary level? To intensify the level of connection between two people, but without the lingering co-dependence. Clearly it was possible to amplify an atmosphere's natural ætheric conduction. If we could saturate a room with a refined version of the chemical compound used to draw æther from the Flow, could it promote this greater level of mental connection? Perhaps even allow us to communicate without words?

What followed were several weeks of frantic design and planning. A wet-room would be constructed in our garden, fitted with a system of pipes and filters connected to electric pumps which would disperse our new solution to temporarily thicken the level of æther in the air and, we hoped, promote the generation of some level of mental conduction between us.

Our plans were not an inexpensive undertaking. We soon came to see that it would cost us more than our combined allowances would bear to finance on our own. We needed to bring in an outside investor to cover the remaining costs. David, being the wealthiest of our colleagues, was the obvious choice. And we knew him well enough to know that he would be keen to be so involved with such a potential development. Accordingly, we invited him for dinner, over which we excitedly outlined our plans. We kept from him the whole extent of our experience, of course. It still felt too outlandish to expect anyone to believe. I also think that some small part of us wished to keep it between ourselves a little longer. It is hard to explain, but such a intimate, unique connection as we shared was not something given away lightly. Instead we gave him a truncated version of the facts; that we had noticed a slight, temporary dip in cognitive function when we worked apart. Despite the outlandish nature of our claims, Daniel knew us well enough to trust that we would not come to him with any idea without cause. It also helped that from long association we knew how to play on his sense of self importance, dangling the possibility of being in on the ground floor of such a discovery. By morning he had agreed to loan us the necessary funds to complete our work. His only provision was that once the wet-room was constructed he was to be included in the first experiments.

How different things might be now if we had decided not to meet that demand. Or if we had had the foresight to seek elsewhere for our funds. But David was the most obvious choice and what reason had we to expect what would occur. But it is too late to dwell on speculative daydreams. What's done is done.

* * *

Thus funded, it did not take long before we completed construction of the wet-room. The night before that fateful experiment David travelled down to stay with us, and the three of us spent the evening detailing our plans for the following day. We thought through every step, determined to ensure that nothing be left to chance. I found myself wondering how similar this must have been to that other night, all those years ago, when David had sat with his uncle thinking through the possibilities for their great experiment. Had they felt this same excitement? Had the atmosphere been as thick with the same sense of anticipation? I wished then that I could ask him, but knew better. David had an anger all too easily roused by any comparisons being made to his uncle's work, however similar the situations might have been.

We woke early the next morning as giddy and excited as schoolboys on the first days of summer. We made a hurried breakfast - Daniel and David both ate hungrily but I was too nervous to take more than a few sips of coffee - before eagerly setting out into the garden. The newly constructed wet-room stood where a disused shed had once been. In outward appearance it could have been a simple garden outhouse; a sturdy wooden construction about five feet by five with a flat roof. The only obvious embellishments - at least that could be seen from the outside - were that the one window had been fitted with frosted glass and the piping that threaded out of one wall. To this we set about fitting the electric motor and the canister of chemical solution we had prepared. Carefully we set the connections and, once satisfied that both were secure, we set the motor running. The loud thumping quickly built, followed by the muted hiss as the ætheric solution began to disperse within.

I stole a look at my companions. Daniel appeared just as excited as I, and while David made a clear effort to appear aloof his own impatience was clear to see. He may not have shared our intimate relationship with this test, but even he could not fail to feel the rush that comes of standing on the precipice of such work.

We waited impatiently as my watch counted down the full five minutes which we judged to be adequate time for the atmosphere within to become fortified with our solution. We disrobed as much as was decent, as any clothing we wore within would quickly become uncomfortably saturated, and at last opened the door and slipped inside.

The air was already thick with humidity, and my mouth and nose quickly filled with moisture as we took our seats on the two plain benches set against each wall. Daniel and I sat facing each other, with David next to me. It was dark, but enough light came through the frosted glass window to see by. Above us, copper piping ran in concentric rings with protruding mesh apertures branching off at regular intervals.

From these floated the fine mist that now filled the room.

Our plan had been agreed the previous night. We would sit in silence, each of us silently counting out ten minutes in our heads. This, we hoped, would work to synchronise our thoughts. We would then begin to repeat - again only in our minds - a set phrase that we had individually chosen and kept secret from the others. It could be nothing familiar, or that the others might guess. Something unique. Our hope was that after a time our thoughts would begin to transfer through the thickened air until one or both of the others could 'hear' them. Under only one condition were we to speak out loud; that being if we began to hear a phrase other than our own in our minds. We would then be permitted to speak it for the other two to confirm or deny.

The silence within that room became as thick as the humidity. Moisture ran down my skin, matting my hair to my scalp. Shutting my eyes I fought against the excitement in my breast and to keep my breath and pulse steady. The conditions were oddly relaxing. Once I grew accustomed to it, the moisture in my throat, nose and mouth was not unpleasant. I could smell nothing, but that did not come as a surprise. I was long used to that strange property of ætheric chemicals. In fact, having worked with them for so long only in this closely confined space was the effect so complete that I found it noticeable.

After seven minutes of diligent counting I felt my mind begin to wander. No, not wander, it was more of a blurring. The countdown in my mind developed a strange echoing quality, almost as if other voices were speaking in time with my own; one counting down in time with me and another instead counting up. My thoughts faltered, and I heard that stumble reflected in those other voices. A burning surge of excitement rose within my chest. I knew these voices almost as well as my own. That which counted in time with me had to be Daniel's, and David's the one contrary to the pair of us. The room may have been silent, save for the beat of the electric pump outside and the gentle hiss of the misters above us, but I could hear them both!

Keeping my eyes shut for fear that to open them would be to wake from a dream, I began to recognise a change in my outward perceptions. Everything felt somehow... duplicated. From one angle everything was giddy, a world filled with youthful delight and open, darting ideas; from another the same sensations came to me, but forced and precise, carefully placed and considered; and between these two separate yet identical perceptions I could recognise my own familiar awareness, made stark through this new comparison. We were three separate minds reacting to the same stimuli simultaneously. I have never been able to satisfactorily explain that experience. The closest comparison I can give is the effect of a beam of light shone through a prism, breaking it into its myriad, glittering components, all different yet each an equal aspect of that same source.

With each moment the new way of perceiving the world grew. Imagine living in a darkened room all your life, learning to survive using nothing but touch, and then encountering the light for the first time. Our minds raced with thoughts that diverged while yet remaining whole. A world of almost limitless possibility seemed to be opening before us. We held in our hands the tool that would shatter borders and boundaries. That would allow humanity to at last truly understand one another. Frank Spilling spoke of communication? He was working blindfolded. A man proclaiming a river as the greatest body of water in the world, without thinking to follow it to the sea.

All of a sudden I felt an external rush of affection. I opened my eyes to see Daniel was gazing across at me. My own feelings responded to his, our emotions echoing through our twinned perceptions; a heady cocktail of the successful culmination of our work and our love for one another. I had never felt anything like it. It is impossible to explain what we felt in that one perfect moment. I do not think it possible for any man who has not been through the experience itself to have any true understanding of *how* it felt. A whole new angle of perception, beyond our restricted viewpoints. Mankind little thinks about how much of every relationship is taken on trust. We believe that those we care about feel the same as we, take their words at face value, yet always there is that nagging possibility that there may be parts that remain hidden. Fears that no level of intimacy or knowledge can wipe away. But in that one moment, that one glorious, life affirming moment, our souls were laid bare. Imagine it! To know, utterly and completely, that the one you love unconditionally loves you in return. To see for a certainty that there are no doubts, no fears, no bubbling resentments, or lingering infidelities. To have pure, irrefutable certainty.

And then a wave of sudden revulsion crashing over us. A sickening realisation that slid over our thoughts like bile. My stomach turned, and for a moment I could feel nothing but deep disgust at the shameful feelings we had just experienced. How could I ever have felt something as unnatural as this could be beautiful? I felt betrayed. Violated. Forced into something horrific without my consent.

I turned and saw David glaring at us with such a look of shock and hatred on his face that I flinched at the sight. With our minds so open, so intimately entwined, nothing could have been hidden in that narrow, humid space even if we had thought to try. Still the connection grew; the passion and shock and lust and disgust and excitement and fear reverberating and multiplying even as we tried to comprehend it. With every passing moment I knew more. Became more... aware. We were all becoming intertwined;

myriad reflections blending together until it took conscious effort to tell one from the other. I could feel David's resentment that he would never outshine his uncle, the great Professor Goldfarn. How it would never matter how much of the work had been his, or how much further he might develop the science in his own lifetime. He would never be more than a great man's nephew. All his insecurities. His fears. His hopes. His pride. His ambition. His drive. Everything. Mixed with this were my fears of inadequacy compared to the advances made by my colleagues. Daniel's contempt for David. David's distrust of Daniel, tainted and fed by the knowledge of that contempt. My shame at having to hide myself from society. Daniel's resentment at the world for the way we were made. My deep fears of rejection. David's anger. Daniel's pride. My desires. Nothing hidden. Every sensation, every emotion, every thought laid open.

And through everything, slick and putrid like stale oil, irrefutable in its intensity, threaded David's disgust.

I cannot say how long this lasted. My perceptions were so altered that I had lost all measure of time. It could have been a moment or it could have been an hour when he stood and, without a word, stormed from the room. As he pushed open the door the thickened atmosphere of the wet-room billowed out into the open air beyond, dispelling the ætheric charge. In one brief, soul wrenching moment I experienced the numbing crash of my senses and emotions snapping back to the mundane sensitivities of the everyday. Bound once more by my own perceptions, I felt blind. I have no idea how long it took before I could gather the wherewithal to stagger out, shivering, into the chill morning air. By the time we managed it David had gone. What would I have said to him anyway? What could there have been to say? There were no secrets between us any more.

* * *

* * *

Our experiment had been a success greater than any of our wildest fantasies, yet who could have predicted that such success could destroy m

y life. There are many things that society will accept, as long as it is permitted to turn a blind eye. But force it to face the unknown or different and it will turn without a thought. I know in my heart that many of my friends and family knew the truth of mine and Daniel's relationship. Those with the wit to see are often the most willing to accept. We hoped that this might be the case with David. That once he had time to realise and process what he had experienced he would come to understand it for the beautiful thing that it was.

We greatly misjudged him. Or rather I should say we willingly deceived ourselves. We had seen his soul and knew what the man could be capable of. Maybe we lived in hope. Or maybe we were simply as ill-equipped to process our new knowledge as he. Either way, instead of trying to speak with him we put off venturing out into society, deciding the best way forward was to present our findings in as academic a fashion as possible. David may have been lost to us, as both a colleague and a friend, but we thought if we presented our work documented and ready for further review than the scientific world would have no choice but to accept it.

Perhaps we made the wrong choice, or perhaps there had been no correct choice. Maybe we were damned from the moment David stormed out of the wet-room. While we worked we found our letters and telegrams were unanswered, and once we did venture out into the world those we had once called friends would not receive us. Establishments and clubs where once we had been welcome refused us entry. In as short a space of time as a week, society had turned its back upon us.

It took a fortnight of trying before anyone would even

speak with us. Frank refused our calls, but at last we received a letter from Terrence Farning agreeing to see us. We met in the private room of a public house in Euston. Busy enough that no one would look twice on three friends wishing privacy. He did not want anyone knowing he was willing speak with us. Over a hasty meal he told us all that David had undertaken over the previous fortnight. While we had isolated ourselves, fooling ourselves into believing the world would judge us on the merits of our achievements alone, David had used every ounce of drive and influence to drag our names and reputations into the dirt. He had spread the story that we had been embezzling him to fund a decadent, immoral lifestyle, and that when confronted we attempted to seduce him with the aim of gaining greater access to his money. He claimed that we had allowed the minor celebrity that had become attached to us through our work to corrupt us, and had used our fame to encourage people to turn a blind eye to our activities. Of our moral shortcomings he had been the most vocal, stirring up a storm of outrage to the point where anyone whom might have been brave enough to speak in our defence would fear being tarred with the same brush. Seeing how quickly the world turned against us, no one wished to bring the same suspicion and hatred on themselves. Our names were already being expunged from any published research by a scientific community fuelled by the righteous indignation of a witch hunt.

We told Terrence everything. All our theories that had led to this, and the true story of what had happened that day. I don't know that he believed us. No doubt he thought the truth lay in some grey area between David's rabid hatred and our fantastical story. He told us he was fighting, as much as possible, to save our work. He, at least, believed that no one's contribution to science should be completely expunged. But David's anger was insoluble, and despite his own fears to the contrary his reputation and pull in society was not unimpressive.

When Terrence left us it was with a request not to try and make contact with him again, lest such communication blight what efforts he would be able to make. I suppose it should be to his credit that he had been at least willing to meet us that once, but I could not help but feel a sense of anger at such abandonment and my final words to him were not kind.

It did not take long for the whole business to spill from the scientific community to the world at large. A week after our meeting with Terrence, Daniel's father arrived at our door. He would not acknowledge me at all, only speaking to order his son to accompany him home. We acted as if he were merely leaving on a quick visit. That he would return within a few days at the most. I think we both knew the truth. No one ever came to collect his belongings, and the scant letters that have arrived since then indicate that his family work to prevent him contacting me. I have heard that he has married. A cousin, selected for him by his family to detract the scandal. I hope he can be happy.

The worst part of it has been that thus parted from Daniel I found myself once more struck by that great affliction of the mind that had inspired this entire ordeal. All attempts at higher thought left me a shaking wreck, with only sleep able to calm my mind. I suppose, had this not been the case, I may have had the chance to undo at least some of David's work, to salvage at least some semblance of reputation that could have saved my life. But with my mind so afflicted I languished alone while the world moved beyond me. Eventually, after several months, the affliction finally began to pass, allowing me to, at last, comprehend what had become of my life. I have no visitors. My one-time friends have abandoned me. What family I have show no interest or concern for my wellbeing. I am alone.

I am at least left a wiser man, shorn of the foolish idealism of youth. I recognise now the true heart of mankind. Men may say we strive for greater knowledge and understanding, but I say they are either the greatest of liars or the supremely ignorant. Humanity is incapable of seeing past its own petty needs and prejudices. In the entirety of human existence only we who shared that moment in the wet-house have experienced the level of intimacy and connection necessary to see deep within the human soul. And see where such understanding has led me. My life shattered. My name forgotten. David, my friend, saw my hopes, my fears, my weaknesses and my loves, and he damned me for it.

I could perhaps live with this. I have money enough to survive for a good many years. But the one lingering note from that day in the wet-room is that I am cursed with the remembrance of how he felt. The echo of that disgust taints the memories of a love I once thought beautiful. Try as I might, I can no longer think of Daniel without some small taste of that intrusive repugnance. I have tried to ignore it. To hide from it. But the truth is that ever since that day this memory has grown until I have begun to detest myself for what I am.

I can only imagine that it is what drives David's furious obsession. Does he feel the echo of the love and affection Daniel and I once shared? Emotions so alien to him, feelings that terrify him so much that he would rather wipe me from the world than face them? How can there be hope for mankind when an experience of love can drive a man to such rage?

Professor Goldfarn believed the world to be filled with discoveries still to be made that would change the way mankind understood themselves. What I have discovered is that mankind doesn't want to to face those changes. We prefer to live with our prejudices and petty beliefs, and to hell for the rest.

There is nothing for me now. Not in life. I have gathered the last existing copies of my work and shall bind them with this account. I barely know why I bother to do so. Neither science nor posterity cares for it. Perhaps there is some small amount of hope in me after all. Hope that one day there might be people willing to regard me with greater compassion than any alive today. Or perhaps my life might provide a cautionary warning for some poor fool who stumbles upon them.

So I shall leave them, as I intend to leave this life. Forgotten and unwanted.

Granville Bannerman,
  18th April, 1911

Timeline

1839 - Birth of Thomas Goldfarn.

1861 - Thomas Goldfarn publishes his first work on ætheric science; *Theoretics of the Ætheric, and their Implications in Modern Science.*

1898 - Professor Thomas Goldfarn first captures æther in a useable form.

1899 - David Goldfarn publishes his uncle's findings in the seminal paper *The Capture and Study of Æther.*

1899 - David Goldfarn, Terrance Farning, and Frank Spilling first begin working together to develop and build the new science.

1900 - Death of Professor Thomas Goldfarn.

1902 - Æther-bowls first used for public illumination.

1905 - First æther communication handset demonstrated by Frank Spilling and Terence Farning.

1906 - While working on refining ætheric chemicals, George Sandringham stumbles upon the process to create æthergraphic images.

1907 - Examples of æthergraphic image reproduction first exhibited.

1910 - There is a minor public scandal when David

Goldfarn reveals two colleagues, Daniel Van Burn and Granville Bannerman, had been attempting to embezzle money by setting up fake experiments.

1915 - Æther communication sets distributed to armies in France, but almost universally fail when used in the field.

1919 - The death of David Goldfarn.

1923 - British Government creates a dedicated ætheric research division. The initial group consists of Ronald Carter, Charles Doyle, Frank Spilling, Bernard Galbraith, and Archibald Spinks.

1925 - Publication of the Spinks Formulae streamlines ætheric communication theory and physical production.

1925 - Archibald Spinks dies in a motorcycle accident.

1925 - First commercial Ashphones go on sale.

1928 - UK Government begins programme of 'Community Communication Hubs', to ensure a secure æther communications network across the country.

1932 - Edith Tanning begins her studies in æther-evolutionary fringe theory.

1933 - Death of Terrance Farning.

1935 - Death of Frank Spilling, the last surviving 'Father of Æther'.

1939 - Edith Tanning killed in an air-raid.

1940 - Failure of ætheric equipment causes the complete breakdown of military communications planning, leading to the evacuation at Dunkirk.

1940 - Formation of Project Forebridge by the UK Government to try and solve the 'Æther Problem'.

1945 - With the end of the war approaching, Project Forebridge officially shut down having failed to solve the problem with æther technology.

1945 - The 'Æther Event' occurs. A connection with the bombing of Hiroshima is never conclusively proven, but the growth of nuclear technology leads many to move away from ætheric research.

1945 - Death of Bernard Galbraith. His work and papers are classified by the UK Government.

1951 - Sandra Green and Hugo Sheridan publish their 'Grand Field' theory, conclusively disproving Michael Ganding's 'Strand Theory'.

1978 - Hannah Chamber's doctorate paper, *Study of Ætherics in Bioneurology and the Reevaluation of Ætheric-Evolutionary Theories*, becomes the centre of controversy and the subject of significant debate.

1980 - The Chambers research team publish their paper *Study of Bioætheric Interactions in Neurology and Medical Diagnosis*.

1981 - Invention of the Chambers Diagnostic Scanner.

1982 - Joanna and Peter Haldine perfect the process of data sharing through what they term the 'æther-net'.

1984 - First commercial 'a-net' units go on sale.

1993 - First reports of Ash, a new designer drug hitting the clubbing scene

Acknowledgements and Thanks

It's been almost three years now since I wrote the first draft of
the first story in this collection, so of course, in that time, there have
been a few people who have advised, discussed, aided or otherwise
encouraged me in the writing of this collection. If I've forgotten
anyone, I apologise. Hopefully, a promise of general gratitude to all
who helped me - whether I remember them or not - will be enough
to placate you.

Firstly, as always, to Frankie. Despite everything she has been
through in the last three years, she has always been there for me.
From reading early (almost unreadable) drafts, offering advice,
proofreading, and otherwise providing everything a writer's wife
could be asked to provide.

To my parents - to whom this collection is dedicated - and my
sisters, one of whom, during the writing of this book, gave me a
nephew, and the other gave my wife a kidney. So much of who I am
is probably due to the people I grew up with, and it all turned out
all right in the end, so I guess I should probably thank them for it.

To Andi, Joni, and Callum, for reading early drafts and giving
excellent notes. As before, thank you for pointing out the things I
hadn't noticed or thought of, which I can now claim credit for.

I would also like to thank Tony. I may not have seen him in
quite a while, but several years ago, I attended a talk he gave in a
pub in Camden about how we use the energy in the world around
us to create 'household gods'. This eventually became the seed of
the idea for this collection. I also learned that all you need to do to
become a druid is pass a multiple-choice questionnaire, but this fact

has not yet made its way into my writing. Maybe someday.

And lastly, I would like to give a massive - seriously, I can't say how big this final thank you should be - to all the doctors, nurses and staff at the renal and transplant units at Hammersmith and Watford General Hospitals. Thankfully we spend a lot less time there now, but the care, concern and professionalism of these people made a terrifying and difficult time of our lives so much easier.

About the Author

Originally from Hampshire, Thomas H. Brand now lives and works in North London. He spends his time sitting staring at the computer screen or notebook page. He loves every moment. When he isn't doing that he can usually be found reading things other people have written instead.

Please visit www.thomashbrand.com for more of information.

If you enjoyed this book, or even if you didn't, please take a couple of moments to leave a review on your online platform of choice. I really appreciate hearing back from my readers. It really does help me out, even if you just leave a rating. Thanks.

www.ingramcontent.com/pod-product-compliance
Lightning Source LLC
Chambersburg PA
CBHW071435200726
48294CB00002B/648